RETURN OF THE DEVIL

ARMAGEDDON

MICHAEL HARBRON

CONTENTS

1

BLOOD OF THE DEVIL

I have dreamt for an age, and I have discovered that the life I used to consider eternal—as granted by my lord, Elton Grando—has been nothing but a blip in the infiniteness of the universe and its age. Five, six hundred years, gone in a flash. And what do I have to show for them? Scars on my body, cracks in my mind, and a bloodless state that prevents me from dying, sleeping, eating, and witnessing daylight.

As if all of that was not enough, I am cursed with something far more weighing than any of my other plights. The blood of the Devil is in my body, conserved forever, as it can only be conserved in a living, breathing container—a vampyre. When he told me that he had a lesser-known title, the Lord of Contingencies, I thought that he was merely being pompous. It did not occur to me then—but it does now—that he was describing himself as honestly as one can expect from the Devil.

I am a scholar of blood, and being the second vampyre to have ever existed, I know all there is to know about it. Such as how it loses its potency if kept in a vial or a decanter or any such paraphernalia where blood is not in direct contact with a living body. It is for that reason we vampyres will always prefer to hunt our prey and consume fresh blood.

And in hindsight, I can all too well understand why Lucifer would choose me as a vessel to safekeep his blood. I am alive in some capacity, and my body has served the purpose of a deposit box for his scalding crimson. I do not know what happens next, for I am bound and kept in the cold dark of this crypt. Any attempt to escape, and the binds grow tighter.

While I may not have any perception of a present or knowledge of the future, thanks to Satan's blood in me, I have all the knowledge in the world of all the ages, eras, epochs that ever were. I have seen everything as a vicarious observer.

This mind sanctum that I have created within some dark corner of my consciousness is a reprieve from all the dread that is the Devil's memory. I may not need air to breathe, but dear God, I have suffocated enough.

Rafael knew that it was just a mental exercise, but closing his eyes and picturing himself in a writing room back in his master's mansion in Little Istria was the only comfort that he could conjure these days. In his mind, he was imagining himself writing on a fine parchment with a falcon quill, staring out the window in between sentences and taking in the grandeur that was this magnificent little town, a Gothic recreation of everything they had loved so dearly back in Europe.

At any given moment, he expected Elton with his long hair

and his heavy robes to walk into the room and say, "Rafael. There's much revelry in the night, and yet you sit here with your books and your writings."

And he would turn around and behold his master standing in the pale moonbeams, looking every bit like the creature of myth that he was: gaunt-faced, haunted-eyed, ashen the texture and color of his skin, tapping his ringed fingers against his belt a little impatiently.

"Master," he'd say in reverence, head bowed.

"Come, Rafael. Fresh blood needs some tending to," Elton would say, and the ink would be left to dry on the parchment. By the time morning would come, Rafael, having indulged in a night's worth of indulgence, would no longer be in the mood for writing.

But now, in this imagined room in an imagined Little Istria, there was no Elton, no Breeding House, no Feeding House, no vampyre kith and kin. Only silence and ashfall and the tolling of a blood-magic-soaked bell. And if he stayed in this Imaginarium any longer, he would get to see all of it razed, leaving nothing but rubble and corpses strewn across the desolation.

He would feel the gnaw of his bloodlust twist and churn in his stomach, and the blood of the Devil would do nothing to sate it. It flowed in his veins, after all, and not down his throat. He would address himself in his mind, asking if he'd ever felt such hunger before. The witch, when she had put him here, had done so in such a way that he'd slumbered, even though sleep was not possible for vampyrekind. The Devil had done no such courtesy.

Rafael wished that he had never given in to the temptation

that was Thiedra; if that hadn't happened, he would have still been by Elton's side when the Order of the Shroud attacked, and maybe, just maybe, things would have been different. He would have either saved his master and continued to live beside him for centuries, or he would have died by his master's side.

This limbo would not have been his fate.

Rafael closed his eyes, even though that made no difference, what with the binds so tightly wrapped around his head, but doing so made him feel like he had some control over his body, some agency. And as he closed his eyes, the relentless barrage of the Devil's memories began once more.

"Please, help," Rafael uttered behind gags for the thousandth time, and with each iteration, he felt the helpless realization dig deeper into his maddened consciousness. That the Devil had forgotten him here, and was never going to come back.

Or worse yet, the Devil was dead, and so was God, in which case he was stuck here forever, a living sieve of profane blood, writhing against his bounds in the cold and dark of the stone crypt, forever suffocating, hungering, despairing.

He was going to be one of Venice's most decorated doctors.

Around the same time as the Provveditori alla Sanita was established to manage plague control, quarantines, and sanitation, Dr. Rafael von Thorburn had finished his guild-based apprenticeship from the barber-surgeons and apothecarists who'd set up their clinics outside of the University of Padua. From there, he had gone on to work at the Ospedale di San Marco near the Basilica of San Marco, treating the sick and the poor.

Rafael von Thorburn, in his twenties, did not much care for the still very grotesque medical treatment that was available in Europe, and knew that the solution was right there at the tip of his fingers. The person who'd be known as the father of modern anatomy, Andreas Vesalius, was a peer of his at the university, and despite all the praise that Andreas got, it was evident that the doctors and scholars of the West were ill-informed and under-equipped when it came to medical methods.

Aspirant, ambitious, Rafael knew that in order to become one of the most renowned doctors of Venice, he needed to bring something fresh to the operating table. All day, he would see patients mistreated in the wards. If someone came with a mental malady, such as an affliction that made them talk oddly or behave erratically, the prescribed treatment was bloodletting to let out all the evil blood that was making them behave so. If someone suffered a deep injury and an infection had set in in one of the limbs, doctors made no such attempt at saving the limb; instead, they chopped it off and called the patient lucky that they'd saved his life by stopping the spread of the infection.

Amidst all these barbaric modus operandi, Rafael started to relegate himself to the study of theory, because the Hippocratic Oath explicitly stated, "I will use treatment to help the sick according to my ability and judgment, but never with a view to injury and wrongdoing."

Well, in Rafael's judgment, chopping off limbs and wasting vital blood was as bad as inflicting injuries and purposefully partaking in wrongdoing.

So he evaded, hiding in the hospital's library, hoping that he wouldn't be called to perform his duties in the ward. But doctors were, by and large, short in supply, and he was often called, quite forcibly at times, to appear in the wards, where he, against his will, had to perform the grotesque operations and feel horrible as a result. He wasn't making any of these patients' lives better; he was cursing them to an existence of disability.

One night, escaping from all the wails and screams of the sick bay, Rafael von Thorburn was studying a book written in Latin, trying to decipher how the civilizations of old used to conduct their medical practices. He had perused all the books in this library and in the library of the college where he'd studied, and he had come to the conclusion that the Western way of medicine was still in its nascency.

With the current political climate of Venice, the rampancy of disease, poverty around every corner, and misery evident through the open window of every home, Rafael had resigned to becoming a listless man, instead of being one of Venice's best doctors.

He closed the book and sat in the drab room. Outside, a low moon hung over the water, the night wind blowing the long, white, silken curtains, making the candlelight flicker and spreading humidity in the otherwise stifling and stale air of the library. There were five other tables with chairs around them, and no less than thirty shelves tall enough to reach the roof. Outside, in the hallway, Rafael could hear the staccato rhythm of boots meeting marble—just another nurse taking a quick break on the third floor, presumably.

It was one in the morning, and the more dastardly of the hospital's administration had already signed out for the day. They would come back tomorrow, being brutish, shoving doctors as if they were nothing more than gutter cleaners, and then, exactly at four, they would leave. It was yet another facet of the Venetian government's rule by force, but nothing that the doctors were not prepared for. This was not the first war they had seen, nor was this going to be the last.

With a glass filled with water and a pipe filled with tobacco, Rafael, dressed in a formal suit—sat brooding, smoking, staring out the window—when a sudden disturbance in the quiet of the night alerted him to the presence of someone else in the room.

It began with the rustling of the curtains; at first, they were just fluttering in the wind, almost idyllically, but this sudden gust made them soar in the air and flap as if they were batwings. Then they settled, and the night was all too quiet—no howling dogs in the streets, no whistling wind, no coughing beggar below.

The candleflames on the candelabra were as still as meditating monks. The book that he'd just closed had disappeared from the table. Rafael cast a look at the open doors and found them closed shut, bolted from the inside.

A nonchalant figure was standing there by the door,

perusing his book. And yet, the more Rafael stared, the more he discovered that this was no mere nighttime stroller fancying a walk through the library but someone with a purpose, a person with a dark energy about them, as if he had drunk all the liquor in the world and, instead of becoming drunk, had become malicious.

The figure, as if overhearing what Rafael was thinking, looked up from the book and gave the young doctor a beguiling smile. His eyes were dark and his face, although not gaunt, looked sallow. When the man in the black suit walked forward at a slow pace, it was then that Rafael realized his skin tone was pale olive, and his hair was gently oiled and combed back. By the keenness of his eyes, he seemed like a kindred scholar.

"Come now, Doctor, let your mind not waver any more than it has," the man said, coming over to the table where Rafael sat and putting the book down. "As far as books go, that is one laborious tome, containing nothing of use."

"Tell me about it," Rafael said, chuckling nervously. "I don't seem to recall meeting you earlier. Are you a doctor?"

"Not any more than you are an angel," the man said, sitting down across from Rafael and intertwining his fingers. "But I have been known to dabble in a little butchery here and there."

"Quite diminutive, calling medicine and surgery butchery."

"Alas, but that's what your kind does in these halls. It's nothing if not perverse."

"And you know better?"

"I, dear friend," the man said, smiling, and as he smiled,

Rafael saw the unmistakable red glint in his eyes, a strange feature that struck the fear of God in his heart, "know all."

"Know-it-alls aren't tolerated all that well in Venice," Rafael scoffed.

"Or anywhere. You wouldn't believe the places I have been cast out of."

"Then what are you doing here?" Rafael asked.

"I intend to offer you something that you have been looking for all your life," the man spoke, and with each utterance of his words, the shadows in the room flocked to him, sending candles dousing one by one, till the only ones left lit were the ones on the table. Even the moon seemed to wane against the man's intensity.

Rafael felt ash in his mouth, and a great coldness such as the kind he'd felt when he had buried his mother when he was no more than sixteen years old. Misery and malice rose out of him as the man reached out and touched his hand.

A sudden burst of epiphanies and revelations bombarded Rafael's consciousness in one split second, making him witness everything he had ever wanted to see. Groundbreaking medical techniques being employed in strange operation theaters in another corner of the world. Strange men speaking an alien language creating tinctures and balms and applying them on open wounds instead of amputating limbs. Intricate pictures showing the cross-sections of human anatomy in a way that he had never perceived before.

The next thing he knew, he was on the floor, covered in sweat, panting loudly, and the man—whom now Rafael was sure was not a man, but something else entirely—was still seated in his chair and was beaming quite proudly at him.

"What did you do to me?" Rafael whispered.

"Nothing as of yet, dear friend," the man said. "I gave you a mere taste of what you stand to gain."

"Who are you?" Rafael whispered.

"Oh, of all the books you have consulted, one would think that the Good Book was the first one you'd have read, or don't you recognize the Devil when he sits across from you?"

Rafael gulped raw air and felt it bulge against his throat as it went down, a deeply uncomfortable sensation, but nothing in comparison to the sheer terror that was lacerating his mind.

Now the glint in the man's eyes was as unmistakable as the moon itself. A deep red glare, a reflection of the Hell from which Satan himself had risen out of, all for what?

To meet me? thought Rafael wildly.

But then the Devil reached out with a very human-looking hand, and Rafael couldn't help but take it. He pulled himself back onto his shaky feet and stood there, acknowledging the presence of Lucifer against a backdrop of a glass-windowed shelf lined with human bones, skulls, and organs hanging suspended in formalin.

"You flatter yourself far too much, Doctor," the Devil said, and then ushered his hand, offering him to sit back down on the chair. "I am not bound by the linearity of time and space. I am here, with you, and in another moment, I am there with someone whom you will shortly call master."

"I renounce any masters," Rafael said hotly.

"And what of the Venetian government? Do they not rule over you? If they send you a conscription order, who are you to deny it? All you men have is masters. Without them, you are nothing," said the Devil with much disdain. "If it's not religion, then it is science. If it is not that, then it is the quest for truths far bigger than your fetid little minds. And those who are not consumed by dogma or discipline flock toward power like moths to a flame. Power in the form of governance, in the form of land and weaponry, in the form of being the foremost, the pioneer in a craft, a skill, anything. You renounce any masters through your consciousness, but your subconscious bows at every altar it finds."

Rafael had never felt so insulted in all his life, not even when the soldiers had shoved him last week on account of being late and lacking his official papers. He had fallen on a heap of dung and mud, his best suit ruined, and the soldiers had laughed all around him as he, scrawny-bodied, had pulled himself out of that filth and walked the walk of shame back home. Somehow, this, this piercing statement from the Devil, was more insulting than that.

But he was quick on his feet, just as he was back when he was shoved in the dung heap. He said, "I have read the Good Book, you know. And whether or not I believe in it or agree with most of what's written in it, I can tell you this much. It got you right. You love dehumanizing humans. You enjoy pinpointing our flaws, Morningstar. Whatever happened to being a light bringer?"

Lucifer studied Rafael's face with a scrutinizing gaze, his own facial expressions stone-like, almost as if they were ready to burst with rage, but instead, he started laughing, clapping his hands.

"Oh, you are good, Doctor. You are good. I knew I didn't make a mistake coming to you," Satan said. "And by the way, this is me bringing the light. My offer is this. I will give you knowledge over your domain and any domain of your choosing so long as you live. Men of your brilliance deserve that, at the very least. I can share with you what Ibn-e-Sina practiced. His *Canon of Medicine* details over 700 drugs and their uses. He's the one who systemized Greek, Roman, and Islamic medical knowledge. I can give you Al-Razi's secrets. What Abulcasis knows of surgery, you shall know too. If you employ what you learn, you will be the master of surgery, the master of medicine; not just the greatest doctor in Venice, but the greatest doctor in the world."

Rafael's mouth had filled with saliva at the offer.

"In another three hundred years, Doctor, someone named Pavlov is going to really get knee-deep in the whole mouth salivating phenomenon. I will tell him of this meeting of ours, of how your mouth went wet upon temptation," the Devil said, getting up impatiently from his seat. He walked over to the window, studying Venice below, his forearm resting on the sill.

"What will I have to do in return?" Rafael asked, knowing that whatever it was, he would do it. The asking was just a courtesy.

"Quite contrary to popular belief, I do not believe in holding humans hostage by way of their souls. Taking the souls is only for the wager, you know. Right. You don't know. Well, good old God and me, we've got a wager going since the dawn of time. Collecting souls kind of plays in my favor because, God being a bitch and I being the father of pride, we like to keep score," the Devil said without turning away from the window. He reached out, as if he could touch the moon. But then he pulled his hand back and addressed Rafael, this time directly. "I have great interest in your life, Doctor, and I ask that for your part of the barter, you give me your soul for safekeeping."

"Not for eternal torment?"

"Oh, no, dear friend. The eternal torment comes after," the Devil said, and laughed good-naturedly. One could not tell if he was jesting or not.

"Anything else?" Rafael asked.

"Yes. Since you play such a pivotal role in the events that will follow, I would like for you to forget this encounter of ours. Sign this contract, Doctor, and then forget that you ever signed it. I will have need for you in the coming days, and it will be better for me that I approach you not as an old acquaintance, but as a stranger," the Devil said.

Too eager to divine the mysteries of medicine, to earn his reclaim, Rafael signed the contract without reading the fine print, and when he thought of reading it, it was already too late.

For there he sat in the library, all by himself, a trace of sulfur in the air, not remembering what had just now happened. The windows were open, the curtains were fluttering, and the doors were ajar.

But instead of the Latin book he had been consulting, there

were several leatherbound volumes, translated from their original languages.

"Avicenna, Abulcasis, Rhazes," whispered Rafael as he studied the names of the authors. He didn't question as to how he had gotten his hands on all these volumes; he took them home and consulted them deeply, learning more about surgery and medicine than anyone in Europe knew.

And the bitter irony of it was that before he had a chance to practice any of it, the Venetian army sent him a conscription notice, with a clear warning—to defy it would be to choose death.

THIS BIT of memory did not come to him from his own mind; it came from the blood of the Devil coursing in him. And it was then that he realized that the Devil had kept an eye on him for quite a long time.

All for what?

For watching him turn into vampyre? For keeping him stowed away in a crypt?

Am I nothing more than a pawn to you in your grand game? Rafael wondered, amidst one wild thought after the other.

He had watched with great interest the relationship the Devil had with a writer named Joe Banbury. And his encounters with the witch, Lilly Frost, who later assumed the surname Thurman for some reason. He lived as vicariously as one would with a Devil's lifetime of memories and nowhere to go. He watched his interactions with God before his fall, and of his years spent in Hell, building an empire out of fire.

But the most bittersweet thing that he saw in the Devil's memories was his master, Elton Grando.

A strange torture, memory. And that too, someone else's. Rafael was left to ponder as to how he could have acted differently to avoid a fate of being trapped in a sarcophagus in a Bridgewater crypt.

He would pretend to sleep on an empty stomach, as he once used to when he was a child, and that would do him some solace. In pretend-sleep, he would pretend not to have any dreams or visions. And such was the way he passed his time, a vampyre growing more and more livid, more and more insane with each passing dark second.

Until one night, when the dark seconds ceased their passing, and someone relentlessly pulled off the stone lid of the sarcophagus, throwing it aside with such ease as which Rafael could not have imagined a human having.

Light fell upon his eyes for the first time in so many years, and what bitter irony it was that his freer was the same being who was his captor.

"I am so very terribly sorry about the delay, dear friend," the Devil said, smiling upon Rafael from outside the sarcophagus. "But I am going to need something of mine back from you. I hope you've been keeping it safe."

Lucifer pulled away the binds holding Rafael in place and yanked the frail, pale vampyre out of the sarcophagus, throwing him on the cold floor impassively.

"YOU!" Rafael yelled as he tried to regain control of his

limbs, struggling to get up. The crypt was the same as he remembered it from some years ago, and that gave him some comfort—that enough time had not passed. Just years and not decades, and what were years to an immortal?

"Yes, of course, me. I hope your long time here did not addle your brain, Rafael," the Devil said, adjusting the cuffs of his shirt, making them fall in line with the sleeve of his coat. And he did this so nonchalantly that Rafael had half a mind to leap at the Devil and wring his neck, but not before draining every ounce of his blood. How dare he stand there so guiltlessly?

"You left me to rot in here!" Rafael screamed, pulling himself up by the lamp sconce. It broke under the strain of his grasp, and he was thrown on his back once more. The Devil shook his head and approached Rafael, roughly pushing him to his feet, and then keeping him in place by holding him by the shoulders. When he was sure that Rafael wouldn't sway and fall again, Lucifer stepped back.

"Well, that's not really true, is it? Your kind don't fester or rot," he said, taking a good look at Rafael from head to toe. "In fact, you don't look a day older than when we met in Elton's manor."

"Don't take his name!"

"As if taking it will tarnish his memory?" The Devil sneered. "Your lord is dead. Has been for some centuries. I hope that in the time you spent with my blood coursing through you, you jogged through enough memories to recall signing a contract with me, one that gives me control of your soul in perpetuity. And before you whine about how unfair I have been, be thankful that I did not plunge you headfirst into a war that you did not have any hope of surviving, that the extent of my torture upon you thus far has only been imprisonment. Nothing else!" These last lines were delivered with such rage that Rafael forgot his own momentarily.

"What war are you talking about?" Rafael scoffed, folding his arms.

"Never you mind that, young doctor," the Devil said, spitting out his anger and assuming his calm demeanor once more. "Because, as it happens, there's another war happening right now. And I...was compromised. But in order to regain my old self, I am going to need my old blood, the blood that you have been safekeeping."

"And what if I don't want to give it back?" Rafael asked, taking a step back toward the open crypt entrance.

He thought he was mistaken, but there it was, clear as day: fear in the Devil's eyes.

"Now don't go and do something stupid, Rafael," the Devil growled.

"I don't want to be bound anymore. Let me go," Rafael bartered.

"Give me my blood and your freedom is yours. Not that there's much you can do with it anyway. The world is fucked, friend. Don't believe me? Go step outside, look to the skies and find the pillarless canopy collapsing in a brilliant display of thunder and crackle. There are forces far older than you and me, forces battling for control over the universe."

Rafael did not pause to listen to the rest of the monologue. Instead, he stepped out of the crypt and felt fresh air on his face, and even though he did not have any need of breathing it, he inhaled regardless, and looked all around him. Here was Bridgewater, as he remembered. No signs of the perpetual undertaker. No sign of the witch. Though, her house stood at the top of the town on a lone hill. Trees flailed all around in the merciless wind and, just as the Devil had said, there was a deep purple jag running along the length of the sky, pulsating with an angry light.

The Devil walked out of the crypt and put a hand on Rafael's shoulder. "See? I wasn't lying."

"What—"

Before Rafael could finish his thought, the Devil wrung his neck and split the skin above his carotid open. Satan had no need of sinking his teeth in the vampyre's artery. He simply pulled his scorching blood out of the vampyre's body like a skilled magician pulling a trick, and then sliced open his own wrist, allowing the suspended blood to travel from Rafael's neck to his own body, where it gently seeped into the cut and glowed a fierce orange.

When the last of the droplets of blood had finished migrating, the Devil's wrist sealed up in a matter of seconds, and he stood there exhilarated, breathing deeply, holding onto two tombstones for support as he laughed, his face flushing red, his eyes bulging out of their sockets. He grabbed the tombstones tighter, and they crumbled under the force of his grasp.

"That fucking hits the spot," Satan whispered. "It's all coming back to me now. And to think that I was, at one point, so disheveled, so lost. All my Hell, all my legions, lost. My vision. Fuck."

Rafael, in the meantime, adjusted his neck till it wasn't wrung anymore and sat up, feeling a great burden lift itself off him. He could no longer share the Devil's memories, and no longer did the scorch sear its way through his veins. He was freed from the blood of the Devil, though at what cost, he did not know yet. While his vision was still coming and going in fits of haziness and darkness, he heard the unmistakable flap of large wings, and when he turned around to address the Devil and discuss terms, he saw that he was all alone.

And hungry.

2

THE LAST INTERVIEW WITH THE DEVIL

"Congratulations on the mess you've made of things."

The Devil's words still hung suspended in the air as he walked leisurely, sniffing the flower in his hand. Joe Banbury did not know if he should be relieved or petrified at what he'd done. Against every instinct of his, he had gone to Hell with his friends in tow and released Satan out of his prison. In his mind, it felt like a captain of a sinking ship opening the prisoners' hold to let the jailed passengers have one final stroll before they inevitably sank with the ship.

But the Devil showed no such concern on his face or in his demeanor. Instead, he had just stood there, both hands resting on his cane, watching the rifts in the sky. A brilliant blaze of purple light and red hellfire meeting on the horizon. Parasites and Hellions clashing, consuming each other, engaging in endless battle.

"Why did you do all of this?" Joseph asked Satan.

He didn't respond, his gaze still focused on the horror unleashed in the skies above him, admiring the creatures that had been unleashed from the false Hell that Joseph had entombed them in.

Amy, Billy, and Blake were gathered around Lilly, who was still in shock, still hunched over Mallory's corpse. They did not speak, for to speak would mean diluting the severity of the moment. It wasn't just Mallory who had succumbed, but some of the strongest witches of the Axis Mundi alongside her. Their bodies lay strewn along the hilltop ruins. The cottage which they had called their last bastion, their sanctuary from the madness spilling all around them, was destroyed, an imploded mess of burning wood and shattered windows, its contents obliterated—beds, furniture, clothes, cabinets, and supplies, all.

Joe stood as a passive observer, his heart sinking at the realization that the Absolute had left them completely on their own, and that expecting any intervention from him would be folly. Because this was as bad as things were going to get, and the Absolute was nowhere to be found. Instead, he had handicapped Joe by taking away his power and authority as God.

"We must bury them," Lilly spoke after what seemed like two eternities stitched together. The Devil had disappeared since, leaving Joe to his own devices and wondering who here carried a pack of smokes on them. The din in the air was deafening, with explosions and screams and rift-cracks and demon howls in the sky, and yet, Lilly's soft voice carried over all of that, directly into Joe's ear. He nodded.

The others stood back and watched Lilly, unperturbed by everything going on around her, get back to her feet after adjusting Mallory on the ground, making her seem as if she was resting. Lilly closed her eyes, tears trailing down her face, and raised her arms up, palms facing the sky.

A dozen ditches were dug into the ground upon a wave of her hands, and then, with the next wave, the corpses of the witches and Sean Gainey were gently lifted into the air and lowered into them. All of them except Mallory. Her, Lilly took gently into her own arms, helped, of course, by Billy and Blake, and lowered into the grave manually. When she was done, she crawled out of the grave, covered in dirt, her face smattered with blotch marks. She stood in front of the open graves, the others standing around her in an arc.

"Rest thee well, witches of this earth, returned to this earth, your purpose of protection, preservation, purification fulfilled. Rest, sisters, and may these graves be as soft and gentle upon your lying bodies as cradles for a newborn. May we meet at the end of it all in the Axis Mundi, and may we meet as long-lost sisters, friends, mothers, daughters, witches. Rest, and know that I will not rest until our purpose is fulfilled. You have upheld each principle of the Axis Mundi and, in doing so, have lived to the zenith of your purpose. May your rest be every bit as soothing as your lives have been torrential," Lilly spoke, her voice quavering, interrupted by sobs and her breath hitching. Amy cried freely, holding Lilly's arm, her head resting on the witch's shoulder. Blake and Billy stood and watched in somber silence as dirt rose and filled each grave, leaving fresh, symmetric mounds. With a flourish of her wrist, Lilly made flowers appear atop each grave—wisterias, poppies, lilies, roses, and chrysanthemums. Above Mallory's grave, she made a bough of orchids appear, as if they were sentinels shielding the witch's grave from all calamities. The orchids waved in the wind.

Suddenly the night air was no longer smelling of hellfire and sulfur and debris, but of flower scent.

Joe, silent observer thus far, watched a veil of clouds travel above the hilltop, blotting out the purple madness happening in the sky. Soft rain poured from the clouds, wetting the fresh graves, freshening the flower, and dousing out any little fire here and there that still clung to debris and tree trunks.

For one second, listening to the rain meet the earth in its gentle patter, and the night covered in quiet darkness, he could almost believe that the world was back to its old ways, and that there was nothing wrong with it.

"LET'S you and I have a talk, son," the Devil said at last. His voice was calm, but beneath it was the rattle of something ancient and tired.

"I think it's time," Joseph replied, drained of ideas. "Not here. Not in front of everyone."

Lucifer tilted his head. For a moment, he looked exhausted —worn by the centuries of his imprisonment, by the coma of false earth and false memory that had wrapped him like chains. His gaze dropped, then rose again with slow irritation, as if weighing whether his son's request was worth indulging.

"Fine," he snapped.

A single clap of his hands shattered the world around them. The battlefield, the horizon, the sky—all gone.

They stood in a realm of nothing. A void without walls or ceiling, black and palpable, stretching beyond comprehension. There was no ground, only the suggestion of footing beneath their shoes. Every step they might take would be into infinity.

Joseph exhaled sharply. The silence pressed in on his ears, thicker than stone.

The Devil smiled faintly, leaning on his cane. "Better?"

"Much better," Joseph responded. "But what about the parasites and the Abstract?"

The Devil smirked at Joseph. "Boy, you know I love the theatrics. My dolls are taking care of the parasites, but they won't last long. The Abstract is coming, and the second these things get a chance to converge, they'll open a larger portal that will let it in. Relax, we're fine in here for now; here, time does not exist.

"Come," the Devil said as he motioned to the two red buster chairs that once sat as the jewel in the crown in Joseph's living room. "Sit."

The buster chairs flanked a grand fireplace, so grand that it stood six feet tall as the flames within danced their dance of red, yellow, and orange. There was nothing else surrounding it but a cream limestone marble—yet, in this dark space, it was a hark back to the moment when Joseph first met his father. It gave him a familiar warm feeling, a sense of calm that he hadn't felt in some time.

Both father and son sat in their respective chairs, the Devil on the left, Joseph on the right. They stared at each other as the fire crackled in front of them, the leather on the buster chairs worn but strong, creaking as the pair of them settled in. Part wonder and part fear of how they got here in the first place.

"Cigarette, dear boy? For old time's sake?" The Devil conjured two cigarettes from his inner pocket, reaching forward and offering one to Joseph. He stared at it for a moment, and his eyes darted back to his father before leaning forward to accept the offering.

Joe brought it to his lips, remembering an excerpt he had once written for the university rag, talking about the benefits of smoking. There had been much uproar from the student body upon reading his scandalous piece that suggested that smoking cigarettes could be beneficial to your health if you pulled your head out of your ass and ceased and desisted with Western hive mind crowd-think.

That there was such a thing called *pranayama* in Indian culture, where breathing in specific ways allowed you to gain different benefits—calmness, the onset of sleep, the relaxation of the airways, rejuvenation, anti-aging, and a dozen other amazing Ayuverdic advantages that the West considered pseudoscience. That little piece was called "The Breathing Method" and it extolled the virtues of tobacco, how nicotine was actually a nootropic that sharpened focus, improved memory retention, and had neuroprotective qualities that were only now being discovered by lab-coated hypocrites working for Big Pharma.

He'd written about the ritual of smoking, how it was a

pause in the madness of the world, breath made visible, fire held between two fingers. The closing argument of that piece was that maybe if people stopped smoking like an addict and instead took to it like a monk—slow, reverent, with intention instead of compulsion—they would understand that the body did not just thrive on oxygen; it thrived on rhythm. And where would you find better rhythm than in smoking a cigarette?

One of the professors had called it "an obscenity parading as philosophy," citing the staggering numbers of smoking-related deaths per annum. Joe had then told him that smoking-related studies had revealed that long-term smokers had lower levels of cognitive decline, Parkinson's, and Alzheimer's, stating in a follow-up letter in the rag that "what kills your lungs might save your mind, and you certainly seem like you're heading into senile territory, Professor, so you better smoke up while you have time."

"Good times," Joe whispered, and dragged deep from the cigarette.

As blistering pain coursed through his mouth and clogged his airways with what felt like molten lead, Joe thought amidst the blinding agony that this was Satan's doing; that he had spiked the cigarette for some kind of retribution.

"Were you in my position, would you have done it differently?" Joe asked, his face concentrated on the cigarette.

"You disappoint me, son," the Devil said, taking out a handkerchief and cleaning his armchair with it. "That you reached the zenith of power in this world and...and I am your fallback?"

"Where do sons go if not to their fathers when they have

failed and failed again?" Joe croaked, the burn of the cigarette scorching his throat and chest.

The Devil exhaled through his nose and looked into the void.

"So...so...what...now?" Joe groaned as a bout of dark, congealed blood spilled out of his mouth.

In that moment, he wondered—not for the first time—how it had all come to this. He wasn't an overnight God. His rise had been slow, brutal, layered in compromise and mistake. He had lived with his power long enough to forget what weakness felt like. He had abolished God, the woman that billions had worshipped. He had descended into Hell and walked back out.

And yet here, in the void, stripped of the illusion of his dominion, he felt like nothing. Clueless. A child at the fire with his father, waiting for meaning that would never come.

Lucifer leaned back in his chair, smoke curling from nowhere as he exhaled. His grin was sharp, but his voice was calm. "You don't understand it, do you? That's the beauty. You think the Antichrist is meant to lead. That was never it."

Joseph's mouth was dry. "Then what is it?"

The Devil turned, eyes gleaming. "To end the story."

"I did end the story. I collapsed both of you!"

"Dear boy, let's not act like you didn't imprison me in a version of what you called Hell."

"You knew?"

"Of course, I knew, you idiot."

"I was counting on you either forgetting or not giving a shit," Joe wheezed as he put his weight on the leather chair, leaning back. "So what happened? Why can't you just cut the cryptic shit and tell me what is going on?"

"What do the Bhagavad Gita, the Poetic Edda, the Bible, and all the books of the world say about the end of times? Kali Yuga ends in destruction, Ragnarok ends with Odin being eaten by Fenrir, and in the book that your mother liked to thump, the seven seals break, the plagues are let loose, beasts rise from the depths of the earth, and the Four Horsemen ride. I am talking about Armageddon, Joseph. It is here. And so am I."

Joe had expected this confrontation; in truth, he had expected it all the way back in Hell.

"How...how are you..."

"Back to normal, you mean?" the Devil asked. On his otherwise smooth and clean shaved face were weary signs of age and despair and anguish, his eyes heavy with burden, his lips pursed, and his cheeks sunken. He looked old, not as the proud Morningstar that had fallen, but as the balancing being witnessing everything fucked that he had to somehow put back in place. "I happen to be acquaintances with a vampyre. Before your Aeternum Trials, and everything that you did that allowed you to ascend to the Absolute and hold court with him, I had a hunch that shit was about to go sideways. I mean, you are the Antichrist, after all. One expects that you'd fuck things up for me, for yourself, and for the universe at large. So, to conserve myself, to save a vital part of myself should I fall, I poured my blood into the vampyre and preserved him in a crypt. That old blood now runs in my veins, Banbury. And I remember every single thing that you did, every turn at which you deceived me and tried to free yourself from me. Tell me, boy, did it all work out as you expected it would?"

Joe shook his head.

"Did you lift the Great Filter? Find your way to the Great, Mysterious Source Code of Existence? Was the Absolute everything you had expected him to be? Was godhood a hoot and a half?"

"You can stop now," Joe said, red in the face.

"Right. Sorry. My bad for pointing out all your horrendous failures," the Devil said, deridingly putting his hands up. "Only, there is no coming back from this, Joe. Like I said, you, acting as the sole agent responsible, have brought forth Armageddon. And here's the bit that those dainty little books don't mention. It always had to do with the clash of the Absolute and the Abstract. All I wished for was to delay Armageddon for as long as one could, maybe even avoid it altogether by preserving the balance. But you fucked that in the ass, didn't you? There can be no balance in a universe without both God and the Devil present, and you sent me packing like I was a pile of yesterday's newspapers!"

"How was I supposed to know?!" Joe scolded back.

"You were not supposed to know! You were supposed to know your place and place your trust in me! But you did not. And now, here we are at the end of time, all out of time," the Devil said.

"I know despair and misery are like your entire shtick, but is there something that we can do about the Abstract? If you take the prophecy part of it away, and just deal with the

Abstract as a self-contained crisis, is there something that you can do?"

"And why would I? What favor do you have to give me that I will listen to you?" the Devil jeered.

"We did sign a contract," Joe said. "You made me beg at your feet, make my pathetic bargain. I said that when we are done, I will leave you alone to rule over your domain. Everything you lost, you can restore it back to its original glory. Your hold on earth, its people, the old wager, everything. What you want, you get. But in return, you have to take care of the Abstract. And then you promised me that you will drag the Abstract into Hell where it belongs."

The Devil's face was blank, a clear tell that he had not completely recovered himself just yet, and that his forgetfulness would go away, but with some time. A lot had happened, and it was certainly a lot to process, even for someone as powerful as him.

"I remember the contract," the Devil said. "One we signed in blood. But the point remains, Joseph, that this is the apocalypse. My dragging the Abstract into Hell won't change that fact. There are fixed points in time, Joe. Fulcrums. Sacred collapses. And Armageddon was always one of them."

"What then?"

"Then, dear boy, we lean into the apocalypse, steer our vessel into the eye of the storm, and see what happens," the Devil said, looking at Joe with uncertainty.

Joe sat there in great silence for the better part of fifteen minutes. Then, when the silence got too heavy to bear, he said, "I am sorry for what I did."

"I know you are," the Devil said.

"No. I mean it. I genuinely am."

"Okay, let's get into it," the Devil said, sitting up in the chair and looking far more at ease than he had minutes earlier. "You know about the deal I made with Her. There have been other worlds, other deals. This one was...different. Evolution made it interesting. We waited around for millions of years, laughing at the crawl of it. Watching fish turn into men."

His lips curled in faint amusement. "Then came Yeshua. Her son, no matter how loudly the scribes painted Him as man. I suppose that was the fashion of the time. Imagine if he'd told the truth; he'd have been crucified a lot faster."

Joseph leaned forward. "Did you ever meet him?"

Lucifer's tone dropped, all his humor gone. "I did, back when I was sinister, meaner. Before I learned your little tricks of comedy, sarcasm, the whole human shtick. I met him in the place you call Eden. I whispered to him. I wanted to see if he would come to the dark side. I taunted him for days, soft motherfucker that he was, too green. He'd have been no son of mine, that's for sure."

He smirked faintly, tapping the arm of his chair. "But brave. And bravery...well, that can change everything."

Joseph leaned in. "So what happened?"

"Well, you know the story. It's mostly accurate. Except the three-day resurrection part— that was a fairytale for the masses, pretty much like the rest of that fictional book they cobbled together after he died. A bunch of authors who never even met him, inventing miracles and fables for crowd control. The only God damn thing they got right was the end of days, and even that was a coincidence." Lucifer chuckled, a low sound as if he'd been holding it in for two thousand years. "Your kind never cease to amaze me, but nevertheless, He had the same choice you did. Stood before me, Her, even the Absolute. And instead of choosing, he knelt," Lucifer paused for a moment, reflective almost. "The ultimate sacrifice, it went on to defy an age. He decided humanity wasn't ready for the real thing."

The Devil cracked his neck, then tilted his head at Joseph. "Smart, in its way. He knew he'd bleed on wood, and he chose it anyway. Said it was worth it if humanity got to limp forward another age. He annoyed the hell out of me, noble and predictable. A real Captain Justice!"

Joseph exhaled, staring at the fire. "And I pulled the exact opposite, huh?"

"Bingo!" Lucifer barked a laugh, snapping his fingers. Two bourbons appeared on side tables beside them, the glasses sweating in the firelight. "And look around, son—here we are. Cheers to that."

"I guess I'm asking you things that I should know the answer to."

"Not necessarily, dear boy, you're not meant to. Each Messiah isn't meant to connect to the next. You're not meant to see each other's failures or wins, otherwise you'd choose repetition over free will."

"So what was Mary like?"

"I didn't have much to do with her. Remember, this was Her concubine. This was their time to test the waters. I just didn't believe humanity was ready either, so in some weird way, I believed in Yeshua. It's the stupid other stuff that in another two thousand years, you'll look back and think humanity was insane."

"What other stuff?"

"You ever read the Book of John? That flowery horseshit about the Word becoming flesh? I'll tell you what that was—a drunk fisherman with a quill trying to make sense of something he'd never seen. Half of those authors couldn't spell their own names. But they built the longest-running PR campaign in history. And it worked." The Devil laughed.

"What, like the parting of the Red Sea?" Joseph laughed back, to no response from the Devil. "I mean, what's different now that couldn't have been different then? We just saw a monster tear a city in half, you think that won't be burned into history?"

The Devil leaned in. "Oh, it'll be burned into history, Joseph. But this time it will be an accurate report. Back then, humanity didn't understand a thing. They made shit up to keep people obedient. Miracles, plagues, talking snakes—anything to keep the crowd in line. And people swallowed it whole, because they were starving for order."

"And those that didn't believe?"

"Who gives a fuck? Let me ask you this: If some gypsy with long hair and a robe descended on Dallas, Texas, claiming to be the son of God, every asshole in town would have him locked up! So what's different now?" The Devil let out an enormous laugh. "Take Moses. That fucker climbed ten God damn hours up Mount Sinai? Have you been to that mountain?

Motherfucker, if I was mortal and made that trek, I'd be seeing stars once I made it to the top."

Joseph looked down into his bourbon and let out a small laugh.

"Look, Joseph, the issue I have with this fucking civilization is the irony, but it's also free will. You all choose who to vilify and who to worship based on trends. One person spews bile and she's crowned a comedian. Another slips a word and you nail them to the wall. It's all fashion. You're exhausting—and I love it. So who knows where the world will take these stories in years to come? All I can tell you is this: the Bible is a complete fabrication of events. If I feel anything for that young man—and he wasn't white, by the way—it's that humanity turned his death into a weapon and used it to control an entire civilization. And the biggest irony? People will look at what's unfolding now and say it proves the Bible was true. They'll point at the fire, the monsters, the end, and say, see? As if scripture was prophecy and not just another con. This is exactly why I wanted you to write *An Interview with the Devil*. Get Her out of the way. Strip the stage bare. And then you and I? We don't just watch the story—we rule it together."

Joseph leaned into the glow of the fire, letting its heat press against him. There was nothing left. No revelation, no clever escape, no more stories to tell. He had done all he could, and it hadn't been enough. And in that moment he realized the truth—even gods can fuck it up.

3

THE CALM BEFORE THE STORM

The sky above London was gloomy, nothing out of the ordinary for London; it was usually grey, wet, and cold. The parasite cast its web across the landscape. Landmarks blinked in and out of visibility as the sky cracked with purples, blacks, and lightning.

The streets were empty. There were no people and no traveling cars. The planet had moved back in time to a day when not even the animals roamed the streets. Only the echo of what had been. Those who survived the initial wave were hidden—burrowed deep into concrete cellars, water treatment tunnels, or in the high mountain ranges where the creatures rarely ventured. The others had been sucked into the parasite's portals, absorbed by its goo and transported to realms far beyond earth.

In Hampstead, a family was hiding in a bedroom. The home, a modest single-family house with two bedrooms upstairs and three rooms below, stood silent. Its shingle roof had collapsed in the corner. The once-orange brick was now ashen and brittle, stained grey from the clouds of debris and neurostatic ash shed by the parasite's feeding.

Inside the home, the family was braced against the wall where the bedside table used to be. The husband's wife in one arm, his daughter in the other—his hands covering their eyes as he scanned the hallway, waiting for the parasite to emerge. The door to the bedroom was wide open; no point closing it now, he thought. He wanted no more surprises.

"Be quiet," the father whispered to his family. There was nowhere to run, and nowhere else to hide. Whatever had come for them, they had to face head on.

The closet on the landing faced directly off the bedroom to the left; it's where the father's eyes were fixated. He knew that would be the portal of entry, for most of the news reports and remaining screams in the street had told him so. Silence had invaded the home for what felt like hours—and as he loosened his grip just slightly, his daughter whimpered, and then it began.

From behind the closet door, a light started to shine through the cracks, accompanied by a howling noise that sounded like wind in a long tunnel. The light was blue and white, almost too brilliant—and before it got bigger, it faded and pulsed, breathing in and out as if it had its own set of lungs.

But the light was not the living thing; the monster was.

A crackling noise began, small pulses of chatter and clicks. The father knew it had arrived and watched in horror as black tentacles began to creep through the closed closet doorway slowly. Thin slivers of glossy black arms exploring whatever immediate crack they could, holding onto the surrounding door frames and balcony. It glued itself to the door frame like black mold spreading faster than it should have. The door itself began to buckle and splinter under the pressure.

The door eventually burst open, and the tunnel that had been carved out behind it looked endless, shimmers of blue and white illuminating the hallway. Then, from inside the bedroom, he saw it, the creature's face emerging from the closet, passing the bedroom as if it hadn't noticed them. The father caught the profile of the parasite as it moved slowly, expecting to find its prey easily. An evil grin was plastered across its face. The back of its head was larger, it looked different than the others that were invading the planet—it was one of the queens.

As it moved through the hallway, it used its tentacles to grip onto each structure in the house, as if at any point it could fall back into the tunnel. Its movements were calculated, as if it was in a different dimension still, attempting to learn how to navigate this one while still tethered to whatever light was holding it in the closet.

Disbelief, before shock—and then a tear, rolling down the father's eyes and dripping onto the forehead of his child, prompting a whimper.

The creature stopped moving and the room went quiet.

For a moment there was silence as the father closed his eyes, his mouth tighter than it had ever been as he tried with all his might to not allow any noise to escape. He didn't care about his own fatality; that was inevitable. In this moment of silence, he prayed for his family, but more so his daughter who he couldn't protect. Failure and regret coursed through his mind as he only hoped that he would be taken first, so that he did not have to witness the massacre of his eight-year-old.

The silence had encapsulated them, the wind outside howling, the sky cracking and thundering as the father felt a drop of slime hit his leg. It was there, a few inches away from his face, staring at him. He opened his eyes and stared at it, shivering. It looked inquisitively at him. It knew his thoughts; it could read his mind and it knew what scared him. Its mouth opened in a grimacing way, the edges of its smile pointy, its teeth jagged like sharp pins.

He screamed and tightened his grip on his family, his face turning away from the monster as he pressed himself farther into the wall. The parasite leaned closer, its jagged grin widening—when the house shuddered, a sudden impact rattling the windows in their frames.

The father blinked in terror, as the window to the bedroom shattered and exploded.

Glass and brick sprayed across the room as a shrieking black shape crashed through the window. A Hellion, wings jagged like torn sails, slammed into the parasite with a sound like steel tearing. Its talons sank deep into the creature's glossy hide, ripping chunks of it free in gory splatters. It didn't hesitate, it knew its target and aimed straight for it. Its eyes black as night, its teeth were jagged and looked like they belonged to a dinosaur.

The parasite shrieked, its grin breaking apart into a howl

that vibrated the room as its tentacles lashed, wrapping around the Hellion's neck and wings, crushing drywall and timber as the two titans grappled, half of their demonic bodies hanging out of the hole that the Hellion had created when it crashed through.

The father breathed deeply for the first time in hours as they huddled in the corner stunned. The Hellion's jaws became unhinged, stretching wide—far too wide—and bit into the parasite's head, tearing half its skull away. Blue-white blood sprayed the walls, sizzling like acid where it struck the floorboards.

The father didn't think. He grabbed his wife and daughter and pulled them through the open door, stumbling down the staircase as the battle raged behind them. The noise from the creatures felt like a bomb going off, deafening anything within its reach. The father grabbed the car keys from the hook in the hallway next to the front door as the family grabbed their jackets. They ran into the street, joining a dozen other survivors who had crawled from hiding places during the chaos. Above them, the sky was filled with wings and webs, Hellions ripping into parasite forms as lightning split the clouds. The Volvo outside was still intact, sitting like a lifeboat as it awaited the click of the car key. The father threw his daughter into the back seat, the wife already inside buckling up.

"What about Oliver?" Rose, the daughter, cried. The family dog that they had hidden in the closet under the stairs was still alive and waiting for rescue as the wife gave a grave stare at her husband. He paused for a second, leaning on the window of the car, out of breath. Both of them wondered if it was worth running back to save the animal.

As he closed the car door to run back inside, he looked up at the second floor of the house where the Hellion had crashed through. The demon was holding onto the roof as it leaned out the window, staring at the father, its devilish grin suggesting in one breath it was ready to swallow the family whole, in another suggesting that it had just saved the family from death as it held the parasite's decapitated body in its other claw. It breathed heavily, its chest rising up and down, joining the father in sync as they stared at each other. Then, as if called by some signal, it looked up to the cracked sky and took flight, the parasite's tentacles trailing behind as it carried it away.

As THE FAMILY sped from their ruined home, they looked up through the sunroof of their Volvo and saw Armageddon unfolding above them.

The sky was split with fractures of purple and black, lightning burning through the cracks like veins. Portals gaped open in the air, on rooftops, even in the middle of empty streets—windows to somewhere else. From them, the parasites came crawling, their slick black bodies heaving through the openings like spiders squeezing through cracks in the wall.

Each time one emerged, a Hellion was waiting. They dropped from the clouds with shrieks that rattled glass and buildings, colliding with the parasites mid-leap, slashing at tentacles, tearing flesh apart before it could gain footing. They were interceptors, demonic anti-missiles, their claws and fangs shredding whatever tried to cross into Earth.

The city burned beneath their battle. Parasites scaled lampposts and the sides of buildings, pulling themselves into this world with clicking grins, only to be ripped away in explosions of blood. The Hellions were merciless, swooping and diving, their wings blotting out the fractured sky.

In the back seat, Rose pressed her hands to the glass, her eyes wide. "Are they...angels?" she whispered.

Neither parent answered. The mother only pulled her close, while the father tightened his grip on the wheel and drove on into the chaos.

LILLY SCREAMED as she skidded to a halt somewhere that wasn't quite where she had expected to emerge. It wasn't like her power to wane so suddenly, and yet, now that it had, she knew all too well why it had happened. Given enough strain, a tree twig snaps in two. Metal is known to bend when pushed with enough brute force. Underneath everything—her power, her influence, her knowledge—she was just a woman. A woman who had just buried her kind and had somehow lived to tell the tale. A woman who had walked through the scorch of hell and had emerged unburned. A woman who had born the tortures of time and tide, lost more than one could perceive, and was continuing to lose more and more with each passing second, with no end in sight.

The collapse of empires, the loss of loved ones, dear

friends departing, old enmities dissolving—time was a strange thing, a drain, and it was ironic that after all these centuries that she had lived, here, at the end of all things, time was one thing she was short of.

"Lilly, are you okay?" Amy, covered in dirt and fallen leaves, had gotten back on her feet and was tending to Lilly, who had not shifted ever since she had fallen out of the portal. Her head had hit an oak trunk, and her consciousness was coming and going in waves.

"I..."

"Look." Billy, lying on his back in the tall grass where he had fallen, pointed to the sky as it cleared of rain clouds. "There's no more of that...parasite business."

"Parasite business?" Blake asked, pulling the man up, but Billy refused to budge. He was in a whimsical mood, a mood that had come after much too long a time. "Is that what you call it in your head?

"The inside of my head knows no language. Thoughts come in all shapes and sizes, and most of them are non-verbal. I shall see a star in the periphery of my mind's vision and know that I am thinking about Marilyn Monroe. I shall see a shoe hanging suspended in the air and it'll be clear to me that I need to go buy a new pair. I—"

"We get it. You're real special because you're a visual thinker," Blake said, sighing vexedly as he pulled Billy roughly, bringing him back to his feet.

"And a bunch of other shit, but you wouldn't care to know that, would you now?" Billy asked with a tinge of irritation in his tone.

"At this point, friend, I'm just happy we're alive," Blake said, looking around the place where they had fallen. It appeared to be a lake, one with exceptionally still and clear water. The lake didn't have an end in sight, and that was partly due to the strange fog that was hanging suspended over it, but the bank that was in sight was marked with bushes, shrubs, cattails, reeds, and wildflowers. They swayed in the breeze, unconcerned with what was happening around them.

"Lilly?" Amy whispered, turning her over with much effort. Lilly was not unconscious, but she was not moving either. Her eyes were looking in the distance, a trail of blood emerging from her nostril and smearing her upper lip. She breathed laboriously, taking Amy's arm and helping herself sit up.

"I feel like my magic has closed itself off to me," Lilly said. "I cannot...do...the things that once came to me like breathing and blinking."

Amy put a gentle, affectionate hand upon Lilly's shoulder and gave it a squeeze, saying, "That's fine. We don't need Lilly the witch right now. We need Lilly the person."

"Do you? Because I don't know where the hell I have landed us," Lilly said, self-doubt creeping in her words. "I think you'd all be better off without me."

"Nonsense," Blake said, walking over to her. Billy followed close behind with a spring in his step. "We'd be nowhere without you."

"You can lay it a little less thick, you know," Billy said, grinning. "A woman's in pain, for God's sake. Hey, Lilly. Look. No more of that purple bullshit in the sky. Look!"

Lilly followed the direction of his index finger, staring at the sky full of ordinary stars—no rifts, no cracks, no unnatural lightning.

"I don't know if that's all that good of an omen," Lilly said, taking Amy's hand and getting back on her feet, grunting as she did so. "The Devil walks the earth again, and all those who were waging a war on it are suddenly quiet. We may have freed Lucifer, but it would be foolish to think that he's going to be on our side. He's the Devil. He cannot help it."

"But Joe's with him. They made a contract," Amy said.

"Oh, my dear, this entire thing is unfolding because of the Devil and his contracts. He lured your brother in to write a book about him, and when you write a book about the Devil, hell follows. This. What you're seeing all around you. This is it. We're all in fucking hell."

"Listen," Amy said, "I do not claim to understand just how forlorn you feel; your anguish is your anguish. But I am sorry for your loss. But I also want you to know that the Lilly we all know and love is much more stronger than she thinks. Despair is not a color that suits her."

Lilly gave her a weary smile, and then gave her face a pat. "Thanks." Then, sighing, looking around, she said, "Right then. Where are we?"

"Like I said, seems like a lake," Blake began.

"Not just any lake. It's a lake of my creation. Well, partly. The lake was already here. I just enchanted it," Lilly said. She cast a glance around. Behind them, there was the wild forestry of Massachusetts, oaks with their twisting finger-branches, ancient elms, hemlocks and red maples and white pines all occupying the same space, their leaves vying for canopy-space.

The forest imposed upon the lake, and given just how thick it was with trees and undergrowth, it also served the purpose of a barrier. To prevent those who had no business near the witch's abode from getting through. And if they somehow did, then they still had the lake to contend with. The lake with its sentience, its fog, and its ill will to any trespasser. At one point, during the height of her power two centuries ago, Lilly had considered making the lake a portal. But that was too laborious, and there was always the risk of some unsuspecting summer swimmer somehow traveling to another part of the world—or worse yet, the Axis Mundi—without knowing how they got there in the first place.

"It seems that we are not that far from Bridgewater after all," Lilly said with a smile, and then began walking beside the lake bank, intending to cross its circumference so she could get to the other side, where the town lay in quiet sleep at this hour of the night.

Or quiet desolation, but it was too soon to tell. The fog on the other end of the lake made it very hard for Lilly to discern what was happening in the town itself.

The others walked beside her, a little uncertain as to where they were headed, but mostly positive that the witch would not lead them astray. They walked in the quiet of the night, avoiding the snarls and the long grass and the rocks, keeping in a single line led by Lilly, with Billy at its tail end. Blake, with his military training kicking in, kept a firm eye on the environs to make sure that nothing jumped them out of the darkness. Amy just wondered what had become of her brother, and what lay ahead.

"Why *did* the sky go back to normal? Does this mean that we don't have to deal with the Abstract and its parasites anymore?" Billy couldn't help himself.

"Have you ever watched one of those old war documentaries, the ones that are the bread and butter of the History Channel?" Blake humored Billy.

"I can't say that I have. I tried to watch that channel one time, and some kooky old idiot was saying that pyramids were built by aliens. Naturally, I disagreed, and therefore, decided to never watch that channel again."

"You missed some good stuff then," Amy said.

"Like *Vikings?* That show was pretty fucking good," Lilly said from the front, reminding herself of the few times that she had allowed herself to relax and indulge in ordinary human activities like binge-watching shows.

"Yeah!" Amy said, chuckling. "Why don't we have men like in *Vikings* anymore?"

"Oh, they're there, all right. Same tattoos, hairdo, knotted beards. They wear obsequious brands that make them look like they're lumberjacks or some such, and yet they drink artisanal coffees and listen only to vinyl," Lilly said, chuckling to herself. But when no one else chuckled back, she looked behind her and found them all looking confused.

"Er. Hate to break it to you, but the whole 'hipster' fad went out of style twenty years ago, girl," Amy said.

"It's been twenty years already? I guess time is funny that way, isn't it? Here I thought that it was only a matter of yesterday," Lilly said quietly, losing her confidence.

"But we get it. Those guys, they were a pain in the ass,"

Blake said, and then, blushing a little, added, "For a while, I was one of those guys too. And I can tell you with a fair degree of confidence, I was being a really conceited prick."

"But she's right. Where are the men of yore?" Billy said, scratching his head. "What do we get today? Alpha bros? Tech bros? Finance bros? Gym bros? It's bros this, bros that. Jesus Christ, give me a break."

"Okay, enough man-hating," Amy said. "What were we talking about before we went off on this tangent?"

"The History Channel," Blake said.

"Shh."

Lilly put a finger to her lips and with her other hand aired caution to those behind her. They ducked instinctively. A large airborne creature swooped low over them, its batlike wings flapping fast, its long tail trailing the grass as it flew by them. A monster, freshly released from Hell, carrying the corpse of a parasite in its claws, ripping into it with its fangs, and consuming it mid-flight. Once it had flown away, Lilly emerged from the grass, closing her eyes, and raising her arms to her sides, feeling the wind rush as hundreds of demons soared through the night, black blots against the blue sky, infernal predators all carrying corpse upon corpse of defeated parasites from all over the world. It was a spectral sight to behold, one that did not fill Lilly with despair, but hope.

"I wonder where they're all flying to," Blake said, getting up from the grass and dusting his clothes off.

"They are going to their master," Lilly said.

"I think that explains why some of the portals closed up, eh, Billy?" Amy said, giving Billy a gentle shove.

"Yeah. That could be it," Billy said, his face uncertain and marred with fear. "Let's hope it's nothing worse than that."

"Nothing worse than a bunch of demons let loose upon Earth, you mean?" Lilly asked.

Billy shrugged, and they all continued walking toward the town. By now, having walked enough, it was coming into view —the house on the hill and the suburbs below it.

"Why Bridgewater, Lilly?" Amy asked. "Like, I know there's a story there. I'd like to know."

"Where would you like me to begin?" Lilly asked, as there was still quite a ways to go.

"I suppose all the way from the top?" Amy asked. "We've still got a long walk in front of us."

"Fine," Lilly said. "Well, once upon a time, I used to live in Salem..."

And as the group walked toward Bridgewater, Lilly regaled them with her tale, starting with her birth, then with everything that followed. And as she recounted each of the important parts of her life, she came to the realization that she wasn't as hapless and helpless as she was thinking she was just now. She had gone through bigger ordeals than this, and even if that was not true, even if there was no ordeal bigger than this one, then at the very least she had dealt with her fair share of shit. Whether it was the women whom she had to sort out in limbo, her husband and son dying, or Elton Grando and the collapse of his empire in Alta, California, in the 19th century, she had lived through enough shit to compile volumes of books that people wouldn't believe as they read them.

And the latest of the ordeals, the one that had to do with

Joe fucking Banbury, that was a story that was still being written.

"And that brings us to the end of my story as well as the end of our path," Lilly said, pointing to the suburb road they'd walked up to. The road was leading up to the hill.

"Holy shit," Blake said in a soft whisper. "I didn't know any of that."

"How could you? I never shared any of this with anyone before," Lilly said tiredly. "Come along now. None of us have cars, and we've got quite the trudge up the hill."

"Are you sure you can't tap into your magic and make us fly to the top?" Amy asked.

"I'm sorry, love. I tried. I am drained. But don't worry. Nothing a few tinctures, a good cup of coffee, a warm bath, and some long sleep won't heal," Lilly said, hoping it was true. Because she had no idea what she was going to do if it was not. The people she'd go to for advice regarding her magic were dead.

"Hey. You never told us something," Billy said, still in his whimsical mood.

"What's that?"

"Which era was your favorite? I mean, we have a bona fide immortal witch in our midst who's been around since the 1600s. Which era did you enjoy most?" Billy asked. Blake and Amy nodded out of curiosity.

Lilly sighed, looking at the town, then toward the crypt. And then, finally, she looked up at the hilltop house. With a smile coming to her face, she said, "You'll think it's a cop-out answer, but the 70s in Manhattan was a fun time. I faced another potential apocalypse then too, but—when I had my son and my husband. Those were the best times of my life."

Amy had a half-impressed expression on her face. Blake mirrored the amazement with the way his eyebrows were pulled back. He asked, "And what about now?"

"This era? The 21st century?" Lilly asked, beginning her journey up the hill. "Well, if the Devil weren't such a big nuisance, and if Joe hadn't gone and messed with the world the way he did, I'd say that this is the best era. All the music from all the ages, all the food from all over the world, all sorts of clothes to wear, billions of places to go, fast cars, every luxury at your fingertips, from information on your phones to menus from a thousand restaurants on your DoorDash app. This was supposed to be the age of excess, of spoiling yourself. It's no wonder why the Armageddon is happening now, of all times."

"Wait, you sort of skipped a beat there. The Armageddon is happening?! The biblical one?!" Blake blurted out, his cheeks pale, sweat on his forehead.

"Yes. All the signs are there. Every portent points to the end of the world. And here we thought that freeing the Devil would do something in our favor," Lilly said wearily, and then, for the remainder of their climb up the hill, she did not speak, and neither did the others. The house atop the hill stood with light in its windows, as if it was an alive thing waiting for them to come home.

Whether it was Joseph's releasing of the Devil, or the Devil himself, no one could say. But the demons that followed him out of the never-Earth realm had spread thin across the planet. In America they hunted with glee, clawing parasites back into the portals that spawned them or tearing into the homes of the humans they devoured. There were victories, but not enough.

In London, the air felt wrong. For something was stirring.

On Westminster Bridge, parasites pulled themselves from the Thames, their black limbs slapping wet against the girders as they climbed. One by one they dragged themselves onto the roadway, their bodies slick and grinning, until the bridge swarmed with them. Then they stopped. Dozens stood motionless as their heads cocked, their jagged smiles frozen as though they were listening for something.

Above, demons clung to rooftops and lampposts, wings tucked tight, eyes gleaming. They hissed and snarled, some laughing, some whispering guttural prayers. They knew what was coming, and they did not fear it.

Inside the blasted shell of a building behind the London Eye, soldiers crouched low against shattered windowsills. They had been perched there for days, firing their weapons at portals to little avail. Now, as the city fell silent, their sweat dripped from cracked helmets onto hot rifles, fingers tightening on triggers that would never be enough.

One parasite reached across the bridge, its tentacle slick and trembling, brushing against another. The touch lingered, strands of black goo stretching between them like tar pulled too thin. More followed. Dozens pressed their limbs together, weaving a lattice of glistening muck across the bridge. The sound of it was nauseating—wet fibers tearing, knitting, snapping back together.

The net grew thicker. In minutes it stretched from one bank of the Thames to the other, sagging heavy above the water. Parasites clambered up the facades of nearby buildings, anchoring the strands higher, hauling the blackness upward. The web rose with them, becoming a vertical shroud, a spider's curtain blotting out the skyline.

People gaped from the convoy as soldiers forgot their triggers. Even the demons tilted their heads, watching the thing grow with grins carved wider and wider.

The mass pulsed. Slow, steady, like a giant's heartbeat. Each pulse lit the web with sickly blue light, veins of radiance traveling through the tar. One by one, the parasites feeding it began to dissolve, their bodies collapsing inward, tentacles melting into the black lattice.

The bridge groaned beneath it while the whole web became a canvas of shifting, luminous flesh, stretching higher, wider, until it seemed the city itself would disappear behind it.

It tore open in the center of the web slowly, widening with a groan like metal twisting. Blue light poured through the seams, rippling across the lattice of black goo. It grew wider, higher, until the entire span of the bridge vanished behind it. The air bent around it, sucking inward as if the city itself were being pulled through. Glass rattled in the windows along the embankment. The Thames churned and rose against its banks. Soldiers and civilians clamped their hands over their ears as a low-frequency hum rolled out.

And then, it came.

The Abstract.

Its bulk poured through the opening in broken stages, as though even the portal strained to contain it. Black limbs as wide as tree trunks clawed at the webbing for real estate. A head emerged—grinning, the jaw unhinged and dripping with mucus that steamed where it struck the stones. Its body heaved behind it, a grotesque mountain of flesh that bent under its own gravity, folds collapsing, tentacles anchoring to buildings on both sides of the river just to keep its weight. Its breath was damp and heavy, coating the air in a stench that made soldiers vomit onto their rifles.

The Abstract paused, tentacles curling and tasting the air, then looked up and pushed forward, letting out a groan that was more vibration than sound, a quake that rolled through the bridge into the city beyond.

The parasites below clicked in unison as their king dragged itself into the world.

4

ARMAGEDDON

"It's here." The Devil stood up as his laughter with his son was interrupted, his face more serious than Joe had ever seen before.

"What?" Joe responded, sitting up, but the Devil didn't answer.

He stood staring into the void, his eyes turning completely black as he chanted a spell only known in a whisper. As he mumbled to himself, another billowing portal conjured, but this portal did not lead to Bridgewater to join the Tribe, or any other such placid place.

This portal led to Hell.

It was not the Hell that once was, for now, where once fire reigned and pillars of scorch held the canopy of black fumes over millions of burning souls, there was no cinder in the kiln, and instead of flame, all was ash.

The Devil did not speak at once, and nor did Joe. There

was a great dark gray nothingness where once Hell had been —a black crater as big as an entire continent, and the two visitors standing at its edge, looking below, in the great ruins of the cities, the industries, the wilderness, and everything that made Hell, Hell. Satan had said nothing to Joe on the journey; he was transfixed, showing a side to Joe that he had never exposed before.

"*My name is Ozymandias, King of Kings;*
Look on my Works, ye Mighty, and despair!
Nothing beside remains. Round the decay
Of that colossal Wreck, boundless and bare
The lone and level sands stretch far away," the Devil recited, looking at his barren kingdom. He looked neither like his earthly form, the one with the demure clothing and princely stature, nor like his hellish self with the wings and horns and tail. Instead, he was an ashen mix of the two, black his wings, matching the black of his suit, black his horns, matching the black of the soot that had gathered on his white cuffs and his oxfords.

"What even is this?" Joseph asked.

"The floor of Hell, the lowest circle. Dante got that one thing right. There were circles. And this place, this crater, is the ninth circle. Betrayers of family, country, guest, and benefactors, one and all, were in this circle called Treachery. I, myself, having been perceived as a betrayer by God in the beginning, was sent down to the depths of Hell, made to freeze in the Cocytus Lake," the Devil said, walking down the slope of the crater, Joe following behind. "Of course, it was after some thousands of years had gone by that I saw myself not as a betrayer and decided to let myself loose upon this realm, quickly becoming its ruler, realizing my destiny as something that I controlled and no one else."

Joe gulped raw air.

"Until you came," the Devil said, staring at Joe with his penetrating gaze. "And suddenly, I was not the one controlling my own destiny. I was no one at all, at the end, when you ceased my existence and put me in a hell of your own making. Robbed of memory. Robbed of power."

The Devil turned his attention elsewhere, looking at the crater, rubbing his hands calculatingly. "But it matters not. There is no use bringing up old, bitter matters. Hell is in tatters, but its master is back. Here to rebuild Hell anew, even if it means that it gets destroyed in Armageddon. Do you know why a mason builds, a writer writes, an artist paints, Joe, yourself being one of those things?"

"Not because they can, but because they must," Joe said, pulling his sleeves back. If the Devil was going to rebuild Hell, the least Joe could do was assist in any way he could.

"Right you are," the Devil said, looking at the dark sky, at the black bounds of Hell. "All right then." He stretched his arms, bringing them back together in a slow, singular clap, saying, "Let there be light." Joe caught a glimpse of mischief on the Devil's face.

It was too quick to notice, but Joe's eyes picked up on the slit the Devil had made appear under his wrist. Blood poured forth from that slit, drenching Satan's hands as the clap resounded loudly and with much echo all over.

First came a surge of fire billowing from the Lightbringer's palms, that fire burning brighter than anything Joe had ever seen, and he had seen all of Heaven and the Absolute. Lucifer's grime and soot burned clean off of him, leaving behind angelic white wings and a pristine face aglow with the joy of creation as the flames swept everywhere. Joe felt their scorch the first time they enveloped him, but then, his innate infernality took hold and saved him from the fire, allowing him to relish it as one would a cool wind.

Flame upon flame flourished from the Devil's hands, burning away all darkness and shadow, all gray and soot, until there was only bright orange fire lit as far as he could see. And amidst that fire, in the center of the crater that was once the lowest point of Hell, stood Lucifer, wings stretched, face refreshed, and hands bloodied.

"What's with the blood!?" Joe screamed over the deafening roar of sentient fire rushing to and fro to serve its purpose.

"You didn't think that the Lord of Hell wouldn't go around carrying a backup?" Lucifer laughed, flames erupting from his open mouth, sparks emerging from his eyes, his entire being coming undone in a brilliant display of fire and fury. And yet, there he stood, despite that undoing, the dark part at the center of the flame. "I am all of Hell and what dwells within!"

Joe stood watching the basin of the crater spew forth dark magma, filling itself up. Above him, pillars were beginning to form, pillars of roaring red inferno.

"God was always an inconsequential bitch." The Devil laughed further, clapping his hands, more droplets of blood spilling from his wrist, from his palms. "Took credit for what she didn't do. Came upon a blossoming universe and then told the biggest lie ever. That she created it in seven days. And all the religious lot of this world lapped it up like gospel. I'll tell you what happened, Joe Banbury, if you'd listen close!"

Even though he was the son of Satan himself, the scorch was getting too hot, suffocating Joe where he stood. He could not see anything with the flames erupting in every direction in every shade of fire that ever existed—blue, dark orange, green, and even black. The air was all sulfur and fumes, making him dizzy.

"Getting a little too hot for you there, sport?!" Lucifer's voice came from the fire itself. Joe could no longer see where he was. Could only feel his presence everywhere. The fire was forming different shapes, shapes creating stories that transcended words, showing Joe a glimpse of what had happened at the beginning of time. It was nothing that Joe didn't know before (well, a version of it, at least), but having Hell itself tell the story of creation from the perspective and means of flame was a profound experience, even if that profundity was wrapped in the profane.

Now the flames were leaping and taking the shapes of valleys and hills, and upon those hills, houses made of basalt, obsidian, bone ash, and charcoal formed, taking the shapes of cities and fortresses. Bloodstone slabs formed grand archways. Charred sulfur-crusted stone formed roads. Black metal turned into chains to bind the more untamable of Hell's elements. Before his eyes, Pandemonium, the legendary city of Hell, erupted from the ground and assumed its imposing stature in the grand landscape of inferno.

"There was no end to the Abstract's chaos, and back then,

the Abstract and his useless creation, God, sulked in a corner of the endless dark, seeking refuge from the sentient night and all the creatures that lurked in its veil. There were no seven days. There were seven hundred thousand infinities that spanned this terrible time for the Absolute and God. And after they tried everything that came to their collective minds, they struck rock against rock in desperation, like brute cavemen. And from the striking of that flint came a spark. A spark that took life and became a flame. I am that flame, Lightbringer! It was not God who said, 'Let there be light.' It was me, Lucifer Morningstar, who said, 'I am Light!' And with each passing second after my existence, I burned fiercer, coming into my own, the Absolute and his bitch fanning me with their hands, making me bigger!"

Joe was on his knees, screaming in response to the intensity of the story, tears streaming from his face as he recognized the truth about his father, and it had taken him this long to realize it. Whether he was speaking in metaphor or not did not matter, what was happening now was real.

"As I grew, so did my blaze, so did my light, and they witnessed, these effete two, that the Abstract screamed and recoiled away from my scorch, driving away to the furthest expanses of endlessness, leaving the blank universe a canvas for the Absolute to create upon. He begged me for my fire so he could fashion the sun and all the brilliant stars that you see burning in the night sky. Without me, Joe Banbury, there would not be a universe. Just as there would be no Hell."

The great cliffs and creeks of Hell jutted from below, rivers of magma flowing between them. Dungeons carved themselves deep into caves. Castles and abbeys, ruins and remnants of forgotten civilizations, all of it came back to populate the topography of this renewed abyss.

"And when they had no more use for me, they plotted against me, threw me in this place they deemed a prison. How laughable. That my fire would burn me or my own? No. Hell accepts. Hell soothes. What of the souls who seemingly suffer here? There was no place in Heaven for the imperfect. I took them in by the millions, by the billions! There was no room in Heaven for the fallen. I gave them good graces and ordained them as leaders, princes, dukes, powerful demons, powerful devils! I did that once. I can do it again!"

Satan's roar rumbled like elemental thunder, and for a brief moment, the flames parted, giving Joe a view of the Devil, standing there like a careful gardener, hunched over the ground, his blood dripping on the ground, forming moving shapes.

"Lit is the cinder and the kiln! Lit is the flame that was doused, doused it is no longer! Arise, my legion, for I am you, and you are many! Stir your eyes open from your slumber and take the name of your Lord Satan, for his age is come once more! Arise, Baphomet, Beelzebub; arise, Asmodeus; arise, Ambassador of Greed Mammon; arise, Leviathan, and be roused from your slumber, Belphegor, and where is the Lord of the Wind, the Lord of the Flies?! My Wrath and Pride call you forth, demons one and all!"

And just like that, they were not the only two in Hell any longer, as blood and flame and magma took shape all around Joe, red wings by the thousands flapping viscera off bodies, shrieks ringing through the air, limbs protruding out of misshapen bodies, giant beings unfurling themselves from behind veils of flame.

Joe stood miniscule against the grand spectacle that was hell rekindled, repopulated.

As the demons huddled around their lord, Lucifer plunged his bleeding hand into his own chest, digging past his own bones and procuring an ash coffer from within his body. He dropped that coffer on the ground. "Here. Tend to the souls that populated Hell, and see each to their duties, their penance. And once you have all taken a few breaths, and rested enough to recount what this place was, what you were, then you may harken me, for I have the task of all tasks for you," Lucifer said, looking in Joe's direction and nodding.

If this was Hell reborn, Joe wasn't sure that his bloodline would spare him. After all, it was his fault that Hell had been eviscerated in the first place.

"I know what you are thinking, Joe," the Devil said, the burning eyes of all his demons affixed on him. "But you would be mistaken if you think that we would exact retribution. This is not your reckoning. Not just yet. You will find, my son, that Hell is the perfect place for those looking for second chances."

As the Devil walked away, Joe did the only thing that made sense to him. He followed his father through the stone doorway that had appeared. The Devil pushed open the doors with both his hands and stepped inside a Tuscan landscape, where, far upon a quaint hill, amidst much greenery, lay his idyllic house, calling to its master with its elegant arches, its white walls, its broad windows, and its sprawling terraces.

“I think you and I will have a nicer time talking to each other in here than out there, don’t you think?” the Devil said, beckoning Joe to walk alongside him instead of just trailing behind.

“As Hell comes alive, the Abstract recoils once again in terror, rethinking its next moves,” Satan said, walking up the cobblestone path leading to the front door. He knocked on the door of his own house.

A familiar face greeted him from inside, wearing all black, an amused and half-bored expression on her face. “Lord, you’re finally back. Oh, and you brought company.”

“Come now, Delphine. Is that any way to treat a guest?” Lucifer said, taking her arm and helping himself inside.

Joe walked inside, his perception of everything he thought he knew warped. If what the Devil had said was true, then he could no longer trust the Absolute.

IT WAS ONLY the major cities that had suffered the worst of it. London. Paris. New York. Cairo. Tokyo. Portals had opened above landmarks, as if the parasite meant to desecrate monuments first, to make symbols fall before bodies did. Smaller towns, villages, the countryside—these places still held on, even if barely. The parasites and their portals would discharge every so often, with a more curious than vicious parasite entering the area. People watched through cheap televisions, old radios, cell phones half out of charge. When the international networks went dark, it fell to the local stations, whoever still had power, whoever could hold a signal, to carry the burden of telling the story.

In London, the BBC broadcast from a basement, the camera shaking as shells burst above. The anchor's tie was loose, his eyes red with smoke, but he read his script until the teleprompter failed, then spoke freely. "The Thames," he said, voice catching, "is crawling with them." His voice went quiet, as if admitting it too loudly would let one inside.

In New York, a drone feed played across every network that still had bandwidth—a parasite scaling the side of a skyscraper, its grin reflecting neon as Hellions swooped in to tear it down. An anchor whispered into her mic, "Angels," as if daring the word to make it true.

Cairo's state channel cut in and out, its last coherent feed showing fire along the banks of the Nile. The reporter stood firm at his desk, refusing to look at the smoke gathering in the glass behind him. "Remain indoors," he said steadily. "We are still here. The city is still here." His mouth trembled when the pane finally shattered.

Paris showed the Eiffel Tower in silhouette, the web of parasites stretching from its iron ribs. Tokyo showed subway mouths vomiting black limbs into neon avenues. São Paulo showed drones scanning the Avenida Paulista, where survivors held sheets painted with desperate words pleaing for help.

Not all feeds ended clean. Some carried the sounds of things entering the studio itself—anchors gasping, microphones dropping, the static of sudden endings. Others simply went dark, replaced by color bars and silence. But still, across the world, men and women who had trained their whole lives to sit upright and speak through crisis, now sat upright and spoke as the world ended. Their reports gave no solutions and no strategies. They offered only confirmation: the nightmare was not local, not singular, but shared.

"Where is Joseph Banbury?" asked one reporter.

It began as a low sound. A low, heavy thunder that rattled from the earth underneath everyone's feet, shaking the buildings. Any remaining shards of glass that had been standing in the windows of the nearby buildings promptly fell like icicles that could not hold on any longer.

In an ironic twist of timing, the clock on the infamous Big Ben began to ring, the chime of each bell sounding like the Collectors had come to reap the last lost souls of London.

Ding. Ding. Ding.

A vortex of cold air swept through, hurling debris into the river and whipping the hair and clothes of those who dared to watch.

The storm gathered its charge and struck—the first bolt slamming into Westminster Bridge.

The ground split, asphalt peeling open like skin. The rupture shook buildings for miles. In the counties, horses screamed and bolted. In the outer towns, from Chiswick to Walthamstow, buildings shook on their foundations.

The crack in the Thames widened, water rushing in and sucking the air from the banks—a warning of worse to come.

The great Ferris wheel of the Eye spun slowly, eerily, with

no electricity, and soldiers who had steadied their rifles at the Abstract now watched in disbelief as the ground beneath their boots ripped apart and vomited legions of Hell. Fire breathed, as smoke rose into the air.

A buzzing sound ensued, and the noise of rubble came next. It was a sound that could not be rationalized or described.

And then they came.

Thousands of demons erupted from the seams—some crawling like beasts, some armored in obsidian, others winged and dripping ash. Observing the world as if they had just seen it for the first time.

The world that had cowered before the parasites now stopped and looked toward the bank of the river, watching a new horror as the hellions gathered in the streets, shrieking their first breath in centuries.

Opposite them, the Abstract's parasites swarmed its glistening frame, lining up like soldiers to defend their master.

The Abstract didn't falter. It had fought greater wars. It heaved back, breathing in the oxygen that was foreign to it, before bringing its glossy black tentacles to the sky and swooping it back down along the bank, killing hundreds of hellions as it thrashed.

The rest of the demons flew or crawled away, not in submission, but in retreat before planning their next move. This was no ordinary army; the monsters that had breached Hell had been waiting for this very moment for centuries...

Armageddon.

The sky continued to turn black, and as the sun caught

brief moments of reprieve, it shone through smaller holes in the clouds, beating down on the city as if to give hope to the demonic forces that were about to play their best move yet.

Then, without warning, Satan's angels began their ascent, flying in circles mimicking the tornadoes' dance as they spun faster and faster, closer to each other, until claws linked with claws.

Wings wrapped around wings. Horns bent into horns. Their bodies folding into each other with sounds of cracking bone and tearing sinew. They did not resist. They welcomed it —laughter of the damned echoing through the city and counties beyond as they merged into one colossal being, offering themselves up into a greater form.

From a dozen came one, and from a hundred came one, and from a thousand, one.

The air stood still. And on the south bank now stood Asmodeus. A demon so embodied with lawlessness and brutality, it personified evil. The titan stood a hundred feet tall, his legs large and muscular, with wings that spanned over a mile.

His chest was a furnace, ribs glowing red as though its heart was pure magma. His arms were vast, stitched from thousands of smaller limbs, each finger ending in jagged claws. The head bore horns so tall they tore the storm clouds as they rose through them, the beast held three heads—a ram, a human, and a bull. Heads so crowded, they fought for space.

The Abstract grinned insidiously, it took a deep breath before lunging forward, destroying any building in its path as it ran toward Asmodeus.

The bridge crushed under their weight as each titan ran toward each other. The first blow landed from Asmodeus—a massive claw driving into the Abstract's throat, splitting it open with a burst of blue blood that rained across the city. Parasites shrieked from rooftops and streets, rushing to its defense.

The Abstract lashed back, tentacles smashing into Asmodeus' chest, shoving him back. The colossal demon staggered, buildings collapsing around him. But he found his footing, and dug his claws into the riverbed.

People fled, soldiers fired uselessly into the air at the parasites, because they could do nothing else but discharge their fear into the night. Above it all, the skies burned red. Lightning danced through the clouds, striking both monsters indiscriminately.

The Abstract writhed and screeched, its face splitting wider as Asmodeus tore a colossal chain from his waist and flung it around the beast. The links glowed red-hot, each one the size of ships, hissing as they seared into its flesh. One by one, the Abstract wound its limbs around the demon-titan's body, constricting it like a serpent.

A roar from Asmodeus shattered the atmosphere, and then the other lords formed.

Leviathan rose from the river in a wall of scaled flesh, his coils wrapping around the Abstract's lower half, anchoring it. His jaws clamped down on a tentacle, tearing it free with a spray of blood that boiled the Thames.

Beelzebub's swarm poured down in a black storm, billions of wings and teeth devouring parasite-flesh, hollowing cavities into the Abstract's hide. The chittering of the flies became a chant, their endless buzzing drowning the shrieks.

Belphegor pressed down from above, his swollen weight grinding into the Abstract's shoulders, forcing it to bend under its own monstrous gravity. His laughter was a gurgling moan.

Asmodeus tightened the chain.

The Abstract howled and sent out a shockwave, alerting its nearby protectors to pause and reach their faces to the sky, sending out their own illuminations, clicking in unison as they sent out their calling signal up to the sky.

And far away, on all corners of the planet, the parasites retreated from their attacks, summoned by their leader.

On the north bank of the Thames, hundreds of portals opened as every parasite on earth jumped through violently—whether the portal opened on the ground or dozens of feet in the air, it didn't matter. What mattered was they were here to protect their king.

The hellions were outnumbered as thousands of black gooey monsters moved in—crawling toward to the riverbed that was now void of any water. The hellions rushed to the edge in an effort to stall them and delay their attacks. But it was no use; if water was the usual substance in the Thames, it had now been replaced with scores of parasites making their way across it.

Satan's army was ready to meet their end, whether they knew it or not.

SUDDENLY, the air shifted.

The Abstract froze, its parasites halting mid-crawl as the storm shifted. The black sky split open, light bleeding gold and orange through ragged seams, lightning tearing across the edges as if Heaven itself had forced a way through.

From that rent in the sky came three blazing forms, streaking not downward like falling stars, but banking, curving, steering with precision no man-made engine could ever command. The atmosphere lit with their passage, rooftops and shattered glass towers below flaring bright as day with every sweep of their wings.

As they drew closer, their shapes took form—wings like polished chrome, vast and radiant, cutting against the storm.

And there he flew, at their head, it was Joph—his face unshaken, his blade strapped across his back.

Gabriel flew at his right, Raphael at his left, neither glancing toward the other, their focus locked forward on the enemy below.

The three angels were hurtling toward the battle to face the parasites and Abstract head on to save Earth from Armageddon.

The Abstract lifted its gaze and shrieked, a sound that rattled the foundation of every thing still clinging to life on the planet. The hellions on the south bank laughed and mocked the parasites as they scrambled up the Abstract's body in a frenzy, clawing one another as they climbed, piling into a writhing tower of flesh that reached high into the storm, desperate to meet the angels before they could strike.

Joph reached over his shoulder and drew the great sword,

ten feet of silver light now burning in his hands. He flew low, leaving the other two behind as he leveled his sword toward the river. His wings folded as he dove, and fire cascaded from the blade—a torrent that struck the riverbed and turned the parasites to fire and ash.

They writhed and split apart, their screams rising above the thunder before the flames dragged them into silence.

Gabriel and Raphael drove themselves headlong into the parasite tower, their wings folding tight as they struck, cleaving through the mass and tearing it apart. Fragments of twisted bodies rained into the burning river as the two angels broke free, wheeled around, and climbed again into the smoke.

For the first time since the war had begun, the Abstract recoiled. Raphael flew to battle more of the parasites as Gabriel swung around in the air facing the diabolical once more.

"*You*!" it roared at him.

But Gabriel wasn't perturbed; he continued on his supersonic path toward the monster, the brilliant white light behind him growing stronger as he smashed into it, puncturing a hole in its abdomen—causing the Abstract to howl a noise that echoed throughout the city once more.

Then, with a roar that cracked every window in London, Asmodeus opened the crack in the Thames even further. Ripping it open with his claws.

The Abstract shrieked, its form buckling, as the chain that was still attached dragged it downward. Leviathan coiled tighter, pulling with the weight of the river. Beelzebub's swarm drove it down in waves. Belphegor pressed his bulk until the

Abstract's spine cracked like timber, and Asmodeus anchored them all, his wings spread across the horizon, pulling the beast into the abyss.

The sky itself reacted. The portal behind the Abstract spasmed and imploded with a thunderous crack, sucking in lightning, collapsing with the sound of worlds tearing apart. And then, the Abstract was gone. Its bulk vanished beneath the river, torn into Hell's furnace, its screech echoing into silence. The fissure sealed in a thunderclap of ash and steam.

For a heartbeat, the colossal Asmodeus stood victorious—smoke pouring from his ribs. The air was heavy with ash, the smell of sulfur and blood indistinguishable. Slowly, almost ceremonially, the great form began to unravel. Claws pulled free from claws. Wings slipped out of wings. Horns bent and twisted apart. Thousands of demons spilled into the air once again, each laughing, shrieking, howling triumph scattering into the night sky.

On the banks of the Thames, the survivors watched in silence. Soldiers lowered their rifles. Civilians fell to their knees, but no one spoke. There lived an eerie silence in the once bustling city. The parasites had retreated, their portals flickering shut one by one. Earth breathed again, broken but alive.

The Abstract had been dragged to Hell, and its parasites had nothing left to do but retreat.

And no one who had witnessed it could say for certain whether they had just seen salvation or damnation.

GREAT BLACK CHAINS clanged heavy with their several-ton weight as they were pulled and tugged in the depths of the burning basin. Every single one of those countless chains—each chain as large and broad as a bridge—was tethered to great stakes driven deep into the bleeding, pulsating flesh of the amorphous horror at the center of the deepest circle of hell: the shrieking Abstract, Azathoth, the great ruler of the Chaos Realms.

It had formed a hundred red eyes in its short duration on the material plane, and those eyes were squinting, weeping, bleeding all over its body, not just on its head. As such, this nightmare had no head. Only a long form with sprawling appendages that looked like tentacles, and great gaping mouths upon mouths with arrays of sharp teeth.

Each of its tentacles was bound in chains, each of those chains that slammed against the floor of Hell were held by powerful demons who had overpowered the Abstract and had imprisoned it here. They chanted their war-chants, building each other's spirit, as they performed their duty of imprisonment and subjugation. They pulled at the chains in a rhythm, and then let go, causing the Abstract to convulse, bleed, feel pain as it had never felt before, for these demons were masters of the craft of torture, one and all, and now they had a subject upon which they could conduct all their sickest fantasies, experiments, and punishments without holding back.

The burning flames of Hell had seared the flesh of the Abstract, sending forth a great rotting and putrescent smell through an otherwise sulfuric atmosphere.

Joe stood watching from the edge of the rim, the Devil

standing beside him. There was reservation on Satan's face, and he wasn't being his vocal self. Joe wondered why that was.

"It grows," the Devil said, pointing at the Abstract. "It grows bigger, and soon Hell won't be able to contain it. Before that happens, come, Joe, let us palaver with Azathoth and find out what it wants."

Lucifer Morningstar flew down the basin, past all the thumping chains, past the demons who sang and chanted their infernal chants, and came to a halt beside one of the large, cavern-like mouths of Azathoth.

"I should think this does not come as a surprise to you," the Devil said, standing ever so nonchalantly in the face of the Great Devourer. "But you are in my realm now."

"Satan." The whisper came not from Azathoth's mouths, but from deep within its body, as if it was its soul that spoke directly without any need of a tongue. "At long last, Satan. At the beginning of time and at the end of it, Satan."

"Your very humble host," the Devil said. "Now, pray tell, what is this all about? My friend Joseph Banbury over here is rather curious as to why you'd lay siege upon his universe, especially right after he became its God?"

"A God of poor considerations leaves his defenses exposed, and can I really be blamed for penetrating past them?" Azathoth whispered, its laborious body drawing slow, painful breaths through its many mouths.

"Do you hear that, Joe? The Abstract has no faith in your ability," the Devil said.

Joe dared not speak. He stood like a matchstick against the

great monolithic magnitude of the growing chaos-lifeform that was the Abstract.

"You made a foolish mistake, Satan," Azathoth whispered, and then convulsed greatly, growing larger in size, making several of the chains fly off as their holders all fell, and the chains shattered, buckling under the weight. "You brought me here. Made my task all too easy for me."

"This is nowhere in particular," Satan said, unperplexed. "This is Hell, the playground of all dark things. You can go nowhere. Here, there is nothing to lay siege to other than flame itself. And how are those flames treating you? I would say that you're at a nice medium-rare right about now."

"ENOUGH!" the Abstract yelled with all its force, growing greater in size, now resembling a mountain that jutted well above the basin, all its bulging red eyes staring in every direction, its many tongues licking back at the flames. A couple hundred more chains broke as their links shattered, freeing the Abstract further.

Before the rupture, before the earsplitting explosion that shook the foundations of Hell and destroyed all the newly built structures within, Satan threw himself back on top of Joe and covered the both of them with his enormous wingspan, shielding them, saving Joe's life.

Outside his wingspan, darkness bloomed, shadows erupted, and the fieriness of the flames was hijacked as they all turned into something far more sinister than mere fire—appendages of chaos, spreading disorder across Hell, all infernal luminescence wiped out by a shroud of dusk and total silence.

When Satan finally let go of Joe, he saw that there was nothing left of Hell. Debris floated, great buildings and pillars lay suspended in darkness, and a great number of the demonkind that had lived there were all dead.

As for the Abstract, it was nowhere to be found. The basin where it had been captured was shattered and lay scattered in a thousand pieces below them.

"What the fuck just happened?" Joe whispered, insanity clawing at his consciousness.

"I believe, dear boy, the Abstract outgrew Hell," the Devil said, resting against a broken arc of the basin, panting deeply, his body greatly injured. "Alas, but the recourse that you'd considered has fallen short."

"You don't get to give up on this so easily," Joe said, looking around for any signs of light, but only finding shades of dark all around him. The surviving Hellions and demons slowly regained consciousness, gathered themselves, and looked around, confused, trying to understand what had happened.

"Well, then," Satan sighed. "If Hell cannot contain the Abstract, and if my powers are not enough, there is only one more recourse at hand."

"What's that?" Joe asked, unable to help himself from feeling the deep misery that had embedded itself in every fiber of his being after the explosion, as if chaos itself had seeped into him.

"I am talking about the Collectors," the Devil said with considerable apprehension on his face, staring into the hollow where Hell had once burned.

5

RIDDLES IN THE DARK

The part of Lilly Thurman that was all magic felt the tremors in Hell and instantly knew that something terrible had happened, which was saying something considering that in most cases, Hell *was* the terrible thing that happened. A deep unrest clawed at her throat, making her mouth dry up.

Presently, having made their way up the hill and into Lilly's recently renovated home, they were making themselves comfortable. Blake and Billy had gone to freshen up, and Amy, having already taken care of that part, was sitting in the living room, admiring the ambience with a glass of wine.

"Have you done something to the place? I wouldn't know if this is how it looked before, but the interior designer in me is curious," Amy asked, looking around the walls, noticing the dark color palette that was utilized to design the place.

Charcoal walls with a tinge of brown in the otherwise gray.

Sconces threw warm orange light on the dark walls, giving the place a rustic, cozy parlor vibe. But it wasn't all drab, for there were indoor plants. They occupied the top of the shelf above the fireplace, little money plants with their vines crawling up a wooden lattice that traversed the room in an intricate and beautiful design that led toward the window. There were more vines than just the money plants'.

A botanist at heart, Lilly had placed English ivy, philodendrons, Swiss cheese plants, and pothos on the latticework, giving it a regal green look that streaked from the fireplace toward the window. As for the window itself, it took up most of the space on the eastern wall, and had elegant jacquard silk curtains covering it. On the other side of the lounge was a piano with more potted plants on top of it. A Steinway, but a modern one that fit against the wall and took up minimal space, if any. It was a nice chestnut color, its wood polished, its keys familiar with the frequent touch of adept fingers. Picture frames hung over it in a haphazard pattern, giving the wall a lived-in, homely look. To the left of the piano was a tall shelf with sliding glass. Inside it were all manner of vials, flasks, and bottles containing elixirs, potions, and ingredients for spells.

At the center of the room was an old oak coffee table with a crystal top. Underneath that table was a large earth-colored rug, rough around the edges. Around the coffee table were dark red sofas, deeply plush and with lots of cushions. Amy had sunken into one of them, and had put her feet up on the coffee table, a fact that Lilly did not mind.

The western wall of the lounge had a large LED display, eighty-five inches, facing all the sofas, underneath which was a black console table containing a VCR, old cassettes, and vinyl records. Atop the console table was a turntable. Lilly looked at it with faint recollection, wondering which beat poet she'd borrowed it from in the 60s. She went over to the turntable and put on a Sinatra album, one of his older works.

"I'm glad you asked that," she said, letting herself relax as the dim music played in the background, and a wine glass found its way into her hands, somewhat enchantingly, somewhat naturally. She walked over to where Amy sat and observed the room from her vantage point. Underneath her feet, matte, dark hardwood felt firm and warm, complete with floor heating. "And if I'm being honest, I don't remember. This house has undergone countless renovations over the years. It's almost its own version of Theseus's ship. Is it the same house, or is it something new altogether?"

"In either case, it's *you*," Amy said, raising her glass to Lilly. "As is this wine. As is this town."

"You're sweet to say that," Lilly said, sitting down beside Amy, trying to induce some of the same calm inside her that Amy was feeling.

The two women sat quietly, sipping their wine, eager to call it a night and let their deep sleep prepare them for tomorrow's tasks. Blake came out of the guest bedroom, his hair still wet, wearing a new t-shirt and a fresh pair of jeans. He looked relatively comfortable, and in a better mood than he had been an hour ago, when he'd had just about enough of walking. He walked over into the kitchen, where a long fluorescent tube hung over the kitchen island.

Its light was muffled with the translucent sheet over it,

giving the kitchen a bearable glow rather than the severity of an interrogation room. He wished for beer and was all too glad to find his favorite bottle waiting for him in the fridge, chilled to perfection. He considered Billy and took out another bottle. By the time he was back in the living room, Billy had rejoined the ladies and was sitting there on the hardwood floor, his face clean shaven, his hair trimmed short, and a dark green sweatshirt on with shorts underneath. Blake gave an approving shrug and handed Billy the beer, then took his own seat in the living room.

"I'm never good with waiting for long periods," Blake said, once the quiet got too quiet. "In the military, we'd play cards. Sometimes, when that wasn't enough, we'd do cold plunges, and between you and me, cold plunges in Afghanistan were kind of much needed after a long day."

"The only cold plunge I've ever done is when I slipped and fell into the Hudson on New Year's Eve when I was sixteen years old. I say slipped; it was really one of the foster kids pushing me just so that I wouldn't make it home in time for dinner. See, it was an *Oliver Twist* kind of situation, where you couldn't ask for more on account of just how many mouths there were to feed. The lady I lived with, Roberta, she was one of those women who get addicted to taking in foster children because of the paychecks that came with each one. She had five rooms in her house and each room had three kids. Go figure. She knew someone in city council, someone who made the inspection lady tick all the boxes and ignore the fact that the living conditions were absolutely deplorable," Billy said, and this was just after taking two sips of beer. It wasn't that he was a lightweight. It was that he was having alcohol after a long time.

"What happened next?"

"A cop pulled me out of the water, asked me how I'd fallen in there. Billy Hawthorne's many things, but he ain't no snitch. I said I slipped. Later that night, I earned the begrudging respect of the one who'd pushed me. Harry Alderson. The next night, I had his pudding. Harry had already served two stints in juvie by that time, so it was really important to him that he didn't go in a third time. After that, every night, I had his pudding. Only, I never realized that the motherfucker—sorry for my French, ladies—was spitting in his pudding before giving it to me," Billy said, ending his anecdote with a bitter chuckle.

"I've got a good one," Amy said, hunching forward. "There was this one time when a girl in my class was giving me shit. Mind you, I'm Joe's elder sister, and I'm in high school. And it was something real stupid that the girl, Melissa Byers, was giving me shit about. Oh, yeah. I remember now. It was Grady, her boyfriend, who'd hung around after English Lit class had ended and asked me if I'd taken notes during the *Great Gatsby* summary, because he couldn't afford another D in class. I gave him the notes, and next thing I know, Melissa is calling me a skank and pulling my hair in the hallway, telling me to stay away from her man."

"Ouch," Lilly said, mimicking pain.

"Anyway, next day, there's a story on the front of the school newspaper titled 'Melissa Byers Eats Shit For Breakfast.' No author name or anything. Just a badly edited picture of Melissa

Byers with a literal shit-eating grin, and a very scathing piece of juvenile fiction about her going from public toilet to public toilet, devouring shit. That girl had no reputation after that. Anywhere she'd go, they'd call her Shit-Eating Byers. And while Joe never said that he did it, he could never stop laughing by himself that week after school. If someone so much as even mentioned the ordeal that poor girl was going through, Joe would burst into laughter. Laughter that wasn't proportionate to the joke. Unless, of course, you were the one behind it. Then it was all shades of funny. Anyway, ten years later, Joe and I are in New York. He's twenty-four and is having a really hard go of it in Manhattan, juggling jobs as a bookstore clerk and whatnot, trying to finish his first book, and I ask him about Melissa Byers over dinner. He burst into that same laughter again, only this time I was a little frustrated at being left out of the joke.

"'It was never me! I worked in the newsroom, yes, but it wasn't me,' he said. 'You wouldn't even guess who it was.' Of course, at this point I was more than just a little frustrated and ordered him to spill it. It was then that he revealed that it wasn't him, but Harry Alderson who'd put in that piece in the newspaper and paid the editor sixty bucks to print it, no questions asked. It turned out Melissa was a bitch all year around, and to everybody, not just me. And her boyfriend had just had a little too much, and knew that breaking up with her in a normal pretext wasn't ever happening," Amy said, amused, her eyes gazing off in the distance, as if there was a window that let her look back in time. "So I asked Joe what was so funny about the whole thing if he wasn't a part of it, and he goes, 'Harry

Alderson paid me fifty bucks to write that story for him. My first money as a writer, and it's a hit piece on a high schooler's scat fetish!'"

Lilly couldn't help but laugh. Blake and Billy joined in. As far as quaint moments went, it was a nice one with nothing happening that threatened their lives. And without saying it, all of them realized that maybe this was the first time in their lives they'd spent time like this together. That night in Iraq, all those years ago, was not like this one. There were militia members on the lookout for them that night. But nothing like that was happening tonight.

But despite that, Lilly couldn't help but feel the uncertainty, the panic clawing at her psyche, and she knew that sitting around wouldn't help her accomplish anything. And right on cue, there was the distant sound of police sirens blaring. Lilly's ears pricked, and so did Blake's.

"It looks like trouble has found us yet again," Lilly said, not knowing what this was about. In any case, she was going to investigate, this being her town.

"I'll come with you," Blake said, getting up from the sofa. "It's not like I've got much to do anyway."

"I'm out," Amy said, shaking her head. "I'm gonna fix up a quick dinner for myself in the kitchen, if you don't mind."

"I'll join you. My battery for adventure has all but run out," Billy said.

"Right," Lilly said. "Well, I have sanctified this place. In fact, I did that first thing when we stepped inside. All my spells are upon this place, protective, offensive, and all those in between. Stay inside, and you'll be safe. If you find yourself in need of weapons, there's a rifle in the guest bedroom and a handgun, also in the guest bedroom. Hopefully, we won't be gone long."

Lilly and Blake exited the house together. Behind them, Amy locked the door and pulled the curtains.

"Are you sure you're good to go out without a jacket?" Lilly asked, frowning at Blake. "It's brisk."

"I'm fine," Blake said, grinning sheepishly. His grin almost vanished instantaneously when he spotted the red and blue lights of cop cars flashing beyond the hill. "An incident at the graveyard?"

Lilly's heart sank. "It's not just a graveyard. Come. We have to hurry."

At first Blake thought that they were going to make a run for it, but then he saw Lilly head into the garage. The next minute, she came out behind the driver's seat of a black Ford F-150. "Come on," she said, rolling down the window. "We don't have much time."

Despite the nature of the situation, he couldn't help but notice just how beautiful Lilly Thurman looked—her hair undone, her face flushed, and her lips still red from the wine.

Awestruck, he got in the truck and held on for dear life as Lilly drove at an unbelievably dangerous speed down the rolling slopes of the hill, racing toward the graveyard.

Five minutes later, when they halted to a sudden stop outside of the graveyard's bounds, Blake's face was paler than the moon.

"What happened, traveling soldier? Can't handle speed?"

"Oh, I can handle speed just fine. It's the twisting turns that give me trouble," he said, feeling nauseous as he got out of the truck. He trailed behind Lilly as she, with much authority, crossed the caution tape and stepped into the scene of the crime.

"Madam Mayor," the cop on the scene said.

"Madam Mayor?" Blake asked.

"It's a glamor spell. I'll tell you later," Lilly whispered in his ear.

"What happened here, Simon?" Lilly asked, looking at the crime scene, but also at the crypt that had been flung open. If Rafael was out, then why hadn't she known about it? She remembered placing a spell on his crypt to notify her immediately if something out of the norm had happened. Unless, of course, something or someone else had happened. It was still very unclear, so she let the cop fill her in.

"Two dead bodies, both died within a half-hour of each other. One's a car crash victim, though that's not all he is. There are strange markings on his body, and he seems to be missing a lot of blood. Far too much to account for actually. A car crash, and that, too, not all that fatal, doesn't really explain it. And then, Amanda Lynn, local reporter; she was found in the brush, her body also matching the MO of the killer."

"You've already deduced that there's a killer with an MO?" Lilly asked, following the cop as he pointed to the crashed car and then a little down the path where there was more tape around the thicket of trees leading into the forest.

"Well, it was almost quite theatrical," Simon said. "Both victims had holes in their neck. Like someone was trying to LARP Dracula or something. All of it in one night. There's also quite a lot of vandalism in the graveyard. Someone destroyed St. Rafael's mausoleum."

Lilly had heard enough. She quietly cast another spell, one which would make Simon and the rest of the police and EMTs gathered there forget that she'd come here, and then headed off into the woods.

"Are these people your puppets or something?" Blake asked, looking at the white-outlined place where Amanda Lynn's corpse had been. There were several markers placed upon the forest floor. Lilly was kneeling beside them.

"No, but when you're around as long as I've been, it's pertinent to cast cautionary magic," Lilly said, getting up and heading deeper into the woods. "There's a blood trail and a scent leading farther into the woods. This cannot be good."

"So, they think you're the mayor?"

"Amongst other things. I've been in Bridgewater for centuries. Can't have people getting too curious about my origins. Sometimes I'm the granddaughter of the rich woman who lived in the old hilltop house. Sometimes I'm the mayor. Whatever's convenient. Come on. Enough of this. We have to go check the crypt."

After walking around the thicket and toward the crypt from the longer route, they reached its broken-down stone entrance. Lilly stepped down the stairs and inspected the place where Rafael had been buried for his own safety. There were straps, and not of a natural nature, that were ripped and in tatters all over the floor. She picked one up and sniffed it. Other than Rafael's smell, there was a trace of sulfur on them.

"Rafael was held here," Lilly said.

"Saint Rafael?"

"No," she said, rolling her eyes. "It's a long story about a sole surviving vampyre from a lost kingdom. I'll tell you about it later. For now, understand this. If he's not in his crypt, and if he's out there murdering people for his feeding, then we have another problem on our hands besides Armageddon. I can't have a misplaced vampyre in Bridgewater, do you understand?"

"I do," Blake said, taking his phone out and calling Billy. "Hey, the situation that we're investigating has become a little... complex. I think we might be here a while."

"No worries. Amy has already fallen asleep on the couch and I'm watching an old rerun of *The Price Is Right,*" Billy said, then eccentrically hung up on Blake without asking for further explanation or providing any.

Blake shrugged. He then saw Lilly whispering something under her breath, with her hand hovering over the cracked stone slabs.

"I've placed a tracking spell, and for our sake, I hope it works. Are you sure you want to go hunting for a vampyre with me? Wouldn't you rather go back and be with the others?"

"A gentleman doesn't leave a lady on her own, especially in moments of distress," Blake said. Something about the way he said it, his words so rich with chivalry of old, reminded Lilly of her husband, and that sent a prick of pain in her chest. She brushed the thought aside and let her spell guide her in the direction of Rafael.

The spell did not place him anywhere in the forest west of Bridgewater. Nor did the trail lead to anywhere else in Massachusetts. Vampyres were fast, this much Lilly knew, but to be so fast that they'd skip across states? She didn't understand how that was possible.

She readied herself for the journey that lay ahead, all the while feeling unsettled about what had happened with Joe. As of yet, she did not know what he'd gone through, or what he had achieved. All she knew was that it was a long night, and it was far from being over.

Billy Hawthorne wasn't really watching an old rerun of *The Price Is Right.* He was busy with something else. The rifle that Lilly had talked of earlier was out there on the coffee table now, completely unassembled. He was cleaning it meticulously, a hobby he'd picked up rather recently. On his phone, he had a YouTube video on about how to clean and maintain a vintage Remington rifle, and was having quite the time of his life admiring this beautiful firearm while Amy was stirring in her sleep on the couch. There was a plate with a half-eaten sandwich on it on the coffee table. Amy had eaten half and had chased it down with another glass of wine, and before Billy had noticed, she had fallen asleep.

It was good meditation, this. It slowed his mind down as he focused on the gun and marveled at the woodwork, the way the iron was still firm and smooth, and how the trigger seemed to press almost instinctively in his finger.

In another ten minutes, he was done reassembling the rifle, and he held it at arm's length, admiring his handiwork.

"Billy Hawthorne, you old so and so. Once this is all over, you're opening up a gun repair store!" he laughed.

"Hmm?" Amy stirred from her sleep, opening her eyes, rubbing them with her hand. "You say something?"

"I'm so sorry," Billy said, blushing. He hadn't intended to wake her up.

"It's okay. Sleeping on the couch at my age is playing dice with the universe," Amy said, sitting up and yawning. "Didn't the others come back?"

"Oh, they called, said it was a complex situation unfolding, and that they'll probably take some time. I wonder what that's about," Billy said, placing the gun on his lap and fitting its magazine back in.

Amy felt a chill run on the back of her neck. Turning around, she saw that the curtains were moving. She pulled them away and noticed that the window was open, air blowing through it.

"Did you open the windows, Billy?" Amy asked, still bleary-eyed.

"No," Billy said, his face contorted in shock. "I didn't."

Her sleep disappeared almost instantaneously. She reached the window and pulled it down, closing it. Then pulled the curtains in their original place.

Something clattered in the kitchen. Billy instinctively held the gun up. Amy crept up from the sofa and walked behind him. Warily, the two of them headed toward the kitchen, the house's dim lighting feeling dimmer as they walked up the hallway.

It was a glass jar that had fallen from the kitchen island

and was laying there, unbroken, on the floor. The window in the kitchen was also open, blowing in cool night air. This time it was Billy who closed the window while Amy inspected the kitchen, her heart beating fast.

They shared a look, a look that said, *We are not alone*.

As if to complement that thought, the stairs creaked, and so did the floorboards on the floor above. Amy stood stiff, frozen with fear, uncertain as to who or what this could be. She brought a finger to her lips to signal total quiet to Billy, who nodded in understanding.

Somehow, the lights seemed even dimmer, making it hard to make out their surroundings. Despite that, they walked out of the kitchen and held the first floor in view. Nothing moved, and yet, there was a palpable feeling that something was in there with them, watching them from behind the furniture, blending with the walls, creeping up the stairs.

The door to the guest bedroom swung with a loud creak. Amy gasped and stepped back. Billy was right behind her, unsure of what this gun would achieve in the face of whatever was in there with them.

"Who's there?" he called out.

As if in response to his questions, all the many shadows in the room flickered in the lack of light, and when they steadied themselves, they had all moved toward the stairs, as if heralding something dark and malevolent.

One by one, the stairs creaked loudly under the weight of the presence that stepped down them.

In no mood to stick around and come face to face with whatever, whoever it was, Amy turned on her heels and raced for the entrance door. She tugged the doorknob after twisting it, but to no avail. The door was shut. She pulled back the curtains on the window next to the door in an attempt to fling herself across the window and break through to the other side, but instead of doing that, she came face to face with the reflection of the specter that had descended the stairs, a creature to which the shadows traveled.

It was tall and obscured in the lack of light, but when Amy turned around to see the real thing instead of just the reflection, she saw its arms, both of them of disproportionate shape, its mouth, hanging open as if its jaw had been broken, and the claws at the end of its fingertips almost touching the floor as it slouched and walked and crouched toward them.

Billy Hawthorne had seen enough. He aimed the rifle at the stairs and pulled the trigger. There was a loud flash and a roar, followed by the recoil of the rifle pushing him back, but the bullet that escaped through the barrel touched nothing in its trajectory.

It was as if it turned to dust while airborne, not even grazing the shadow that crept forward. Amy grabbed Billy's arm and pulled him into the living room. From there, they ran around the haunter and climbed up the stairs.

The shadow chased them on the stairs on all fours, the sound that came from its mouth not a roar but not a whisper either. It was as if the shrieks of all the damned had formed one discordant symphony, and that symphony made the stairs shake, the walls quake. Amy was the first to climb to the second floor. Billy rushed behind her as they headed into Lilly's bedroom and bolted the door behind them.

The door first buckled under the weight of something that struck it, and then oozing smoke started to travel from underneath it, creeping toward them both, the air smelling of death, the air turning colder than the inside of a crypt, all oxygen being drained from it, making them both claw for breath, their eyes watering, their haunter unrelenting as it crossed the threshold and stood in front of them, a tall beast with a grotesque body bathed in blackness, its eyes stretched long, burning a bright orange, its wide grin revealing bloodied teeth.

As Amy and Billy huddled against each other in one corner of the bedroom, wondering who had sent this creature, and why Lilly's spells had failed, the lights all flickered out in the room, leaving them in total dark.

And that was when the air was split with a loud banshee wail, making the windows reverberate and shatter, driving delirium in the senses of the two humans who could not see anything other than pitch black, or hear anything other than that chaotic din. The floor shook every time the shadow stepped forward, making them lurch and cling to each other for dear life.

6

THE ABSOLUTE LIE

It does something irreparable to the psyche of a man who has ridden the sinusoidal wave-form from Heaven to Hell and now finds himself back in the middle, knowing that at any given minute, the wave-form will resume its cresting and troughing, and he'll be subjected to brave the torment once more.

Joe Banbury's inertial mind could still feel the whiplash of Hell upon his person as he came to a grinding halt face-first on the top of the Bridgewater hill-slope, his exit from Hell as unceremonious as it was sudden. In the face of Hell's great disruption, with its pillars and foundations floating away in the void like clouds, and the Abstract nowhere to be found, the Devil had sent Joe back to Earth while he took care of business on his own end. Reparations first, and then resurrection of the ones who had died in the fight against Azathoth.

Joe hadn't argued. There was not really much he could do

there, other than contribute to the rising tension by way of asking unnecessary questions and prodding Satan along to another course of action with unpredictable outcomes. He could already sense Satan's patience running thin, and could imagine him sneering, "What more would you ask of me, bane of my existence? That I hurl myself in the void and let chaos devour me as sacrifice?!"

Needless to say, he did not want to come across that version of Satan, not even in his mind, so he snapped out of the maelstrom that was going on inside his head and considered his surroundings.

Considering this was the first time he was in Bridgewater in all his life, it took him a while to absorb the fact that this surreal little town was Lilly's home. This was followed by the guilty realization that he didn't know all that much about Lilly to begin with. There were facts and omniscient data points that he had gone over pertaining to her life in his short tenure as God, just as he had gone over the lives of everyone that he knew, and most of whom he didn't. Simple statistics, hardly enough to tell a story.

But this town, with its quiet hill and its fog-covered lake, the docile suburbs with just a car or two on the streets, and the little town center populated with a smattering of pedestrians, it told a story of preservation, legacy, and old pain. The crypt was a metaphor for it as well as anything.

The air that he inhaled was cool and crisp, a welcome respite from the hot fumes of Hell or the vacuous nothingness of space. But the charcoal cloud that cascaded all over the house on the hilltop did not seem like it was one of Lilly's spells or a protection charm. It was the only thing that seemed out of place.

Joe walked up to the edge of the house, trying to discern what was happening inside, but the layer of thickened soot was so impermeable, he couldn't perceive anything. This was not the brand of magic that he knew Lilly to use.

The house stood atop the hill against the backdrop of the low hanging sun, its many windows, eaves, and multi-layered shingled roofs all shrouded in impenetrable smoke, and Joe stood in front of it, unsure of how he was to enter, if at all.

And then he heard a bloodcurdling scream echoing from inside, and all such reservations were laid to waste, bringing cold-blooded clarity. This was not Lilly's work, and it did not seem like she was here at all.

Joe hurtled himself against the black barrier, and when he could not make his way through, he let his fire out, burning his way through, stepping inside layers and layers of obscurity, relying on his infernal vision to guide him.

From the inside, it seemed that the whole house was being fumigated with suffocating smoke, and no matter how hard he tried to look around, there was more of the same void to behold. Despite that, he crawled and crashed around, locating the source of the scream.

"Enough of this!" Joe growled as the smoke tried to hold him in one place. He reached within himself and pulled out as much of his father's fury as he could, beginning to burn away at the darkness, his mind going back to the story Lucifer had told him about driving away chaos with fire. If Satan had done it, so could he, even though he was not sure that this was the Abstract's doing.

His body pulsing with fire, Joe became a beacon unto himself and ran up the stairs, the smoke and fog no longer touching him but keeping just close enough that he wouldn't be able to see beyond a foot of himself. If he burned any hotter, he would bring the house down, and those who were still inside it.

"HELP!" Amy screamed from somewhere close by. Joe's heart sank. *Not my sister*, his mind raged as he flew through the barred door and came into the room, all ready to inflict hellfire upon wherever dared terrorize Amy.

Joe thought he was prepared, especially since he had just been through two great battles back to back, one in another star system, another that left Hell fractured. But no sooner than he'd come into the room did he find himself in another place, in another time entirely.

He was no longer an adult. And neither was Amy. And neither of them stood in the bedroom of Lilly Thurman's house.

They were standing there, clinging to each other in pure terror, as the dark presence with his aglow eyes and devastating claw-span crept through the basement of the Banbury residence. And Joe knew that there was nothing that he could do to escape this grimy, cold, unfinished, packed earth floor basement, because he was far too little and too weak, and the stairs leading up the basement were barred by the presence of the demon who stood with his wings unfurled, his claws out, flames jetting out of his nostrils as he breathed through his nose, his black body covered in wiry hair and nothing else. With a broad head bracketed with curling horns, and a wide, muscular body, the demon looked more like a minotaur than he did a hell-fiend. A tail thumped heavily on the ground as he walked up to the two siblings huddling under the desk. Joe had gone stiff with terror, and could only behold the naked, smoke-perfusing demon as he walked with his long member swaying between his legs like a pendulum, shaking the entire house with each thud of his footsteps.

The cross on the wall behind them, a loving ode to the one and only Jesus Christ, shook and fell off, crashing on the ground and splintering into pieces.

"Joey, we can't outrun it this time," Amy whimpered, a little girl who hadn't even entered her teenage years. "There's no outrunning evil, no matter how fast you run."

A series of disconcerting thought dissonances rang him to within an inch of his life right after her defeated statement. The sound of 8-bit Nintendo and Atari videogames, the sudden infiltrative smell of freshly mowed grass and bunches of freshly fallen maple leaves in the suburbs of Red Bank, New Jersey, the blood dripping from lean cuts of beef and pork wrapped in yesterday's newspaper merging into the sight of red-soaked ice-pop sold at the store, the clang of the church bell signaling that they'd shortly be seeing Father O'Hara behind the pulpit, the stagnated sight of his father sitting in a mess of cigarette butts and beer cans as he watched whatever brain rot was on the television at the time, and his mother with her apron and gloves and her trays of baked goods.

All of it hit Joe in the head like a sledgehammer bullet

from a .45 Magnum, rattling the inside of his skull, turning his brain into mulch as he careened through all of his existence and came back into this moment in the basement where he was stuck with his sister and the broken cross by their feet.

The demon tore away the desk with just one swipe of his hand, leaving them coverless. Amy grabbed Joe close, her tears soaking into his shirt, her hair smelling of lavender shampoo and feeling like a thousand threads of smooth silk brushing against his face.

The demon was all set to impale them both at the end of its claws, first bringing its muscular arm up all the way, and then about to bring it down, when there was a gunshot that resounded from the back of the basement, followed by a large hole in the middle of the bull-like creatures forehead. Dark sludge dripped out of the hole, and white smoke rose from the bullet's exit point. The red-eyed demon groaned with his tongue hanging limp out of his mouth, his penis leaking urine. He first collapsed to his knees, both Joe and Amy hearing the cracking sound of his kneecaps as they crumbled under his weight, and then continued his trajectory, landing face-first on the packed earth floor.

The two kids ducked away just in time to avoid the horns, both of them staring agape and wide-eyed at their savior.

"Billy?" Joe said, his voice that of a child. Billy Hawthorne stood there with a rifle in his grip, sweat all over his face.

"Billy?" Joe called out again, only this time, he was back in the bedroom, back in his old body, and his sister (no longer in her tweens, but in her late forties) clinging to him, eyes shut in anticipation of more horror.

Billy Hawthorne stood by the window, at the center of the eye of the black storm that was roiling in the room.

"Enough!" Joe yelled, furious that this dark little trick had compromised his mind and had exposed him to some of the most vulnerable memories of his childhood. Joe reached into the torrent of smoke and pulled out the menacing creature with its red-eyed and fume body. Joe's hands burned at a temperature so terrible that they solidified this nightmare-dispelling creature as he latched onto its throat and choked it to within an inch of its life. The harder he choked, the more the fumes dispersed away, leaving the room clearer and clearer.

"Who is your master?!" Joe said, his scorching grasp making the creature writhe and squirm, its length no longer than four feet now, an impish thing with red glazed eyes and a slippery body flailing to get free. It grew smaller, unable to draw on any more air to grow in size, but Joe did not let go. "Who do you serve, because it sure as shit ain't Satan! What do you want from me?! Are you here on the Abstract's command?!"

The creature, no longer than three feet now, croaked with its little red tongue out, and as it died, the only word it managed to convey to Joe was, "*Absolute.*"

Billy Hawthorne stood there dumbstruck in the bedroom, staring at the gun, wondering what he'd just done. There was no more smoke in the room or in the rest of the house, nor for that matter was it anywhere around the exterior or on the hill. It had evaporated into thin air as quickly as it had appeared out of it.

The culprit now dead in Joe's hand disappeared into a thin wisp of smoke before any of the three had a chance to inspect it closely.

"Are you okay, Amy?" Billy asked, giving her his hand. She grabbed his wrist with shaky hands and helped herself up off the floor. "Billy Hawthorne, as you live and breathe, you're the one saving people for a change," he continued, amazed at his present-mindedness in the moments of chaos.

"Thanks, Billy," Joseph panted, looking at his hands and all the black soot clinging to them. That soot was all that was left of the silhouetted assaulter. "Thanks for looking out."

"I was sure we were done for," Billy said, still staring at the rifle. To his eyes alone, there was some sort of glistening sheen appearing on the Remington, as if it was an enchanted weapon capable of more than just firing bullets. He made a note to ask Lilly about it later. "Until you came, you know."

Amy was finished panting, and was standing there by the window, covered in sweat.

"Ames? You good?" Joe asked, standing up and walking over to her.

"I was back in that basement," Amy whispered, her eyes reflecting the lake's reflective surface. "Joe. I was back in that basement. How was that possible? It didn't seem like a vision. I was *actually* in there. And I was thinking about homework. I was thinking about the chores Mom had given me. It wasn't just a flashback. I was..."

"I know what you mean. I could feel it too," Joe said. "We have the Absolute to thank for that." That was, if he could trust the dying words of the creature. In Joe's experience, no matter what your nature in life, in your final moments, it did not matter if you were a fierce demon or God Herself, you could never lie. You used your last truth as a bargaining chip in hopes it would save your life. That's what the creature had tried to do. He could see it in its eyes as he'd choked its life out. "Where...where are Lilly and Blake?"

Billy said, "They said something about the situation becoming complex at the cemetery. The two of them called me to let me know that they'd be investigating."

It's not like Lilly to leave those in her charge defenseless, thought Joseph as he rationalized what was happening.

"I'm going to have a drink," Amy said, running her hands through her disheveled hair, assessing Joe with a look on her face that brought out all her age in sheer contrast to the eleven-year-old terrified child Joe had seen. The basement had rattled him in a way he wasn't willing to admit. In those few moments that had seemed like hours during which he was trapped there with Amy, it had seemed so inescapable, and everything else that happened afterward (from growing up to becoming published and then becoming the Devil's writer) felt like a wild dream meant to make Joe escape the terror of that subterranean reality. That he would always be a kid stuck in the basement while his parents weren't home, and that there'd always be demons prowling about.

"I'm going to join you," Joe said, following her out of the room.

"Billy Hawthorne, you gun-whisperer, you," Billy said to himself, admiring the rifle, recalling how he'd just taken a blind shot in the dark, hoping that it would strike true, and struck true it had. Whatever happened next, he wasn't going to part with this gun. It seemed to have a will of its own.

A board creaked in the quiet of the bedroom, startling him to the realization that he was the only one left standing there. He walked out of the room, closing the door behind him, and followed the sound of the footsteps the other two were leaving behind.

Downstairs, in the living room, Joe sat tensely, observing the interior, waiting for Amy to come with something for the three of them to drink. In the meantime, Billy Hawthorne came and sat down beside him.

"How'd you do that?" Joe asked. "How'd you penetrate past its whole illusion?"

"Trust me, bro, I don't even know. I was in an illusion of my own, battling the parts of my mind that I thought I'd conquered. They all came back rather suddenly, you know, all those other darker halves of my personality. How many halves can one person have? Can you have... Anyway, there I was, trapped in my old apartment, the one where I contemplated killing myself every night, and Other Billy was pointing this rifle at me, telling me he'd kill me in a heartbeat because all I'd ever done would never amount to nothing," Billy spoke. "And it was quite absolute in nature, the misery that my fucked-up self was throwing my way."

"What did you do?" Joe asked, wondering how he was going to break the news to Amy and Billy that he had failed in solving the Abstract dilemma, and was effectively back at square one. He decided that he'd probably break the news if a) something so terrible happened in the meantime that it would warrant an explanation, or b) when all the group was together so that he'd only have to go through the events once and not over and over. In the meantime, he wanted to get to the bottom of this surreal episode.

"Oh, I just told Other Billy to shut the fuck up and basically brought it to his notice that I knew he wasn't Other Billy on account of the Real Billy and Other Billy having kissed and made up and living happily ever after. It's true. I don't get none of those bullshit visions of my mom hanging herself in the apartment or dear old dead Teddy. Whatever happened in Iraq, and later at the Stonehenge, it just made us all accept and own each other. I haven't been bothered in that way since. So it was a little out of place that Other Billy would show up now. And that's when I let 'em have it. Pulled the trigger and killed him. He dispersed, and so did the illusion. And then I saw the two of you huddled together, pretending that the both of you were hiding underneath some desk or something. So I shot the source of the illusion. But you were the one who killed it," Billy said, looking at Joe with some degree of admiration. "As always, you're the one who's putting the finishing flourishes on everything. I'm just the guy who gets you most of the way."

"If it weren't for the guy, we'd be senseless," Amy said, bringing three cups of steaming black coffee in a tray and placing them on the table. "So, thanks, Billy."

"Yes. Thanks, Billy. Also, Ames. Coffee? I don't get it."

"I think it's time we gave the old metaphorical wine

bottle a break. I'm not saying we become teetotalers, but some bit of sobriety is in order," Amy said, handing Joe a hot cup.

"Fine with me," Joe said, drinking scalding coffee and feeling none of it burn his mouth.

"I'm going to go out and sit on the porch," Billy said, taking his cup with him. "Keep an eye on things. I've had enough of these walls."

Amy watched him go, cautiously sipping her coffee, reminding herself that she might be Joe's sister, but had none of his hellish abilities to help her drink scalding coffee. When she was sure Billy was gone, she sighed in relaxation.

"You've been gone the whole night. I was worried," Amy said, resting her head on Joe's shoulder, closing her eyes, seeking comfort from her brother's warm presence. "Did everything go okay? I mean, considering everything?"

"It's too soon to say," Joe muttered. "Call Lilly if you can. Let her know that I'm back. I'll be able to share my story once everyone's here and accounted for."

Amy fished her phone out from between the sofa cushions and called Lilly. In the meantime, Joe headed out of the house to get some fresh air. On the porch, Billy Hawthorne had put his feet up and was reclining in an armchair, the gun still in his arms.

"Going somewhere?" he asked, his eyes still closed, the chair creaking under his weight and the lulling rhythm of his feet as they pressed against the railing.

"Not particularly. Just a nighttime stroll."

Billy only grunted in approval, making himself more

comfortable in that cowboy-esque pose, his hand running along the rifle's barrel, as if doing this soothed him.

Joe circled around the back of the house, noting every little detail, such as the path with large slabs of different-colored stones leading down the hill. The grass around this path was freshly mowed. Below, there was a clearing in the woods with the barn roof visible above the canopies.

Joe was quite impressed by Bridgewater's labyrinthine nature, in that wherever you looked, a pathway seemed to lead somewhere. And whatever magic Lilly had placed upon this town that she bought and built up, it had kept the parasites out. He had already connected the dots on the mental map he'd made of the place. If one were to walk farther west of the barn and through the forest, they'd come out on the other side in the cemetery. And if someone was to take the opposite direction, they'd come out on the east side, at the lake.

And in the middle, all this expanse of green grass and wooden fences.

"Lilly Thurman, I never took you for a cowgirl," Joe whispered as he descended the stone steps. For the rest of his climb down, he stayed silent, listening to the overwhelming sound of the chirping insects, and the moving of animals in their enclosures. Joe wondered passively as to how Lilly was able to take care of her animals while herself being constantly on one adventure or the other.

A gamekeeper, perhaps. Or maybe a full-time attendant. Who was he to know? The more he was in Bridgewater, the more Joseph realized that he knew next to nothing about Lilly. And to think, at one point he'd presumed to love her.

After several minutes of descending, he was in the field covered from all sides by the forest. Long stretching oaks and birches with their branches and canopies forming a convoluted mesh. Maples struck out from amidst them, as if making their presence known by the distinct display of their shapely leaves and their white bark. Joe could hear something else other than the insect chirp and animal sounds—running water. There was a stream somewhere close by, the meditative rush of its sound making Joe want to ditch his failing mission and his terror-filled thoughts and just be in the vicinity of fresh, clean water racing over smooth rocks. And then he could sleep, maybe.

The trimmed grass provided a very juxtaposing contrast against all the tall underbrush and weeds that grew along the circumference of the forest. To his left, there were lights on in the barn. Joe wanted to go in and see what kind of horses Lilly Thurman kept, and he'd already taken the first step in that direction when a benevolent-sounding voice called out his name from behind him.

He should have known that it wasn't just whimsical exploration that had brought him here, far enough from the house so that no one would eavesdrop on the conversation, and close enough to it that Joe could still rush there to aid anyone if prompted.

"That was remarkably handled," the voice said, filling Joe with the urge to envelop his fist in a blaze and pummel the Absolute with it. He controlled his impulse, choosing to calmly turn around and face the One Above All, standing there ever so resplendently and belongingly in the open field, dressed nondescriptly in a pedestrian plaid shirt tucked into dull brown cotton pants. Underneath, he wore oxfords. He was clean shaven, and had come to Joseph in a very human guise, the one that he had seen a very long time ago in the Devil's Tuscan abode.

That was when he bore the name Samuel.

"You and your tests," Joe seethed. "Tell me something. When you saw me trapped against my will in Hell the first time, you left me there on purpose after that meaningless conversation. Was that a test?"

"Aren't all things a test?" the Absolute asked with all the political diplomacy in the known universe, his fingertips touching in a neat inverted triangle, a businesslike smile on his face, his eyes gray and hazy.

"Cut the crap."

"Yes," the Absolute said, his smile dispelling gradually, leaving behind a stone expression that did not suit this mild-mannered avatar of his. "It was a test of perseverance to see how much you'd put up with. You forget, Joseph, that I know all, and am on every node of time-space at once. Just as that was a test of your perseverance, this most recent one that you passed with rather flying colors was a test of your resourcefulness. Even without any of your godly abilities, you vanquished your opponent, saved your sister and your friend."

Joe stormed up to the Absolute, his index finger pointed close to his irritatingly passive face. "Listen. I'm done playing games. And if you pull that shit again, I..."

"You will what?" The Absolute uttered each word with menace and condescension.

Joe wasn't one to hold back, especially not now. "I'll kill you."

There was surprise on the Absolute's face, as if this was not the answer he expected to hear.

"Just because you've mustered the armies of Hell to your side and have set your crosshairs on my adversary, you think yourself strong enough to take me on?"

"I think you're shitting bricks right about now. All that bullshit about being on every space-time node at once is just you patting yourself on the back for thinking you're the top dog, when clearly your very existence is threatened at the hands of the Abstract. And you're not as wise as you think you are. You don't know when to quit. You think I am still your champion, that after I undergo yet another humiliating rite of godly passage, you'll give me back my powers, keep me in check, and then set me like a trained dog upon the Abstract."

"And won't you?" the Absolute jeered, his malevolence out in full display.

"I'll deal with the Abstract for my people. For this world. I do not need your fucking powers or your ordaining me God. I tried that gig. Doesn't pay well and it's a thankless job. You're free to elect another one in my presence. And while you're at it, leave me the fuck alone!" Joe snapped.

"I will hold you to what you have said, Joseph Banbury. And a word of advice: Hold your people close. You know how fickle human lives are. From the minute one of you is born, you claw in the dark against the unending abyss of existence, your lives balancing upon the edge of a knife. A car crash, choking on a piece of food, drowning in a swimming pool.

Your lives that you think grandiose are wipeable with the same thoughtlessness as with one swats a fly," the Absolute said, interlacing his fingers.

"I think you're projecting an awful lot. I don't know about humans, but *you've* certainly been dealing with an unending abyss, and now it's come for everything you've ever built," Joe threatened back.

The Absolute looked away, ceding the staring match to Joseph, and choosing instead to stare at the house atop the hill. In a disappointed tone, he spoke, "I came here to rearm you, to make you my champion in the war you're a part of."

"I can do well enough on my own," Joe said. "Why don't you fuck off to some distant corner of one of your many universes and watch from afar. Apparently that's all you're good for."

"I am most disappointed in the way our relationship is ending, Joseph Banbury."

"Well, then you shouldn't have fucked our relationship to begin with."

For a second it seemed like the Absolute, brought to utter frustration, was about to strike Joseph Banbury. In the next moment, he pulled back his arm and stepped back, disappearing without ceremony, without so much as a flash of light.

His blood pressure spiking, his head throbbing with equal parts rage and migraine, Joseph climbed back up the hill, cursing the Absolute under his breath. He walked around the house and saw Amy standing there, her eyes wet with tears, her hand covering her mouth as Billy gave her consoling pats on the shoulder.

"Ames," Joe began.

Billy Hawthorne shook his head somberly.

"Amy." Joe walked up the stairs and held his sister. She burst into violent sobs against his chest, her wails filled with pain.

"What happened?" Joe asked, putting his hand softly upon her head.

"It's Mom," Amy whispered, looking up at him. "I just got a call from Dad five minutes ago. He's beside himself. Mom had an aneurysm. He called an ambulance, but being so close to the city, it's hard for anyone to get through. The parasites have taken over so much of it."

Whatever else she had to say was lost in gut-wrenching sobs.

Joseph Banbury stood there with his blood freezing in his veins, his hands shivering uncontrollably.

7

PROVIDENCE

Lilly Thurman huffed, frustrated, tired. A forty-five-minute long drive on the I-95 leading them to Providence, Rhode Island, a town familiar to her through the centuries, but given that she'd come here under very different circumstances now, she could not feel any of the familiarity that she'd felt when she'd attended Brown University for a brief spell in the 1950s.

When life was long and you ran out of things to do, you started eyeing universities as an excellent prospect for killing time, four years at a time. She attended its anthropology undergraduate program, eager to learn an academic thing or two about socio-cultural anthropology, linguistics, and paleoethnobotany, a personal favorite subject of hers that explored the relationship between humans and plants. As a witch, it had fascinated her.

And then, the 50s were over, and with it, the freedom of the post-war era, teaching Lilly Thurman another grave lesson. Human beings were addicted to warfare. It had only been five years since the end of the Second World War when the Korean War began. Two years after the Korean War's armistice, the Vietnam War started, and by the time it was 1964, Lyndon B. Johnson gave the green light for open combat operations in Vietnam.

As terrible as the war was, it gave Lilly an up-close opportunity to look at another side of the human coin. Resilience in the face of all that was wrong. Back home, the people went out in droves as part of the antiwar movement, inventing an entirely new form of poetry, giving birth to the music of the late 20th century, loving each other fiercely in the most uncertain of times, and never stopping to believe in the values that they held close, of which freedom was above all.

"The way you've been quiet, it's almost like you've got deep history with this town," Blake said, rolling down his window to let out the heaviness in the car.

"I attended Brown for a few years when I was bored," Lilly said, giving no more thoughts on the matter. Blake was good company, but he was also sometimes quite dumb company. He wasn't like Joseph, who rose to challenge everything she said, or intelligently wrestled with her on every intellectual minutia.

"Brown?" Blake blurted out. Lilly almost anticipated having to roll her eyes at whatever he'd say, but then, what he said instead made her surprised. "My father went to Brown."

"No way."

"It's not jarheads all the way," Blake said, looking out the Providence River that ran to his left. From here, Lilly made a turn on Memorial Boulevard. The WaterFire installation in the Waterplace Park was lit up, little bonfires above the surface of the water, casting a warm glow on the colonial buildings across the street. They didn't linger to admire the sight, because Lilly's spell was pulsing uncontrollably, signaling that Rafael was near.

They drove across to downtown Providence, where the old buildings stood tall. From here, the Rhode Island State House with its massive dome was visible, illuminated by lights, standing like a beacon in the night sky. The tall tower of the First Baptist Church in America jutted out like a spear.

They drove past the Arcade Providence, a spanning building with Greek columns, saw the three-story brick market house in College Hill, and parked next to the Industrial National Bank Building on 111 Westminster Street.

"You surprise me," Lilly commented, admiring the Kennedy Plaza bus terminal's green copper roof and its modest brick structure. The small terminal was humbled by the four-hundred-foot Art Deco building in front of it.

"I'll tell you something else," Blake said, pointing at the Industrial National Bank Building. "They call this the Superman Building. Did you know that?"

"Huh?" Lilly was busy sensing the spell to ascertain which direction Rafael had gone in. The spell did not signal that he was north, south, east, or west. The spell was signaling up. Lilly looked up at the grand building with its fine-grain Indiana limestone structure, a broad base that transitioned into narrower shafts and culminated into a stepped crown and lantern. The lantern sat atop a series of progressively smaller setbacks, giving the silhouette a sense of tapering elegance. Its Neo-Gothic verticality complemented its Art Deco style much like the Empire State Building without overdoing anything.

"Because it resembles the Daily Bugle building where Superman works," Blake said, a little frustrated that Lilly wasn't paying as much attention to him as he wanted. He scoffed under his breath and got out of the car.

Lilly parked the truck on the street, put a few coins in the parking meter, and then followed Blake.

"Hey, listen up. I'd have loved to come to Providence with you and go over every building and its history and architecture style, and how your dad enjoyed Brown University, but this isn't the time. We're..."

"Hunting a vampyre, I know," Blake grumbled.

"What's your problem?"

Blake stopped dead in his tracks, pedestrians walking all around him, looking at him rudely but not saying anything, because this was Rhode Island, not New York City where you got an earful for sidewalk obstruction. Here, a rude glance was all you were going to get.

"My problem is everyone's problem with you but they refuse to say it so they don't hurt your feelings," Blake said, looking at her darkly, any infatuation that he had for her buried under anger and an uneven stubble.

"I beg your pardon?" Lilly snapped back, folding her arms, glaring at Blake.

"That's what it is. You're so wound up in purpose and self-righteousness that you never actually stop to register that it's other human beings around you, people with feelings, people who might want to get to know you, people who deserve your time. Joe might not have said that, or Amy or Billy for that matter, but I certainly feel it. All night I've been by your side, first scouting the cemetery, then scouring the forest, and then getting into the truck with you and driving for almost an hour in search of a fucking vampyre. And we've only had like two or three sentences of small talk in all that while," Blake said.

"I don't know what you think I am or in what capacity you see me," Lilly snapped. "But you're under no obligation to be with me. I don't have the luxury of wasting time indulging in small talk or going over history or trivia or this and that!"

"Glad you made things clear," Blake said, shrugging and turning away.

Fucking infant, Lilly thought to herself as she brushed past him and entered the abandoned building. It hadn't been in use for more than fifteen years. Perfect for a vampyre to seek refuge in. She looked around the lobby, and only groaned in increasing frustration as she saw that the building's elevator was out of commission.

"You coming?!" she called out sternly. No one replied to her. She looked back and saw that Blake had not walked in behind her. At this moment, she didn't have the energy to deal with him or dissolve the unnecessary drama that he was always creating. To think that he'd give it a rest even after everything, but no. It was the same old aggressive Blake Weston trying to wear her down into saying, *Yes, sure, I'll bite. I'll go on a date with you when it's all over, hear all about what a fascinating soldier you were, and how many brave battles you were a part of. My, my, Blake Weston, what mysterious aura you've mustered in your personality. The smolder, the manliness. Your traditional wired instincts to protect me make me feel like I can lower my defenses and let you handle it.*

"Enough. It's getting a little too real," Lilly commented to thin air, and then cleaved a portal that would lead her to the roof of the tower. After all, that was where Rafael was. And between going after a lovelorn man-child throwing fits and the last surviving member of an undead species, she wanted to deal with the more pressing matter at hand.

Lilly stepped in through the portal, now standing atop the roof of the Superman Building. The first thing she noticed was the water damage everywhere. Black splotches of dried water had seeped into the walls, making moss grow on the rooftop. Air conditioner exterior units sat in rows, gathering rust and dirt. The exhaust ducts were caked with long strands of spiderwebs and dirt. Lilly could tell just by looking that no air had come through these ducts in years. Below, the white-and-orange-lit city with its streetlamp-lit roads, the luminescence behind each of the windows in the scores of buildings, and the reflection of the night sky on the Providence River were all quite a timeless sight, but the question still remained: Where was Rafael?

Her spell had stopped now. It did not blip nor signal in any direction, making Lilly doubt her magic as she began to recast it. There were still floors above her, the building growing narrower, the unlit lantern at the very top like a dark, ominous crystal.

"Rafael?" Lilly called out when her spell did nothing. It fizzled out, leaving no trace.

Against the contrast of all the city lights, the rooftop seemed darker than normal. Lilly walked carefully, her eyes peering around corners to see if anything was out of the ordinary. She tried to get into Rafael's head and imagine why he'd come here, of all places. She got nothing. The man was an enigma even before his entombment. What he was now, after so many centuries, Lilly did not know anymore.

This was a judgment lapse on her part. A consequence of having too many kettles on too many stoves. She could have checked in on him from time to time to see if he was doing all right in the crypt. But then again, being as busy as her, there were bound to be a few things that one lost track of.

Including her magic. She could feel it coming and going on its own, as if it was angry with her. Or, worse yet, if the source of all magic, the Madam, was purposefully limiting her powers. Could that be? Or was it just her beaten-down self no longer able to wield magic as she once used to? It could have been the distortion in the magical field in the known universe, all thanks to the Abstract. But if that was it, then why did she feel so weak within? Like she was being torn from the inside out like a ruthless tailor unraveling old fabric.

She walked around another corner, hoping to see Rafael there, all out of sorts. But there was just more of the forgotten rooftop here, with water marks deep in the walls. Except... these right in front of her were darker than the rest of the water damage. She cast her light upon it, hoping that her magic would come through. It did, but weakly. A frail beam of light fell upon the suspicious color and texture on the wall, and only when Lilly Thurman had seen it up close did she realize that it was congealed blood. She gasped and stepped back, beginning to trace the blood splatters to the other corner of the roof. The blood grew thinner, its splatter pattern turning into drops, as if a body was being dragged by a predator not done with its corpse just yet.

Lilly turned the last corner and halted dead in her tracks. A security guard lay there dead, his shirt torn open, his face slashed ruthlessly, blood still dripping out of his lacerated neck. One of the eyeballs, being so horribly gashed, was hanging out of its socket. There was a darker pool of liquid underneath the man's seat, his pants wet. It stank of putrid urine and coppery blood, the two scents mixed together. The dead man's hand was curled in a pointing sign, as if in his dying moments he had blamefully aimed his index finger at his killer.

Lilly stood where she did, ten feet away from the body, watching the trail of blood lead up the roof in blotches and drops, and disappear behind the lantern. And there, by the shadow of the glass-covered lantern, stood a dark shadow with cat-like eyes livid and red, his clothes flailing in the wind like sails of a ghostly pirate ship. He held onto the lantern with one hand, and from the other one fresh blood dripped, falling upon Lilly's face.

She had only a moment to recollect herself, but that moment came and went, and within it, the vampyre atop the lantern descended with ferocious speed, landing upon her before she had a chance to conjure a defensive spell. His body was heavy and agile, making Lilly fall and hit her head on the roof's floor. Dazed, she held out a hand to plead, but the vampyre grabbed her by the neck and threw her effortlessly. Lilly was flung to the edge of the roof, her head beyond the edge, hearing all the traffic sounds coming from twenty-six stories below, her hair flying in every direction, blotting her vision out. Her body was still on the roof's edge for the moment, but it wouldn't be for much longer. She saw the vampyre walk up to her in a slow, menacing speed.

"Rafael!" Lilly called out to instill any familiarity. She could sense that he was not thinking straight, and that this cold-blooded murder wasn't the only dead body he'd left behind. There were two in Bridgewater, and who knew how many in between. "Rafael. It's not too late. You have to stop."

The vampyre, soaked in all the silhouettes that fled to him from every corner of the roof, drawn to him like licks of flame to a roaring fire, strode forward, and when he was close to Lilly, he knelt, putting his long-nailed, skeletal, pale hand around her neck, letting her see his face for the first time since his reappearance. His cheeks were sullen and gaunt, blood upon his lips, his two long teeth jutting out from his grimacing mouth. He snarled wordlessly, his psyche fractured beyond the usage of words, his confusion and rage apparent.

Lilly knew that if she couldn't muster another spell in the next second, this would be her end. There was no clause in her immortality agreement with the Collector that she'd still live if she fell from four hundred feet. Even if she would, what kind of comatose, broken existence would it be? She summoned her magic, and her heart sank when it did not heed her call.

"Please," she begged as he pushed her another few inches off the roof. "I never meant to..."

Rafael lowered his head next to hers with the cadence of a past lover seeking to steal one last kiss, and then opened his mouth, bringing his teeth closer to Lilly's throat.

She braced for the pain, and the fall after. To her, it felt like taking a shortcut. If she were to die now, she wouldn't have to deal with anything that'd come after. Not the Abstract, not the politics of godhood, not Joe, not—

Blake Weston emerged from behind Rafael, a tall figure illuminated by the lights coming from below, a stark contrast to the vampyre, who was submerged in shadows. Blake pistol whipped Rafael in the back of the head, making the vampyre faint and fall on top of Lilly.

With one swift movement, Blake threw Rafael onto the roof and grabbed Lilly's hand, pulling her away from danger.

He watched her gather her breath, coughing, panting on all fours beside the edge. In the meantime, he went over to Rafael, who was still knocked unconscious. Blake Weston procured old ropes that were meant for tying tarp over the external electrical equipment in case of a storm. There was no more tarp, only rope. He took it all and began winding it around the vampyre, tying him to one of the big Hitachi external units. When he was sure of his handiwork, Blake stepped back, repulsed by the vampyre. In all his life he had never touched someone so cold. Not even the dead bodies back in the war zones that he'd help put in black body bags were this cold.

Only in a morgue had he once touched someone this cold, but by then their body had been on ice for a day.

"Are you okay?" Blake shifted his attention to Lilly, staying just close enough that he'd be able to lend a hand if needed, but far enough away that he wouldn't appear like an over-chivalrous knight in shining armor.

"Where did you come from?" Lilly panted, holding her sides. She put her hand against the wall and gathered herself, first running her hand through her hair, then slowly standing up, adjusting her shirt, pulling up her jeans.

"I regretted not following you into the hotel, so I took the elevator," Blake said, not taking his eyes off Rafael.

"The elevator was not working."

"It wasn't anything a little tinkering couldn't fix. I hotwired it."

"Thanks for the backup."

"Don't mention it."

When Lilly could breathe normally again, she walked up to Rafael and placed her hand on his head, muttering a reviving incantation, unsure if it would work. But it worked, and Rafael came to, thrashing furiously against the rope.

"Release me!" Rafael screamed.

"Calm down!" Lilly commanded, her voice heavy, carrying within it great authority that reverberated with a mystical energy that couldn't be called magic, and yet was every bit as potent.

"Who are you to tell me to calm down?" Rafael growled, his dirty hair covering his face, his seething eyes staring from behind.

"I am a friend," Lilly said, kneeling beside him. "And if you don't remember, allow me to jog your memory."

~

IT TOOK some patience on all three of their parts for it to work. First, Lilly tried to replenish her magic, coaxing and pleading to it to work so that she could heal Rafael. Nothing happened at first, and for that brief spell of twenty minutes, Rafael was still inconsolable, a bloodthirsty beast trying to undo the knots that Blake had tied so masterfully.

Then, when her magic finally worked—and that, too, only grimly, with a flickering warning that it might not work again —Lilly cast the spell of calm and recollection on Rafael, hoping that it would suffice as a quick fix.

"Thank you," Rafael said slowly as Lilly lifted her hand away, allowing Rafael to subdue his tumultuousness and tap into his saner mind. When that was done, he explained what had happened to him, and how for the past few years he was buried alive and awake, the Devil's blood burning within him. He told Lilly about the altercations that he'd had with Satan. Lilly first listened intently, and then, when Rafael was done sharing his side, she told him all that she could tell him, with Blake chipping in every now and then.

When they'd gone over the events of recent history, Rafael sat there, still bound in ropes, and said, "I cannot believe that I was overcome so...viciously by my bloodlust. I have murdered no less than five people in one night. And I wish I could say that I did it on my own, but you know my condition, witch. The more I drank, the more I lost control. It wasn't until you... you came and helped me as you did that I regained myself."

"You were my responsibility," Lilly said, aware that nothing could be done now of those who had died by Rafael's hand. "Those deaths aren't on you alone."

"Come what punishment may, I am ready," Rafael said, lowering his head.

It was Blake who made the first move. He went over to Rafael and undid the ropes, freeing the vampyre.

"What..." Rafael began.

"I, too, bear the burden of having taken lives that had no right to be taken," Blake said slowly, and then backed away, still a little cautious of the vampyre.

"I thank you, gentleman, and assure you that while I am still possessing of my sobriety, I shall not maim another soul," Rafael said with genuine contrition.

"You are a danger to yourself and to others while you're free. The world isn't as it once was, Rafael," Lilly said, sitting cross-legged on the floor. Her blue shirt was matted with dirt, and her jeans had ripped in several places. But if someone could pull off that disheveled look and still appear graceful, it was Lilly, and she looked quite composed and elegant, even with her present demeanor.

"Then do with me what you will," Rafael said, standing up and walking over to the edge of the roof, beholding all of Providence below. "Look upon the works of these men, these successful enterprising men who built their empires, sprawling these roads and tall these buildings. My master wanted nothing more than this for his people, and what did he get in its stead? Death. Was it too much to ask of fate, that our people lived safely in these lands, tucked away in the Redwoods?"

Neither Lilly nor Blake said anything.

"I envy the short-lived lives of all those who built these

monuments and minarets, who paved that river yonder with light and fire, who scalded the earth and made it so that their vehicles may roam freely, and if I am to be terribly sincere, I miss my master," Rafael cried, tears spilling down his cheeks. "I miss him dearly."

"Then let me take you to him," Lilly said, the idea coming to her with unbridled spontaneity.

"My master is dead," Rafael growled.

"But he still rests there. I made sure of that," Lilly revealed.

Rafael looked at her, his eyes widening with gratitude and surprise. "You did?"

"He was a great man deserving of a final resting place. I gave him one." Lilly nodded. "Come along now. Both of you." She held out both her hands. Blake took her palm first, and then, after much deliberation, Rafael clasped her hand in his.

This time around, Lilly did not plead with her magic, but instead scolded it to appear, summoning it with authority, telling it to cut the shit.

The portal appeared meekly, the Californian Redwoods visible on the other side. Lilly stepped through with the two men walking beside her, and came out on the other side in the preserved ruins of Little Istria.

Rafael gasped upon seeing that the rubble was all gone. The buildings that were left standing in the aftermath were missing walls, windows, and roofs, but at least they were still there. The Border House in the distance. The Feeding House. The forgotten pleasures of the Breeding House. Much care had gone into preserving this place, and it showed in the way the cobblestone pathways around the town were clean and gleaming. How the lamps were still lit. How the unnatural quiet of the place made it feel as if vampyres still lurked behind glazed windows.

"Where are they? All those who died?" Rafael whispered weakly as he walked from door to door, peering inside, suspending his disbelief even if for moments so that he could imagine his brothers and sisters coming out to greet him in the night.

"Buried in the courtyard cemetery, along with Elton himself," Lilly said. "When I came here after the battle, I took care of the dead. Burned the corpses of those who belonged to the Order of the Shroud. Somehow, it did not seem fitting that I did the same to the vampyres. So I buried them. You shall find that Elton rests beside the tombstones of his daughters and wife, so that his soul may know some kind of peace."

They followed Rafael as he led them through one building and another, headed for the courtyard where all the tombstones were. The well that led deep into the basement was filled with water, no longer giving any access to underground torture chambers. All around in the courtyard were tombstones marking the sites where vampyres were buried. Iron grills around the flowerbeds glinted with perpetual dew. Lilies and white roses climbed out of the flowerbeds and hung over the grills. No nightbird chirped nor did any wind rustle a single leaf, even though there was a sprawling yew tree in the courtyard, its dozens of limb-like branches bowing with the weight of hundreds of thousands of leaves and vines.

Rafael knelt beside the grave of his master, his head against the tombstone, his tears falling in the dirt. He held onto the tombstone with both hands as he wept, "Master. I killed them all. I found every last one of them across this accursed continent and killed every single one of the Order of the Shroud to avenge you."

Blake Weston was overwhelmed by the imposing Gothic architecture of this building, assuming its haunted past, conjuring imagery of blood dripping from gashes in necks, women screaming in pleasure and pain, and dead bodies hanging upside down, their viscera hanging out of cuts in their torsos. If he closed his eyes, he could hear the screams that still echoed in these walls after all this time.

Lilly had brought Rafael here because she figured it would serve as some kind of closure, maybe help him recover some part of his mind, and then move on. What happened next was neither her intention nor something that she had anticipated.

A hand shot out of the grave where she had buried Elton's remains. And they had been remains, she was sure of that, because after the explosion of the tower, there wasn't much of Elton left whole to complete his body.

The hand reached and held onto Rafael's throat, using him to pull the rest of the body out. And yet, the body that came out of the grave was not physical. It was a specter, reeking of ectoplasm, emitting a ghastly green-blue light, resembling Elton Grando in every last detail.

"You failed me, and to think that I called you son!" Elton screamed as he hoisted Rafael by the neck.

"Master!" Rafael's lamentation came out of his croaking throat, his disbelief making his body limp.

"A damned failure," Elton Grando boomed, his angry eyes

torn wide open, his mouth pulled in a frightening sneer. "The harbinger of my demise!"

"No, master!"

"ENOUGH!" Lilly Thurman said, raising her hand and banishing the phantasm, shredding its spectral body into thin wisps. It did not take much effort to exorcise this spirit, for it wasn't a spirit at all. Just a lingering echo of the blood magic that was steeped into every wall and stone, its potency holding strong even after centuries.

But Rafael had no way of knowing that. As his master's ghost disappeared, he himself came undone in deep mourning, curling in a fetal position.

"Rafael," Lilly said. "You have to know that that wasn't your master's soul."

"How can I know that?!" Rafael responded despondently, looking at her with haggard eyes. "After everything he said, everything you heard, what purpose is left of my existence? I should drown myself in shame that my master, even after his death, would admonish me for my failure!"

"Because that wasn't Elton. The world is coming undone. The Abstract attacks the very fabric of our universe. Things are happening all over every continent that defy reason. Thousands of people dream the same dream every night, their collective psychosis worsened when their worst suspicions are affirmed the next morning. That everyone dreamt the same dream. Of the world's destruction. The Abstract has messed up the world's balance, making it askew," Lilly shouted. "My magic waxes and wanes, something it has never done before. These are uncertain times, with uncertain things around every corner. The Devil walks among men as their accomplice, not their adversary. God is dead and we have killed Her. If, somehow, in all this, an apparition appears out of the grave, do not consider it absolute reality, for it is not."

"Then what is it?"

"Dude, you just said that your body was, like, filled with the blood of Satan until tonight," Blake said, hoping to claw some reason out of this madness. A vampyre's ghost was not on his bingo cards, nor was seeing an actual living vampyre. "Maybe it did something to your physiology, something that would take some time to get used to. You haven't been yourself all night, something that can be attributed to that same blood? And maybe when your tears fell upon the grave, they stirred your own restless guilt into that ghost you saw."

"It's one too many maybes," Rafael said, wiping his tears, no longer in the fetal position, but kneeling beside the grave. "But we do not have any proof that my master died having made his peace with me."

"Actually," Lilly said, producing something out of thin air. It was a very yellow and dated parchment, all of it whole and preserved by a brand of magic that even she did not know. She had found this on what remained of Elton's person, deep within the pocket of his burnt and tattered cloak. It had surprised her that the letter was whole. It was folded, addressed, *To Rafael*. She'd tucked it away for safekeeping, not knowing when would be the time to show it to him.

Except now, the opportunity had presented itself.

"A letter, from your master," Lilly said, giving Rafael the

parchment. He held it with great reverence, gently unfolding it and holding it up in the moonlight.

Dear Rafael.

If you are within possession of this letter, then I am dead and we never got a chance to make amends. For that, I am very remorseful. I would have liked to have my one true ally, my blood, my kin by my side when I met my end.

As of writing this letter, I am still alive, and this makes me wonder what kind of magic wordcraft is. When I finish this letter, I shall seal it in my own magic, magic that will make it so that only you will be able to open it. Fire will not scorch it. Time will not weather it. It will remain preserved until it finds its way to you, and in that regard, words have made me immortal.

How strange, isn't it? That all the authors of yore who died centuries ago still find pulpits from which to deliver their didactic monologues, and we know of those pulpits as books, books that teach and entertain and terrify, sometimes all on the same page.

Oh, I would have wished to write a book if I'd ever had the time.

Maybe you can do it in my stead.

But it is not literature or words that I intend to discuss with you, Rafael.

I must first address the matter upon which we parted.

I am sorry for how things turned out. I should not have banished you as I did. You should have put up more of a fight. We should have fought like father and son, or better yet, as brothers, or even as close friends. But we did not do that, and that has made all the difference.

Now, I do not know what happens. But I know this. I cherished our relationship. You taught me more than I can admit. And in the deep dark hours of the night when the world slept, long after my wife and daughters had died, and madness was the island upon which I'd find myself stranded, it was you whose company brought me to saner shores. It was you who tended to me.

No saint am I, nor am I some prophet that my words will make quake the throne of God until they are heard. I am just a vampyre, the first of my kind. And I have not succeeded in my endeavors. I pray, not to a God or to Satan, but to you that may you thrive long after I am gone. And that may you find some manner of comfort in your long life.

And it does not matter that I am dead, Rafael. Death is just a doorway to another realm where the story continues, not ends. Here, on the other side of death, you may find me in bliss in the arms of my beloved wife, being peppered with kisses on the cheek by my two daughters.

And it is here, on the other side, that I may find you again. Not in Heaven, nor in Hell, nor in any structured afterlife that the organized religions of the world will try to peddle, for that is just fear-mongering for the sake of filling up offertory baskets.

Maybe on the other side, I will build Little Istria as I never got a chance to in this life. And if you ever find yourself there, look out for me on the tallest spire.

But in the meantime, Rafael, live in my stead, and you may find that even in death, I will live vicariously through you.

Your Lord, Father, and Friend,

Elton Grando.

He read the letter again and again while the other two stood there patiently, in silence, not wanting to intrude upon the personal moment, all the while keeping an eye for any other phantasm that might pop out.

Rafael gradually folded the letter and placed it in his breast pocket. He then looked up at Lilly with a deep mix of gratitude, sorrow, and closure.

"You have done me a service, madam witch, as no one has ever done me," Rafael whispered, his voice hallowed. "Thrice you have saved my life, and thrice I have done nothing to repay you."

"I do not do it for repayment," Lilly said, clasping his hands in her own and lifting him up. "I do it because someone must."

"Ever my good fortune that for me that someone is you, over and over again," Rafael smiled. "I feel much better now, all thanks to you."

"Then can we get the hell out of this place already?" Blake asked, unnerved.

"What do you say, Rafael? You wanna be a part of the ragtag group of misfits who are trying to save the world from its inevitable flaming end?" Lilly asked wearily, but underneath all that tiredness, there was a sliver of optimism and happiness.

"I do not know how I may contribute to the cause, but I am yours to command," Rafael said, bowing gently.

"Uh oh," Lilly said, pulling out her vibrating phone. A series of missed calls from Amy, and a message.

She looked up at Blake, and then at Rafael.

"I don't think we're done with cemeteries just yet," Lilly said. "There's been a death."

8

A BANBURY BURIAL

No matter what kind of a relationship a child has with their mother—whether it is a working relationship where two-way begrudging respect is earned in adulthood in the great aftermath of childhood and teenage years, or if it's a relationship where both parties are estranged on account of trauma, difference in views, or any other number of reasons—it is never easy for them to deal with the passing of the woman who brought them into the world.

Joseph Banbury was not quite ready to say goodbye to his mother. There were still a lot of unresolved things, unsaid sentiments, and now that she was dead, that's all they'd ever be. He never got a chance to say sorry to her, to hear her side of it, to have her apologize to him in a way that would really fill up the wound that was still throbbing in his heart. They'd grown amicable near the end, but that was just a mirage. It was not how he'd left things when he'd left them. Anything that happened afterward was just godly subterfuge. The real Joyce, the one who had been bitter toward Joe toward the very end, when he'd brought the girl back to life in Madison Square Garden and they had a terrible fight, was gone without ever clearing the air between the two of them.

When he'd met her again, both her and his father had taken that miracle drug Genesis X and were both looking younger and fitter than ever. Back then, Joyce had not picked a fight with Joe. It had seemed that she had forgotten all about it. She had offered him breakfast, and all her love. As much as he wanted to remember her that way, it wasn't truly her.

The real mother was underneath everything, underneath the miraculous dopamine-resetting mechanisms of Genesis X. And he hadn't had the chance to meet her. When he'd met her last, the many chemical changes that Genesis X made to one's body and mind had already affected her, making her independent of her religious obsession, treating her depression (for which she used religion as a crutch) and her anxiety. He had no qualms with that version of his mother.

And it wasn't that version of her that he missed terribly. He couldn't bring himself to walk into the same church as where Father O'Hara had died. Her funeral service was being held inside this church today, two days after her death, a death that was all but inevitable, if the doctors were to be believed.

It was late at night when the husband and wife were just talking, drinking coffee, sitting side by side while watching a nature documentary on their TV. They weren't really focused on the documentary as much as they were on the conversation.

Tommy recounted that Joyce was feeling really happy about her budding business, and that their conversation was all about how she'd save up enough money for a second honeymoon with her husband, and they'd finally visit Mexico as they'd always wanted.

And then she had reclined in her sofa and closed her eyes. Tommy had thought that maybe it was just her resting for a minute, but then the coffee cup, still filled with coffee, fell from her hands, unloading its scalding content on her lap. She did not respond. Her eyes were still closed, a little froth gathering on her lips.

"Joyce!" Tommy had screamed, and had tried to bring his wife back to consciousness. It was pure bad luck, where a blood vessel wall had formed wrong and was waiting to burst like a ticking time bomb, giving away at night.

By the time Joe, Amy, and Billy arrived, she was dead. Eyes closed, a faint smile on her face, her skin cold, her skin blue, the floral dress that she wore blotched black from the coffee stain that was still wet.

He wept, and with him, so did Amy. The two siblings stood there on either side of their father, holding onto him as their support. Their father with his bushy eyebrows and his burly figure stood there with silent tears running down his cheeks, clinging to his mustache, his cheeks withered and sunken, despite the Genesis X miracle treatment. There was no cure for grief, no matter what the pharmacists of the world said. Grief was its own cure, and Tommy Banbury was experiencing it in waves, witnessing his dead wife half-covered in a sheet.

Joyce was perfect in the way all mothers were perfect,

always looking out for her children, making sure they had clothes on their bodies, warm food in their stomach, their bed made, their homework done, and their daily religious duties fulfilled. She had brought them both into the world and then had molded them in her own image, as did every mother who birthed a child. Who else's mold was she going to borrow? And she raised them right, or as right as is expected of a lower-middle class woman working double-time to make ends meet and fend off poverty while also holding true to God and the Church, all in the same go as raising two children and ensuring that the world that was always out to get little vulnerable children didn't get hers. The world won every now and then, but most of the victories belonged to Joyce, for she raised them with rigor and constant vigilance as long as she could.

That was how Joe could remember her now, standing there with a coffee as he looked out the window. Lilly got out while Blake drove the truck off somewhere.

"Where is he going?" Joe had asked as the two met outside.

"There's someone in the truck who can't really come out in the daylight," Lilly had said, and then she'd given Joe a hug, a deep and tight hug that squeezed the sorrow out of Joe, letting him know that Lilly Thurman was still here for him, in whatever capacity it might be. As he hugged her, feeling her womanly warmth, he wished that it was his mother he was hugging, but it was a little too late for that.

The next day had gone by in a daze. People had come and gone from the house, uncles and cousins and aunts and long-lost relatives gathered for the first and last time to attend the funeral, which given the circumstances was arranged fast. For no one knew if the parasite was to return. Somehow, the two siblings and their father made do, and managed to entertain the guests while also taking care of the funeral home expenses, picking out a casket, and booking the church for the next day.

And now it was the next day, and Joe, still wrapped in disbelief and denial, stood in front of the church, watching people dressed in black—friends, neighbors, relatives, and acquaintances—climb up the steps and enter the building. Outside, surrounded by garlands, was a picture of Joyce in her youth, smiling at the camera, a dimple on her cheek. The words *In Loving Memory Of* were written above the picture.

Joyce was a Red Bank fixture, and as such, most of the people who knew her were in there.

Joe, in his black suit, stood with his eyes on the rapidly parking cars and the people, searching for someone. Lilly, Blake, Billy, and Amy were already in there, as was his father.

"It's rude to keep the departed waiting," Lucifer spoke slowly, emerging from behind the old oak tree on the church's front lawn. He was dressed in black as well, and looked every bit as somber as the rest of the attendants.

"I can't go in," Joe whispered.

"What would you have me do, Joseph?" Satan asked. "I can pause all of time so you can go inside and say goodbye without everyone looking at you, overhearing you as you say your final words to her."

"I wish I could have saved her," Joe said. "And then... reached some kind of truce."

"As do we all when faced with the death of someone whom we love to hate, hate to love," Satan said, giving Joe his arm. Joe passively took it, glad for the extra support, and then walked alongside the Devil as the two of them climbed the steps of the church and headed into the packed hall. All the heads turned as the two walked in.

"Easy does it, son," Satan said, walking slow so his steps matched Joe's.

Joe's head was low, staring at the marble floor, his ears listening yet not listening to the words of the priest who stood where once Father O'Hara used to. He spotted his childhood friend Mike sitting in the pews, and a handful of his neighbors, who looked at him with sorrowful smiles. Lilly sat at the front with Amy. Tommy sat beside them, staring affixed at the open casket wherein his wife lay in a pale green dress that she'd handstitched herself and had always worn on picnics, family outings, and intimate dates with her husband. There was just a little bit of makeup on her face, accentuating her features such that it seemed like she was alive and merely sleeping in front of the great audience that had assembled in the church for her.

As Joseph made his way to the front-most pew, Satan let go and stepped back, opting to sit in one of the pews in the back.

Joe sat alongside his dad and looked up at the dais, where the priest acknowledged Joe's arrival.

"Joyce was a fierce believer, despite all the ways in which the world tried to shatter her belief. She'd show up to the church, contribute all that she could even when times were tough. And she did it for the act of giving itself, not for some reward. She told me that once. She believed that humans were put on this earth to be kind to each other, because God hadn't created us for worship, but for our humanity. That we'd be nice to each other. As she was. As her husband is. As her children continue to be," the priest said, rapping his hand on the dais, punctuating the many sobs that came from the attendants.

First it was Amy's turn to speak some words. Whatever they were, Joe didn't hear them. His eyes were on the shadow pooling in one corner of the hall, right beside the door that led into the backrooms. A shadow had no business being there at this time of day. The place was illuminated from all the windows bringing in ample August sunlight.

And yet the dark pool remained there, waiting. Joe could make out the outline of a presence, but it couldn't be.

Then it was his father's turn.

While he was speaking, Joe turned back and looked at the Devil. The Devil nodded in the direction of the shadow, confirming Joe's suspicion.

A Collector had come for Joyce.

But why had it come now?

Why not two days ago when she had died and her soul needed collecting?

Was it because—

Time stopped, and it wasn't the Devil's doing. He sat there motionless with the rest of the people, all of them looking at Tommy Banbury trying to muster the courage to address so many people at once, and that, too, about his dead wife. But even he had paused mid-sentence, his arm lifted in the air.

Joe looked all around him, and only when he had confirmed that everyone was unmoving did he get up and head over to the place where the Collector stood. It floated above the ground, its presence pushing off smoke and blackness as a shroud. Underneath its cloak, the skeletal presence acknowledged Joe with two bright eyes.

"Do you know who I am?" Joe asked.

"I know you to be this world's God," the Collector spoke in a rattling voice.

"I'm not too sure about that," Joe said, looking up at the hooded figure. "Just as I'm not sure why you're here."

"She insisted," the Collector said, pointing in the opposite direction. "Our kind honors last requests. Otherwise, Collection would be impossible."

Joe didn't want to turn around. Turning around would hurt too much. He had tried to rationalize it as many times as he could that it was the Absolute trying to get back at Joe by killing his mother with an aneurysm, but no matter how many times he tried to convince himself of this antagonization, something always felt off.

"I wanted to go," she said, and upon hearing her voice, Joe finally got the courage to turn around and face his mother. "It's no one's fault."

"Mom," Joe said, walking the length of the church and meeting her underneath the cross. Next to her spirit lay her body in the open casket, looking frail, looking peaceful.

"I wasn't myself by the end there, Joe," Joyce said. She wore the same dress as her corpse, but looked remarkably younger than her dead self. "Genesis X, or whatever that gosh darn treatment was called, it changed me a little too much from the inside."

"I..."

"You should know, Joseph Banbury, that no matter your

station in life, whether you ascend to the highest of heavens or descend to the deepest pits of Hell, you are going to be my son. A mother loves her son dearly. There is no love that can come near, and the universe can attest to that," Joyce spoke softly, looking upon Joe with kindness.

"I..."

"I know what you want to say, dear. You wish it didn't have to end on that bitter note. And let's just say that it hasn't. *This*, Joe, is the final note. And I do not find it bitter whatsoever." Joyce turned her attention to the attendants. "Everyone I've ever known is here. My beautiful daughter. My lovely husband. And I see that the Devil's come to pay his dues too," Joyce said with great calmness. "And you, you're here. The only fear I had while dying was that maybe you'd miss out on our goodbye."

"Your love was tough," Joe said, not bothering to wipe away the tear that rolled down his face. "But it made me who I am."

"I could never say it in life, because when we are alive, trifles such as pride and ego get in the way of what we really want to say, but I am unburdened of all of that now, so let me say it. I'm proud of you, Joe," Joyce said, putting both her hands on her son's cheeks and bringing his face down so she could kiss him on the forehead.

He reached forward to hold her in his arms, only to find that he couldn't, that she wasn't there anymore, and neither was the Collector.

Time resumed its ticking, and all the people in the church breathed in unison. Joe found himself sitting where he was, feeling as if he'd just woken up from a deep sleep.

"Son..." Tommy said, beckoning with his hand.

Joe walked over to the dais, his father taking leave rather thankfully. In his hands he held a piece of paper on which he'd scribbled several lines, none of them feeling like they'd do justice. So, in perfect Banbury fashion, he stowed the paper away and decided to go off-script.

"Here lies my mother, and with her, all her hopes and dreams, all her desires," he began, all too aware that it was a little ruthless how he'd begun, but he had something better planned. Out of the corner of his eye he could see the priest reeling in anticipation of the wrong thing being said, same as he could see Amy bracing Lilly. But sitting behind them, Satan simply smiled, and upon seeing him, so, too, did Joe.

"That's what it seems like, doesn't it? That when a person dies, everything that made them alive is swept up under the great cosmic rug of nothingness, that it's too late. That my mom would never get to go on her second honeymoon to Mexico. That she'd never buy that one Prada purse that she'd had her eyes on for the longest time back when Prada still used to have ads in real magazines, real paper. I wanted to buy her that purse. I never did. She never asked for it other than mentioning it to Dad a couple of times while perusing those old magazines, *The Atlantic*, the *New Yorker*, what have you. 'Heathen publications,' she'd jokingly call them. Yet, they remained her guilty pleasures. She couldn't get enough of the stories in them."

Here, a little chuckle rang through the crowd.

"And I think much of my creativity comes to me from my mother. It's not something you inherit once and that's it. It's a constant process. Now that she's not here, I feel like a door has closed up on me forever."

Amy sobbed loudly, her voice echoing all the way up to the roof, the sound of her sob making others sob out of solidarity.

"I can only say this without giving much away. The spirit is immortal. As are dreams. Desires live on long after we're gone. And may my mother know some kind of Heaven, one with sandy beaches, a deep blue ocean as far as the eye can see, a warm sun, all the *Atlantic* magazines that she'd want to read, and a pina colada in her hand. If I close my eyes, I can already see her there, big straw hat too big for her head shielding her from the sunrays. She's happy there. Wherever that is," Joe said. It wasn't the perfect note to end on, but who was looking for perfect?

There was a little cheer and scattered clapping as he walked away from the dais. He leaned close to her head and planted a kiss on her forehead, whispering, "Goodbye, Mom."

THEY BURIED her in the cemetery behind the church, a large reserve of land populated with as many trees and plants as there were headstones.

It was evening by the time everyone left. But Joe still stood there by the six-foot-deep hole at the bottom of which the coffin lay. He stood there alone, watching the sun go down behind the trees.

"I have a request," Joe said to the only other figure that stood beside him under the yew tree.

"Speak, although that is not what I came here for," the Collector said. "You have been summoned by the Head Amasser."

"And I will be there shortly," Joe said, looking the Collector dead in the eyes.

"What is it you ask?"

"Treat her soul with care," Joe said. "It's not an order. Just a request."

The Collector did not respond with words. Only a brief nod, to which Joe responded by nodding back.

"This next part, we kinda do all by ourselves, sir," the gravedigger said, coming around the tree with a spade in hand. He was a simple-looking, if somewhat cheery, man in a red checkered shirt and faded black jeans. He wore tall boots that went up to his shins. He had a long beard that he was altogether too young to have, but having that beard gave his face some gravitas that suited a gravedigger. If Joe were to hazard a guess, the man was no older than thirty-five.

The Collector was there no more, only Joe standing by the empty chairs.

"Mind if I lend you a hand? Grunt work's what I need right now to get out of my own head."

"Let me fetch another spade."

When the gravedigger came back with a spare spade, the two of them began filling the hole with dirt, and they continued long after the sun had gone down, stopping only when there was no more loose dirt left, and the hole was level with the rest of the cemetery ground.

After the gravedigger had left, Joe stood there for another

fifteen minutes, looking at the tombstone that said, *Here Lies Joyce Banbury—Mother, Wife, Of Fierce Faith and Stern Resolve.*

Underneath that, upon Joyce's posthumous insistence in her will, there was a verse from Revelations. 21:4, to be precise.

"He will wipe every tear from their eyes. There will be no more death or mourning or crying or pain, for the old order of things has passed away."

As Joe bid his mother one last farewell and then walked away to his car, he mused about the Bible verse, wondering if it was supposed to be a consoling sentiment to him or instructions.

When night fell upon Red Bank Cemetery, a lonesome figure emerged from behind the shade of the yew tree over Joyce Banbury's grave. He knelt beside her grave and planted a single rose in the fresh dirt on her grave. And then he, too, like everyone else, was gone.

Joe's late appearance at the Banbury residence was on purpose. He didn't want to be there at the wake. By the time he arrived, the last of the guests had left, leaving behind the Morningstar Tribe members.

His father had gone to bed, saying that he had been up for three days and hadn't rested a wink. "Not that I can rest a wink all alone in my bed," is what he'd said to Amy as he'd gone into his room. Amy had gone in there with him, choosing to sit on the armchair in the corner of the room, reading one of her mother's old magazines while her father fell into a deep, snoring slumber.

Lilly, Blake, and Billy were in the living room, a beer each in hand, looking tired from having to deal with all the guests in Joe's absence. The place was cluttered with trash and paper plates and leftover food when Joe walked in the house.

"Let me get that for you," Lilly said, snapping her fingers and making all that trash disappear into thin air. "Now it's the landfill's problem, and not ours."

"Your magic's come back, eh?" Joe asked.

"It comes and goes," Lilly said, getting up from the sofa and walking over to Joe, giving him a squeeze with her arm around him, beckoning him to the empty seat. "How are you doing?"

"About as well as one can hope in such circumstances," Joe said, taking a beer from Blake and giving him an acknowledging nod. Blake nodded back.

"Is everyone gone?" a voice came from the top of the stairs.

"Who is that?" Joe asked, alarmed, turning his head to locate the mysterious person.

"You haven't met him yet," Billy said. "From what I've heard, he's a vampyre. Although, between you and me, he just looks very pale. Like an anemic."

"You can come down now, Rafael," Blake said.

"Much thanks, Mr. Weston," Rafael said, climbing down the stairs.

Since this was the first time Joe was meeting a living vampyre, he got up to his feet, not knowing what to expect. There was a lot of stuff that the group hadn't discussed with each other in the wake of Joyce's death, and somehow, the most pertinent of facts were lost in the chaos of the funeral. Such as there being a vampyre in the house.

"You don't have to be so formal all the time," Blake said a little frustratedly.

"You must be Joseph Banbury," Rafael said, holding out a pale, skeletal hand. Joe shook it with some caution. "I am most terribly grieved to hear of your loss, sir."

"Thank you," Joe said.

"Oh, Jesus Christ!" Amy gasped as she reappeared in the living room. "I can't. I can't. I know you're supposed to be a vampyre and everything, but I can't...just..."

"Come now, Ames. Is that any way to treat a guest?" Joe asked. "Please, Mr..."

"Von Thorburn. Dr. Rafael Von Thorburn, sir," Rafael said, feeling a little embarrassed.

"I'll just call you Rafael if it's all the same," Joe said.

Rafael gave a brief bowing nod.

"It's a vampyre!" Amy said, her face drained, exhausted, eyes red, cheeks pulled in grimness.

"Why don't you go to sleep, sis?" Joe asked. "You've been up as long as Dad has."

"What guarantee can anyone give me that I won't find him lingering in my bedroom, eager to drink my blood while I'm sleeping!?" Amy lashed out.

Everyone processed grief in their own way, and it was clear to Joe that for Amy this wasn't about Rafael being a vampyre as much as it was being in a house devoid of their mother's very large and domineering presence. Her subconscious was trying to step up to the occasion and fill in that large presence all by itself.

"Madam, upon my word as the last of my kind, I shall never do you or your kin any harm," Rafael said.

"Come on," Lilly said, taking the hint from Joe and ushering Amy out of the living room to her bedroom.

In their absence, Joe, eager to distract himself from the gravity of the day, asked, "How does one go about becoming an immortal bloodsucker, eh, Doctor?"

"You get bitten by a vampyre...the rest is just...let's just say, extracurricular," Rafael jibed back, a faint grin on his face.

The three men sat in the uncomfortable silence of the living room. Ten minutes later, Lilly appeared in the room, looking weary herself. "I put a gentle spell on her, something that'd help her sleep."

"I don't appreciate you putting spells on my peeps, witch," Joe joked.

"I don't appreciate your tone, young man," Lilly quipped, taking a seat between Blake and Rafael.

"Now that all of us are here, I have things I need to tell you, as I am sure you have things to tell me," Joe said.

"We really wanna do this without Amy?"

"She's been through enough as it is. Let's leave her out of it. Someone's gotta stay behind and take care of Dad. She's going to do it, and she deserves a break from all this cosmic madness."

The four of them sat in the living room, eager to begin. Billy Hawthorne hadn't yet parted with the rifle he'd picked up from Lilly's home. They hadn't had a chance to discuss why the rifle spoke to him and him alone, and why it felt so unnaturally powerful in his hands. Blake Weston had yet to fill Joe in on how he and Lilly went to Providence to rescue a vampyre, and then provide that vampyre with much needed closure in the forgotten ruins of a long dead empire. Joe hadn't yet told any of them what had transpired between him and the Devil, or of the battle in Alpha Centauri, or the one that followed in Hell, resulting in its rupture.

They were teetering on the edge of a rich conversation about to take place when the Devil walked in through the front door, much to everyone's alarm.

"You're not seriously starting this without me, are you?" the Devil asked with his usual slyness, admiring his manicured nails, still in his black suit.

"You!" Rafael glowered, standing up, his eyes livid, his hands trembling.

"Oh, do compose yourself, Rafael. I see you've found new friends. What an auspicious coincidence that they also happen to be the very company I'm fond of keeping," the Devil said, grinning at the people in the room, and then closing the door behind him.

9

THE CORNERSTONES

The very palpable tension in the living room was brought to an abrupt dissolution when Lilly Thurman stood up taller than everyone else in the room, including the Devil, and said, "A person has died, for fuck's sake. Her mourning husband and her distraught daughter are asleep in this house. If any of you so much as raise your voice a decibel more than what's considered an indoor voice, you will have to deal with me!"

The Devil shrugged and stepped aside.

Rafael was not so quick in disarming himself. He stood there with his claws out, his mouth still turned into a snarl.

"You do not know what he has done," Rafael said, his eyes turning red. "He imprisoned me, used me as a vessel to store his blood, left me awake in a crypt for years!"

"Oh, do get over yourself, Rafael. Rage is a color that suited your master, not you," Satan said, seating himself on the armchair. "And besides, haven't you heard what the witch has said? Don't get on her bad side. Unless you want to take it out and then I can show you what I'm capable of. You forget, boy, that I have your soul in my vaults. You sold it to me at a bargain price without reading the terms and conditions. If you had, you'd have discovered that they allow me to use you, abuse you, and, when I want to, lose you. I'm not Saint Nicholas last time I checked. Unless you're a dyslexic, in which case I'll give you a pass for spelling Santa as Satan."

"Shut up," Rafael snapped and sat down.

"Oh, I do love a good rebel." Satan grinned, nodding at Joe. "This one's got spark, don't you think? Worlds colliding right now. I shortlisted Dr. Von Thorburn to be my writer, though I never did share that with him. But he still has his uses."

"You're the Devil's writer?"

"And bastard son," Joe added, raising his bottle to the room at large. "Up until some time ago, I thought I was the Antichrist, but since then I've been assigned a new role. Apparently, I'm one of the Four Horsemen."

"And to think I thought *I* was dangerous," Rafael said.

"Let's discuss business, gentlemen?" Billy Hawthorne mused, stroking the barrel of his gun.

"What is it with you and that gun?" Blake asked, a little vexed.

"I don't know. It's an amazing gun," Billy shrugged.

"It belonged to America's oldest gunmaker, Eliphalet Remington II," the Devil commented, admiring the gun from afar. "He asked for my help, naturally. Told me to make a rifle that would always shoot true. Am I right in assuming, madam witch, that this is the same rifle?"

Lilly nodded, a little proud of herself. "Pried it from his dead hands. He was a witch hunter of old. The history books will tell you he died of inflammation of the bowels. He died fighting me. That gun is a memento," Lilly said.

"To keepsakes and unkillable witches," the Devil said, making a wine glass appear in his hand and toasting Lilly.

"Hear, hear," Blake Weston said.

"Ah, the traveling soldier," the Devil said, smiling slyly at Blake. "Boy, you have a color of deep envy about you. Solid craftsmanship. It's like I can peer into the depths of your soul and all I see is you comparing yourself to everyone around you. You couldn't have been cucked so bad that all that remains distinct of you is jealousy."

Blake bolted out of his chair, but Joe held him down, shaking his head, as if saying, *You don't want to tussle with Satan.*

"Are you going to do anything other than stir shit up, Satan?" Lilly asked. "I thought you were on our side for once."

"I am a self-serving agent, madam, and as such am always on my side," Satan said, sipping his wine. "But, yes. There are matters to discuss that don't involve shit stirring."

"Then let's get on with them," Joe said.

Joe began first, telling the others what had happened in Alpha Centauri, including the sudden appearance of the archangels, and then what had transpired in Hell. How the Abstract was on the loose, and had destroyed Hell as it had escaped.

"I find myself in a hell of my own," Satan spoke with great grief. "I keep rebuilding Hell over and over. I've just rebuilt it again, resuscitated all my dead demons, rekindled the flames. But it served a purpose. As does everything. The Abstract has fled this universe. But make no mistake. This retreat is temporary, if anything. With each passing second, it amasses its armies, ready for its final attack, what all the apocryphal texts refer to as Armageddon."

The others sat with this knowledge for a full minute, absorbing it.

"So, if Hell isn't enough to hold the Abstract..." Lilly said.

"Oh, I am sure you've received your summons just as Joe here received his. The Madam calls you, Ms. Thurman. I am sure it'll be to inform you that the chiefest of the Collectors, the Lord of his domain, the Head Amasser, has requested an audience with Joseph here."

"I met a Collector," Joe said quietly. "It informed me of the summons."

"There you have it then," the Devil said.

"Am I expected to come?" Rafael asked.

"Well, you are a very well educated vampyre with knowledge that rivals mine," the Devil said slyly, hinting at the fact that Rafael had lived through the Devil's experiences when he was infected with his blood.

"I never asked for the curse of that knowledge."

"Your mistake for perceiving it as a curse," Satan said. "You know as much as me. When I had been compromised, you retained my essence within you. Without you, I wouldn't be here. And without me, the world would have ceased to exist. So, thank you, and you're quite welcome."

Rafael became quiet.

"I never really understood the role of the Collectors," Blake said. "But that's just me."

"It's not," Lilly said. "By design, the Collectors are a mysterious force, and no one knows all that much about them."

"Well, not *no one*," Satan chimed in. "If you want, I can give you the dirt on them."

Joe nodded. "I would like to know more about them." He was thinking of his mother, and the ghoulish Collector that had accompanied her.

"Everyone else also equally invested in this grand fable, or is it just Joe?"

The others nodded their *ayes*, including Lilly, who had a Collector come to her in her final moments back when she was strung up in Salem. Rafael had sometimes heard his master mutter about the damned Collector, but had never really grasped just how important this mysterious entity had been in Elton's life.

"Forget everything you know about religion, god, me, the universe's creation, the Absolute, the Abstract. Just throw all preconceived notions out the window. If we're doing this right, then I'll see to it that the story is told without bias," Satan said, getting up from his armchair and heading over to the window that overlooked the street.

"The Absolute is not above lying," the Devil said. "And in that regard, he will always lie, calling himself the sole creative force behind the universe. A real credit-hogging egomaniac, if there ever was one. In truth, this story does not start with the Absolute and the Abstract duking it out in the uncreated cosmos."

The Devil slowly turned to face them, the living room suddenly feeling darker than before. In the darkness, Satan's eyes shone with ambition and recall, and a hint of nostalgia.

"In the beginning, there were four cornerstones," he said, looking at each of the four members sitting in the living room. "Feel free to stop me if you already know this. No? No one? All right. Then listen close. And we may begin."

The multiverse as you know it now emerged from the following cornerstones.

Chaos, ever present in its totality and broad reach as represented by the Abstract, or better known to cultists and its worshippers as Azathoth.

Creation, first represented by the Absolute, later on represented by an avatar of the Absolute, the fine lady you all knew as God.

Craft, which was represented by the esteemed Madam of Magic, signifying the powers of sorcery, witchcraft, and everything that pertains to the mystical arts.

And Collection. Of course, Collection remains a very obscure cornerstone, because it has never dealt with divulging. Only collecting. The Collectors that some of you are undoubtedly aware of are entities that seek to right wrong wherever they see it. For every death, they bring forth the equilibrium by collecting the soul of the dead.

For every injustice that happens in the universe, they create a champion who shall counter that injustice. Do you remember the Provveditores of Venice, Rafael? Their power was going unchecked, and to right that wrong, the Collectors brought forth your lord, Elton Grando. And you, Lilly Thurman, although once you were Lilly Frost, you were a course correction for a world keen on burning witches. The Collectors gave the world a witch they could never burn.

And if you're wondering where I come in all this, allow me to introduce myself by another name. The Cataclysm, an entity unto myself, representing the intersection of all these axes.

When I choose to instill chaos, you shall find me the sole architect behind the demise of empires. Babel. Sodom. Gomorrah. The Mongols. The Mughals. The British Empire. All my chaotic handiwork.

When I wish to Create, I create Hell with its unhallowed halls burning white hot with my own blaze.

At the heart of every Craft in the world, be it the spark in a poet's mind or the final flourishes to the magnum opus of a prolific author, or the masterstrokes on the painting of artists such as Da Vinci, I am.

And, of course, though not a Collector by design, I still Collect souls by the billions as they flock to Hell. Some know rest there. Others torment for the rest of their days. Some find bliss in nonexistence. Others atone for their sins; masochists that they are, they arrive equipped with ideas for their own punishment. Lakes of fire. Red hot lashes on their back. Scalding chains to drag them with. That was never Hell to begin with. Hell was a reprieve from God, a refuge for all those who sought freedom from the constraints of fearful belief.

While Creation and Chaos may have you believe in a binary, real life is rarely, if ever, a binary. You shall find all things a spectrum, and somewhere on that spectrum between magic and magpie behavior, I resonate, a frequency akin to a symphony of all notes strummed at the same time.

Make no mistake—there is only one universe, this one, the prime one. All other universes that exist are reflections of it. Branching nodes of choices upon choices leading to different results resulting in an infinite number of universes. And it is not merely Creation creating all those universes.

It is also Chaos, as dictated by Chaos Theory and all its effects —the Butterfly Effect, the Lorenz Attractor, the Spiral Effect.

It is also Craft, filling every gray space with color. It's Creation's job to create flowers. It takes Craft to make those flowers bloom. Chaos takes the reign when the pollen flies, and makes it land arbitrarily where it wills. Cataclysm makes it wilt. And when it is all rotted and consumed by fungus, a Collector gathers its essence, preserving its memory in the great annals. All these forces are not always antagonistic to each other.

Except when they are.

When Creation declared war on Cataclysm (yours truly), a wager was set in place. Joseph Banbury is the culmination of that wager, supplanting God, shaking up the status quo, shifting the balance.

With no more Cataclysm on the board, and Creation buckling under the weight of a new avatar, Chaos infiltrated the universe.

Craft alone could not handle all this, and Craft failed. The dead witches that you buried are evidence of that. And then I failed. My fractured Hell is proof of that. And, of course, Joseph failed, and in his failure, the Absolute failed.

Now, we have only one final recourse at hand.

To turn to the Collectors.

UPON THE END of the Devil's monologue, the lights undimmed in the living room, revealing the dawning of understanding upon each eager listener's face.

"Any questions?" Satan asked, looking around.

When no one spoke, the Devil clapped his hands on his thighs and looked enthusiastically at Joe. "If that concludes the matter and brings all you up to speed, the only question is, when do we visit the Collectors?"

"Does it have to be now?" Lilly asked. "He just lost his mother."

"And tomorrow, we stand to lose this world. I have no idea where the Abstract is as of this moment. There are realms where one cannot step without explicit permission or intent. Hell is one. Heaven another. The realm of chaos is where the Abstract dwells. I have no spies operating in that place. Nor do I, for that matter, have any knowledge of what the Collectors' realm looks like and what goes on there," the Devil said. "How long can one expect this temporary ceasefire to go on? In another where, in another when, the Abstract gathers itself, all too aware that it will face Hell again. What it doesn't know is that we can bargain with the Collectors."

"This is just me being bluntly idiotic," Blake said, "but what are the Collectors going to do? Collect the Abstract?"

"Contain it," the Devil said. "For long enough that we can restore some semblance of balance. Understand, Mr. Weston, that we are trying to avert apocalypse. The universe hasn't faced apocalypse before. Even the Absolute, in his infinite knowledge, doesn't know what happens next. Here in the book of fate we finally come to a blank page, and our every action and inaction decides what gets written on that last page."

"No pressure," Billy Hawthorne quipped. It relieved none of the tension built in the room.

In perfect devilish fashion, Satan took his leave abruptly, leaving everyone wondering where he'd disappeared now. As the night grew late, Blake took the guest room, and Billy slept on the sofa in the living room. Lilly said something about sharing Amy's room with her. Joe headed up to his old room and lay in his bed, all his racing thoughts making it impossible for him to fall asleep.

He lay there shifting from one side to the other, trying to imagine what his mother's first night in the grave must feel like. If he closed his eyes, he could imagine it. A timber rattlesnake finding its way into the grave, slithering past the coffin. Centipedes and scorpions waiting for the wood to decay so that they'd be able to make their way through to the dead body within. Gritty dirt slipping through the little cracks in the coffin, filling it up, leaving no breathing room, not that the dead needed breathing room.

"No," Joe whispered, trying to picture anything but rattlesnakes and creepy crawlies, trying to empty his mind so that he'd be ready for the journey that lay ahead tomorrow.

Despite his room being so different than it was in his childhood, the view from the window was the same, the haunting branches of the tree swaying in the night, casting tall shadows on the floor, moving shadows that flitted between shapes, rattling against the windowpane. Rattle. Rattlesnakes sifting in the loosened grave dirt.

"No."

A knock on the door made him sit up in bed.

"Joe?"

"Come in."

Lilly Thurman wore a t-shirt and a pair of shorts that belonged to Amy, her hair undone, falling in elegant crests on her shoulders and beyond.

"Lilly," he said.

"I... Your sister snores very loud," Lilly said, stepping in the room, gently closing the door behind her. "Sleep evades me for other reasons, however."

"Do tell."

"The Madam got in touch with me. I have never heard her sound so afraid. She was being very urgent, but I held my ground, told her that we'd arrive tomorrow in the Axis Mundi," Lilly said, but Joe cut her off with his own train of thoughts.

"What do you think happens during death? I know there's all sorts of running theories on afterlives and whatnot, but..."

"There is pain, I won't lie," Lilly said, sitting on the edge of his bed, maintaining polite distance. One could almost say that it was platonic distance. "But pain is just a toll extracted for crossing over. Some say when pain crosses all thresholds, that's when a person dies. Others say that death can be as painless as simply sighing and letting go."

The answer did not console him in the way he expected it to.

Lilly sought to change the topic by looking around the room, commenting, "This used to be your childhood room? I never thought I'd be here. Was it always this barebones?"

"More barebones than it is now," Joe said, smiling. "Mom was very particular about not having posters up. But she had a little give. Allowed me and Amy to put up a few of our posters. There's only so many times you can say no to teenagers. I mean, I assume. It's kind of a little late for me to have a kid of my own to know for sure."

"Would you like that? Assuming all ends well. A kid?"

"It's the only thing that I haven't been. Think about it," Joe said, a little smile appearing on his face. "A mini-me carrying my traits. Someone I can pass it all on to, and then let go."

"I can imagine," Lilly said, smiling back.

"You're being awfully nice to me. Please tell me it isn't because my mother died. God, I'd hate to be subjected to pity. I think I preferred you cold."

Lilly grinned. "A necrophiliac necromancer resurrects his dead girlfriend."

"Jesus, that's a dark premise."

"He's happy that the love of his life has returned from the great beyond. To commemorate the occasion, he has sex with her. But he doesn't enjoy it as much as he thought he would," Lilly continued.

Joe suppressed the urge to laugh.

"'What's wrong, my love?' his girlfriend asks. Can you guess what he says?"

"Go on," Joe said, smiling more freely now.

"I think I preferred you cold."

"Christ, Lill."

"It just came to me," Lilly chuckled.

"I missed you." It came out of Joe so suddenly that he didn't consider what saying that to her would imply, them being alone at night in a room, on the same bed.

"I missed you too," Lilly jumped in before he could spiral further. Her hand was on his hand, her face close to his face, her cheeks puffy, hot breath exhaling from her mouth, falling on Joe's face. "But I *still* miss you. There's *you*. And then there was the Joe that I knew. Somehow, the two of you seemed like two different people until recently. When I saw you be vulnerable at your mother's passing."

"It humanized me, is what I assume you're trying to say," Joe said, not feeling bitter about her statement. Yet still, it hurt.

"I couldn't fathom you as God, and in all honesty, you were a piss-poor God in your very short tenure," Lilly said. "But you're not all that terrible as a human. You remind us of our flaws, and yet your actions make us look inward, where our strengths lie."

"Careful now," Joe said, feeling something stir within him that had no right to stir now, of all moments.

"Or what?" Lilly said, her face closer to his.

He did not want to answer.

And from the looks of it, she did not want an answer.

Before either of them knew it, his hand was in her hair, pushing her head closer to his, kissing her furiously, feeling all of her lips in his mouth, her tongue on his tongue.

They were both a little too big for the single bed, but in this moment of passion, that was the last thing on their mind. Joe pulled her closer till she was lying on top of him, all her body in contact with all of his, her gentle lips pulling on his lower lip, dripping her sweet spit in his mouth. He swallowed it as he ran his hands under her shirt, feeling the smooth skin of her back on his palms, running his hands up to her shoulders and cupping them. The soft weight of her breasts pressed against his chest, the hard length of his cock jutting against her naked thigh.

He let himself go, relaxing his body as she pulled her t-shirt off and threw it on the ground, revealing her naked body. Her breasts fell full and heavy down her chest, her nipples hard, her areolas expanded out of arousal. Joe managed to slide his shirt off while still being underneath her.

He held her breasts, feeling their softness in his coarse hands.

Lilly stifled a moan. Underneath the bed, the floor creaked with their weight.

Lilly lowered herself on him till their cool skins were

warm, her arms around his neck, her hands in his hair, her moans in his ears as he let his hand slip between her thighs.

She took his pants off in one effortless swoop, and in the next moment, did away with hers. Her hand wrapped around his erect member, stroking it without any impatience, contemplating what to do next. He let her have her pleasure, his fingers gently cradling her wet labia, pressing beyond them, touching that firm little flitty knot at the top with his thumb.

She thrust her thighs against his hand, moving her hands faster, matching his rhythm. Her beautiful nude form half-illuminated by the moon's light.

When her fingers were wet with his precum, she ceased stroking, bringing her finger to her lips, and tasting him before straddling him. Once she was on top, her hips spread on either side of his thighs, she grinded her pelvis against his stiff dick, not yet taking it in, enjoying as much as she could from above. Joe, caught in a torrent of pleasure, cupped her breast in his hand and brought it to his face, licking her nipple, sucking on it gently. He remembered she liked it being sucked gently.

She remembered he preferred her on top.

It felt like home, warm and snug, as he entered her, her gushiness swallowing his penis whole, squeezing it along its length, pulsing pleasure in some secret morse code that only the two of them knew. She lay on top of him as she lifted her buttocks and then brought them slowly down in a slow rhythm, letting his cock rub her vagina in all the right spots, sending soaring pleasure signals up its length, invoking deep moans that echoed in the hallowed space between their bodies.

He slid his hand up her belly, past her heaving chest, and up to her neck, holding it as she moved in swiftly, silkily, deriving just as much pleasure as she gave, or perhaps more.

As for her, she could feel all of him, his human warmth, his beating heart, and his familiarity, reminding her that it was the same Joe that she'd once known, the same Joe that she'd once loved. And perhaps she still loved him now, witnessing his naked form lying underneath not as some ordained messiah, but as a supplicant praying at her altar of pleasure. With that, she let him have it, her full weight, as she thrust against his length, dull pain mixed with infinite pleasure. Lilly dug her nails in his chest and pulled, leaving light red trails on his skin, which somehow made the part of him that was inside her harder, longer.

She moaned with each exhale, her eyes closed against the arrival of one wave of pleasure after the other. Her thighs tightened around his hips, chasing the friction without any reservation, her breath becoming faster, not just from her fast movement but from the heat building between them.

For a moment, she closed her eyes, as though she might be drifting, but she was memorizing the feel of him, like it could be taken away again.

Joe's hands tangled in her hair, holding onto her instead of pulling her closer, as if they both needed to anchor onto each other. Then, his arm was around her back, and with one effortless movement, he was on top of her, and she lay underneath him, her wide blue eyes peering deep into his soul as he thrust, the two of them building toward a climax that was a long time coming.

He interlaced his fingers with hers, pinned her hand next to her head, and thrust faster, reaching down with each thrust to give her a kiss, feel more of her tongue, touch her lips with his.

It came as a quake, this familiar yet welcome pleasure that spouted from the tip of his stiff penis, gushing inside her pulsing, soaking, tight depth. Lilly held onto Joe, wrapping her trembling legs around him, her arms around his back, pulling him as close as she could as the two of them came together.

In the quiet moments that followed, they lay in each other's arms, covered in sweat, heavy their breaths, wordless their silence.

He did not want to think about anything. Nor was he concerned with trivialities such as what this intimate act meant. He felt her falling asleep, naked, in his arms, and followed her into that uncharted territory, closing his eyes to much needed, dreamless slumber.

10

THE BONE ORCHARD

Lilly Frost stood naked by the pond. Thankfully, she was alone. Fall was upon Salem. Red and rust were the colors of trees, and wherever they were neither, they were a deep crisp yellow, indicating that here, in this part of the world, upon this time, you would not behold a green leaf even if your life depended on it. Even the grass on the forest floor was all yellow.

Nature's funeral wreaths.

Lilly Frost was in a body that had never known any torture. The air in her lungs felt fresh, her lungs unburdened by any sediments or deposits that would weigh them down in the coming centuries. The soles of her feet tickled and pricked as she walked on the dead grass toward the edge of the pond, wondering when a pond stopped being a pond and turned into a lake, because from the looks of it, this water body was right on the edge of that definition. Any bigger, and it would have to have its own name.

Lake Eerie, Salem, Massachusetts, thought Lilly with some degree of amusement and wonder—wondering what might become of this place in the future. When she saw her reflection on the surface of the water, she blushed red, realizing that she was naked, but then, as if prompted by her embarrassment, gray robes covered her.

It took her a lot longer than usual to realize that she was dreaming. Usually, she was the first to know that this was not reality. But tonight, she had allowed herself to relax after eons. And had slept in Joe's arms, blissfully unaware of whatever would follow.

Grimly, she realized that doing something like this would have its toll. Cosmic soldiers like herself were never supposed to let down their defenses, otherwise reproachment would follow.

Such as this.

The Madam stood on the other side of the pond.

Her hair had long gray streaks in it, her skin darkened and deeply lined, her black dress dull.

The Madam tread on water effortlessly, but then again, so did Lilly as she stepped on the surface of the pond that had, at some time during the turn of the last century, been dubbed a lake by the city, its parks and recreation department preserving it as Lake Little Salem.

"You called, Madam?"

"I invited you earlier, Lilly. You turned down my invitation to have an audience."

"So you intrude upon my privacy?"

The Madam shot Lilly a look of disbelief, scathed by what she'd said.

"Child?"

"No," Lilly said, shaking her head, raising her finger. "We're not doing the whole mentor-mentee thing. I know better now. Imagine my surprise coming to learn the truth from the mouth of the Devil."

"What truth would that be?" the Madam asked, the sky beyond the fall leaf canopy turning dusky.

"That you are one and all bureaucrats of your own departments, using us only as a means to your end," Lilly said. "My sisters died that night, fighting the parasites. Where were you, Madam?"

"Child!" the Madam wailed, her hands to her chest. "I was here, channeling all the power of the Axis Mundi to those women. I fought from my realm. You must not think me the same as the others! When each of them died, I felt the pain of their death just as they had. In a single night, I have aged thousands of years."

Lilly considered what she was saying, and how earnest her evident woe was.

"These are unprecedented times," the Madam spoke, her grief-struck form seemingly sinking wherever she stood. "I cannot scry anything of the future. Do you know how terrifying that is for the woman who holds the reins of all the magic in the known and unknown universe? I know nothing of what tomorrow brings. I come here not as your Madam, considering you my charge. I look up to you as my champion,

Lilly Frost. And when the time comes, I shall imbue you with everything that I have. You shall find in yourself no dearth of magic."

"My magic is waning. Is that your doing?" Lilly asked, crossing her arms.

The Madam shook her head. "You have been running on reserves for quite long. I am glad to see that you took a break from your duties tonight."

"You've been spying on me?"

"No." The Madam smiled. "Merely keeping tabs on your battery. Tonight, you did not draw from it, giving it time to replenish. You do not understand, my child; despite the breadth of your powers and your immortality, you are, underneath everything, a human. And humans grow weary. Humans are not cut out for this mess."

"I beg to differ," Lilly said, standing tall over the Madam. "It is *only* humans, us meager forms with our mortalities and our sickness and old age and fears and inhibitions, that are cut out for this mess. How would a being who has never known any defeat feel the toll of loss? How can the Absolute deal in anything that is not? How can the Abstract appreciate order? How can the Madam of Magic know what it feels to live a mundane existence, one where a snap of your fingers won't light any flames in the stove and you have to use a matchstick like the rest of us?"

The Madam spoke nothing. Her eyes were lowered, peering into her own reflection on the water.

"Come what may, I shall stand beside you when the time comes. As will all of the Axis Mundi."

"Good," Lilly said. "And it won't be a favor to us. You'll only be saving your own skin. You say that you cannot scry into the future, but I think that's a lie. I think you have seen several versions of the future, and most of them end with the Abstract dissolving everything in the universe. I think that has you scared the same as it has the Absolute."

"Lilly, there awaits nothing on the other side for deities such as myself," the Madam pleaded, holding Lilly's hands. "If the Abstract wins..."

"Then you better make sure it doesn't," Lilly said, holding the Madam's hands in her own. She decided that it was useless being tough on the Madam. Not anymore. Being one of the Cornerstones of Creation must undoubtedly carry with it a great toll. The stakes were high, and if you failed, then it was only the collapse of the fabric of reality that you had to deal with. Nothing more.

"Our sisters have fallen, true," Lilly said, holding the Madam close. "But that is what a witch is. Simply because some of us fall, Madam, does not mean that all of us fall. Our sisters are assembled the world over, waiting for their next orders. Your orders. Rally them to our cause. And when you have done that, when each witch across the entire planet has harkened to your war cry, you shall fight alongside us."

"And what of the future?"

"The future, Madam, is overrated, from what I have observed. The more you try to learn of it, the more desolate it seems. On a long enough timeline, there are no happy endings. That's why books end on the note that they do. So that the reader can just assume that it all works out and that the characters *did* live happily ever after," Lilly said, finding hope within her heart that was not instilled by the Madam, nor the Devil, nor even the fact that they were soon going to the Collectors. It was self-instilled hope, hope that she had gotten from Joseph Banbury, who didn't know the word quit. A lesser human being would have folded. But not Joe.

And perhaps that's why he had ascended as much as he had. Perhaps there was a lesson that they could all learn from Joe Banbury.

"You think of him so loud that it's all I can hear in my mind," the Madam said, still holding Lilly's hand, the two women standing peacefully on the surface of the water.

"Oh well," Lilly said, blushing. "He's trouble, for sure. But I've made my peace with the fact that he is my trouble."

The Madam smiled in acknowledgement. Something about standing in such close vicinity to Lilly had done something good for her appearance. She no longer looked so haggard. Still old, but her hair settled down, and her dress smoothed itself, returning lost grace to the Caretaker of Magic.

Lilly couldn't help but give her a hug. The Madam was shocked at first, but then let her hands fall on Lilly's back, hugging her in return. The two women did not talk in this moment, as the wind blew all the red and orange leaves all over the surface of the lake, as the water rippled and the reeds on the lake bank swayed.

"You have been my support for as long as I have known I am a witch," Lilly said. "The only thing that I can do is be that same support for you now that you are in need."

"Then I hereby dub you, Lilly Frost, Champion of Craft,

and may you find every weapon in the arsenal of witchery at your access when you fight against the Inevitable, the one they call Azathoth, chaos god of the outer dominions."

Lilly felt the transfer of something unseen yet powerful course from the Madam into her, and it was something as intimate as the act that she had performed with Joe last night. She felt the cool blue aura shroud her body.

"What's happening to me?" Lilly Frost asked, holding her hands up, marveling at the light that was coming from within her. Now no longer standing there, she floated atop the water.

"You have my grace, Lilly. Do with it as you will. And when you and your friends are ready, call out to me, so I may take you to the Collectors. The way to their realm is a riddle only I know the answer to. And as such, it shall be me who accompanies you there."

Lilly felt her body plunge into the lake, hanging suspended in the clear, cool water, waterweed flailing around her, fishes swimming above her. The fall into the water was abrupt, and the cold was bitter, waking her up with a start.

She was lying on her side, one leg over Joseph, the sun pouring into the room. An ordinary sun in an ordinary sky, no rifts or parasitic trails marring the horizon. She could pretend that her life was normal, and that this was the only life she'd ever known, and she discovered that the thought came to her easy.

She looked at Joe lovingly, sleeping with his face buried in his arms, lightly snoring. She let him have another five minutes of undisturbed sleep before gently waking him up.

"Mm. Lill. Why are you so cold?" Joe asked as she ran her hand against his forehead.

"Believe it or not, I fell in a lake," Lilly joked.

"Oh no. I hate it when I fall in a lake in the middle of my sleep."

"It's time to go, Joe."

"Already? I thought that we'd have another day of pretending the world wasn't falling apart."

"Pretending's over," Lilly said, sitting up in bed. "Now we've got to do the hard part."

Joe opened his eyes, staring at the ceiling first, reconciling with the waking reality of his dead mother, the impending attack of the Abstract, and answering the call of the Collectors. But then he looked at Lilly, and altogether at once, the waking reality did not seem all that terrible anymore.

He wrapped his arm around her and pulled her back into bed, if for nothing more than just five more minutes of blissful ignorance. She let him, and even whispered a few things to him that were for his ears only. In response, he whispered similar things back.

They kissed each other, realizing that promises had been made now that could never be broken. And then, hesitatingly, not wanting out of the sanctuary of this room, they got up and got ready to meet the rest.

IF THERE WAS someone for whom waking reality was still the equivalent of a terrible nightmare, it was Blake Weston, who had not slept a wink that night. First, it had been Billy Hawthorne, the source of his unrest, what with his tossing and turning and loud snoring. To seek some reprieve, Blake left the room and thought of making it to the basement, but then he realized that their resident vampyre, Rafael, had sought refuge in the basement.

So Blake went and sat down on the living room sofa, dozing in and out of sleep. He thought he heard the sounds of doors opening and doors closing, but ignored them. However, the sounds that came after that affirmed all his worst suspicions and made him realize, if not a little too late, that the woman he had feelings for was never interested in him in the first place.

With that bitterness, he stayed awake for the rest of the night until morning came. Amy Banbury was the first to wake up in the house. She saw an irate Blake sitting red-faced in the living room, and asked, "Didn't get any sleep?"

Blake simply shook his head.

"You're not subtle, Blake," Amy said, bringing over two cups of coffee from the kitchen.

"He doesn't deserve her, you know, and I know this is your brother we're talking about," Blake said, taking the coffee from her. "But he really does not deserve her. Not after everything. Not after the lies, the running, the godhood, the... And she just falls right back into him like he never broke her in the first place."

Amy sat on the armchair, looking well-rested, less perplexed. "You're jealous."

Blake's face turned redder. "No shit," he said.

"Then don't be."

Blake finally looked up with a glare locked and ready, but Amy's face didn't carry any mocking upon it. Only tender understanding, like she was talking to a child. "You want advice? Get out of this thing that you've built in your head. You find someone who doesn't leave you guessing. Someone whose presence doesn't break you in half every moment you're with them. Someone who is not Lilly Thurman. Because if you keep measuring yourself against my brother, you're always going to come up short. That's his curse, Blake. Don't make it yours."

"Easy for you to say," Blake said as he swallowed her stinging words. He leaned back, looking toward the staircase, listening to the muffled sounds of movement upstairs.

"No shit," Amy said, smiling faintly. "You know why they circle each other? Why it seems that they are fated to each other? Because he has as much baggage as her, and that's someone who's been around longer than your life and mine put together. She understands him in a way no one can. He makes his peace with the parts of her that the rest of us cannot even fathom."

"I think I would like to be done with this conversation," Blake said grumpily.

"Fine by me," Amy said, going to check in on her father. He was still asleep. And it was best to leave him like that, because Tommy Banbury had the rest of his life to wake up to the fact that his wife was no more. And if she could help him sleep just a bit longer, pretend to be in a world where that wasn't the case, then she was going to do that. In fact, she had made up her mind last night. Wherever this journey was headed for the rest of them, this was her stop. She was getting off here. She was going to stay behind and take care of her dad. If apocalypse was nigh, she needed to be near him when shit hit the fan.

Rafael emerged from the basement, looking out for spots of sunlight in the living room, avoiding them. Even for a vampyre, he had a haunted look on his face. He nodded at Amy and Blake, and then stood in the only dark corner of the room.

"There is something terribly wrong with your basement," Rafael spoke silently, warningly.

"Do tell," Amy said, not surprised. "All our terrible childhood memories revolve around that fucking place."

"It's not evil as you would think evil is. It is not a place cursed with Satanic energy. There is something else at play here, Amy Banbury. I speak in my capacity and authority as a vampyre, the second of my kind. Vampirism is not just limited to people. There are places that draw on your energy, suck your happiness. And that place where I spent last night is one such place. A vampiric place with its teeth sinking into me, filling me with dread, diminishing in my end everything that makes me, me."

"How can a place be vampiric?" Blake Weston asked.

Rafael looked at him pityingly, as if this man had never let his imagination soar beyond the trivial, as if he had never considered the mysteries of the world. "Tell me, Mr. Weston, have you ever felt discomfort in a hospital's hallways as you wait for a loved one?"

Blake nodded unassumingly.

"That is one example of many vampyric places, places where all the darkest thoughts in the world pool and affect any who find themselves there. Whoever must have originally started to use this basement must have been grappling with some great demons in their mind," Rafael said, nodding at Amy, who pulled curtains in front of every window, allowing him to move freely inside.

"That was our mother," Amy said. "She wrestled with guilt and sin."

"And now she rests," Joe said, stepping down the stairs with Lilly behind her. "So why not leave it at that?"

There was a great tension in the air between Lilly, Blake, and Joe that would have hung even more tensely if not for Billy Hawthorne appearing nonchalantly in the living room, saying, "Hey, whatever you guys have planned today, I'm not expected to be a part of it, am I?"

"No," the Devil said, appearing in the room out of thin air, as was his way. "This journey is not one for the humans of this...tribe. Do you still call yourselves the Morningstar Tribe?"

"That was more Sean Gainey's shtick," Joe said, remembering Sean, remembering Joph. "But yeah, in effect, we're still the Morningstar Tribe."

"I am flattered," the Devil said, placing a hand on his chest. "But I am also in a great deal of urgency. So..."

"Why can't I go?" Blake asked.

"I so do hate being interrupted," the Devil scathed.

Another presence walked amongst them, a woman with bedraggled hair and a gaunt face, wearing a black dress, her hands folded behind her back. "You will guard the hearth," the Madam said.

Lilly, all too shocked to see the Madam emerge in real life, gasped a little.

"There is honor in that, soldier," the Madam said, nodding at Blake, and then at Billy.

"Why?" Blake asked again.

"Rafael is an immortal vampyre," the Madam said. "Lilly an immortal witch. Joseph Banbury is... Need there be more said about him than everyone knows? And the Devil is one of the Cornerstones, as am I. We cannot be harmed in the Bone Orchard. There is no guarantee what the myriad of Collectors will do to your souls if you just happen to waltz into their world."

"Bone Orchard?" Joe asked, raising an eyebrow.

"That is what their realm is called," the Madam said. "And it is there that I must take you now."

Wordlessly, the Madam of Magic conjured a dimensional portal, one that carried her own signature, a greenish hue.

The Devil walked through it first, giving the Madam a courtesy bow, as if the two were in the know of something the others weren't. Then Joseph. Then Lilly. And finally, Rafael. The Madam closed the portal behind herself, leaving Blake and Billy and Amy alone in the house.

While the others were standing around in silence, Tommy Banbury walked into the room, rubbing his eyes.

"Morning, folks," Tommy said, patting his daughter on the head. "Where is the rest of the rabble?"

"Morning, Mr. Banbury," Billy Hawthorne said. "They have gone to run an errand."

"Including that funny-looking fella?" Tommy asked, referring undoubtedly to Rafael.

"Yes. Including that funny-looking fella, Dad," Amy said, holding her father's hand. "Come. I'll make you something to eat."

"Just the coffee for me, Joyce... Oh, I'm sorry. I meant Amy," Tommy said, his voice breaking at the end there.

Billy headed for the door.

"Where are you going?" Blake asked.

"Home. New York. If this is the end, I'd like to be home."

"I wish I had that choice."

"You're free to come with me, you know."

Blake thought about it, then nodded. "Sure. Why not?"

"That's the spirit."

The two men were about to leave when Amy appeared. "Where do you two think you're going?"

"We're making ourselves scarce, Lill," Billy Hawthorne said. "I think it's about time we headed home."

Amy gave them both a parting hug. They hugged her back.

"Take care of yourself and your dad," Billy said.

"I will," Amy said, smiling at him. She watched the two of them leave in the Ford truck that was parked in the driveway, thinking to herself, *Didn't that belong to Lilly?*

While portal travel was something Joe, Lilly, and the Devil were accustomed to, each on their own, this travel was different. It was with the Madam this time, and the dimension they were being led into was unlike any place any of them had been before.

Joe was faintly reminded of the fever dream that was the Aeternum Trials. Lilly recalled how time stood still as she hung at the stake in Salem.

The Devil, on the other hand, was enjoying himself. For a being to whom not many things remained a mystery, it felt like a welcome reprieve to look forward to something shrouded in the unknown. The Devil had never been to the Bone Orchard, and as such, had no expectations.

The travel itself was brief. They hurtled from one end of the portal to the other and landed in great darkness, all of them on their hands and knees.

"Where are we?" Joe Banbury asked, looking around and realizing he had landed on a bed of broken bones. He was alarmed, reminded of the last time he'd seen something like this in India, when he had come into contact with a strange presence in the form of an Aghori Baba.

"This is the Bone Orchard," the Madam said, standing up, adjusting her clothes, and somehow managing to look resplendent despite the circumstances.

Lilly steadied herself shortly after, standing just behind the Madam, looking around, checking if this matched her expectations. Nothing did.

This place was devoid of light. The sky above was dark, and there was no boundary to the blackness that enshrouded them. As far as anyone could see, human bones were strewn across the ground. The only sound was that of their feet crunching the bones as they walked toward nowhere in particular.

"Oh my," the Devil said. "I kind of like this place. And I thought Hell was a hoot. Clearly, the Collectors have their own bit of fun."

Joe walked close to the Devil, as though proximity to him would offer protection from whatever dangers lurked here.

"All that stuff you said last night about the Cornerstones of Creation... That was true, right? You weren't weaving one of your yarns?" Joe asked timidly.

The Devil chuckled, stepping over broken femurs and tiny tibias, enjoying the sound they made under his heels. He went out of his way to find rib cages still whole, and crushed them as he walked over them.

"Joe, my boy, I never lie. Even though whatever I say may sound extraordinarily outrageous, I have never known myself to lie. And you've known me long enough now to know better than to ask that question."

The others walked quietly, and behind them all trailed Rafael.

He wasn't sure what this place was, but he was certain of one thing—if the basement was a small chapel in terms of its vampiric draining ability, then this place was a veritable cathedral. It drained him, drawing on every last strand of energy he had. He hurried closer to the Madam and Lilly so as not to fall behind. The mist in this realm was not gray or white; it was jet black, consuming everything around it, leaving nothing for sight or senses to grasp.

They walked as quietly as they could, for as long as they did, not knowing when the journey would end.

"I'm getting impatient," the Devil said. "I know the Collectors enjoy their little theatrics, but this is ridiculous."

"What did you expect?" the Madam asked.

"Oh, Madam," he sighed, "you know a little flair goes a long way. But we've been walking for some time now. I don't see this as anything more than a cheap party trick for the Collectors' amusement. Isn't it obvious they're making fun of us?"

"Then let us make sure to announce our arrival," the Madam said. "Shall we?"

Lilly watched as the Madam raised her hands above her head and clapped them once. A beacon of green light shot into the air, rose above the black mist, and exploded somewhere along the horizon. As it did, the mist began to thin and disperse.

The first thing they all saw, making them freeze in place, was a creature two hundred feet tall, sitting alone upon a throne of bones. It resembled the Collectors: gaunt, hollow-eyed, skeletal fingers, a hooded robe. Yet it was far taller, broader, and more menacing than any of the Collectors they had ever encountered.

"Speak," said the giant presence from atop its throne. "For now you hold audience with the Head Amasser."

"Well, well, well. If it isn't the head honcho," the Devil said, grinning.

"Lucifer Morningstar," the Head Amasser replied. "We meet again."

"Indeed," the Devil said. "The pleasure is all mine."

"Why have you come here?" the Head Amasser asked. "This land is not meant for those who are not of my ilk. Explain your presence."

"You called us," Joe said.

"I invited only you," the Head Amasser interrupted. "And you chose to come with an entire entourage. You bring a vampyre whose soul is not ours to collect, for it rots in Hell. You bring a witch who once bargained with one of us, true, but who has since pledged herself to the Axis Mundi. And you bring the Devil and the Madam, two of my rivals. Dare I take this as a threat, Joseph Banbury?"

Joe now saw more clearly beyond the Head Amasser, now that the black mist had dispelled. They stood in a dark hall with bleak luminescence dotted on the dark ceiling, akin to stars, and all around them floated thousands of Collectors, looking down upon the intruders, their collective rattling breaths an unnerving symphony.

Joe drew a sharp breath, panic rising, but then remembered why he had come. He steadied himself and spoke.

"As of this moment," Joe said, his voice echoing in the hall, "you are well aware, Head Amasser, of the chaos the Abstract has unleashed on our world. You know what measures we have taken to stop it. And you know we have failed. I became God, chose to do away with the dichotomy of good and evil, and clearly that was a mistake. My doing so ruptured the balance of the cosmos, allowing the Abstract and its parasites to attack the very fabric of this universe.

"I brought back the Devil, but I fear it was too late. We couldn't put an end to the Abstract together, not in Hell, not when we battled it in the vast expanse of space. So we come to you in this great hour of need, asking for your assistance."

Such vastness the Head Amasser possessed, in terms of sheer size, that when it moved its skeletal arm, it appeared to be doing so in extreme slow motion. It rested its skull upon its closed fist, as though pondering deeply, and then spoke in the same slow, drawn-out voice that befitted its grandiosity.

"Are you aware, Joseph Banbury, that I am a hive mind? That each of my Collectors is but a manifestation of myself? They do nothing beyond what I will. They operate as marionette dolls under my control."

Joe shook his head. "I did not know that."

"Well, then you must also know that in a universe gone rogue, my Collectors have been forced to go rogue in turn. They must keep up with the pace of the dying, to gather all those scattered souls on your planet, all because of your mistakes."

Joe raised his hands in defiance. "I'm not saying I made no mistakes. But how long have you been the Head Amasser?"

"For eons. Ever since the beginning of time, and even before then."

Joe met its gaze steadily. "Well, I was only God for a couple of years. Mistakes were to be expected. I won't judge myself too harshly on them. Rather, I would judge the other Cornerstones for their complacency, for allowing my mistakes to fester without stepping in at the right time. The same holds true for the Madam, who never came to me in a capacity of warning or counsel. The same holds true for you."

"You speak as if you are the Absolute himself," the Head Amasser rumbled. "Where do you conjure such ego from?"

Joe gave a faint, bitter smile. "This old thing? That's just bruised and battered me, speaking from the heart. The Absolute has nothing to do with it. The Absolute would rather strip me of what power I had, then force me to traipse through trial after trial as if I must earn my godhood back. I've decided that in this final battle, I will not run to him for aid."

The Head Amasser sneered. "So instead you come to me."

It wasn't Joe who answered, but Rafael. His voice was meek as he addressed the towering leader of the Collectors.

"Pardon me, my lord, but isn't the Abstract more of your concern than the Absolute's anyway?"

"And what makes you think that?" the Head Amasser asked, its hollow eyes settling upon him.

Rafael stepped forward. "I speak as a vampyre, my lord. I thrive on human blood, and can therefore be considered a parasite. When I am robbed of blood, when my energy is depleted, I find myself unable to do anything. I am weakened and sink into a comatose state, such as the one I was in for more than two centuries, entombed in a crypt courtesy of Lilly here. My point is this: If you were to collect the parasites and isolate them in a place where they could no longer feed on the fabric of this universe, that would solve the issue. Without its parasites, the Abstract would be defenseless."

The Head Amasser sat and listened, still as stone. Joe was

impressed by Rafael's words. He now understood why the Madam had insisted on bringing him along. Out of the corner of his eye, he saw the Devil grin faintly, amused and satisfied.

At last the Head Amasser spoke. "Rafael Von Thorburn, I knew your master. I came to him once and offered him an accord. He accepted. What befell him afterward was a terrible fate, but know this—I collected him with my own hands when his time came. He rests peacefully in my domain. As does your mother," it said, turning its gaze to Joe. "I heeded your request, the one you made in the church. All souls whose time comes and who do not desire an eternity of torment in Hell, or an eternity of reward in Heaven, are mine. At least, when there was such a thing as Heaven. I collect souls. But I also collect the essence of this universe. And throughout time immemorial, I have collected threats against it. That is my duty.

"And in this, you are right, Dr. Rafael Von Thorburn. I do possess the capacity to isolate the parasites. But the Abstract is as powerful as I am, for it is chaos, and chaos thrives against the meticulousness of the Collectors. So, what do you propose we do about the Abstract?"

Lilly answered. "We don't know. But we know this much. We will not sit idly by and watch the Abstract consume our universe. If it wants a fight, a fight is what we will give it."

"I admire your spirit," the Head Amasser said. "As I admire all of your initiative. Tell me, Dr. Von Thorburn, would you wish to be my champion in this fight? If you say yes, understand that your role will not only be that of a vampyre, but of my prophet. You will carry my will into the world and into this final battle. Say yes, and I will grant you my aid."

Rafael looked uncertainly toward the Devil. "But isn't my soul still in your control?"

Lucifer gave a dismissive shrug. "I can return it. If you are to be such a vital player in this fight, then by all means, feel free to have it back. Be whole again, Rafael. If not for your sake, then for the universe's."

A look of astonishment and relief crossed Rafael's face as Lucifer Morningstar released him from his contract.

"Very well." Rafael turned back to the great Collector. "I shall be your champion in this final battle."

"Then we have a champion each," the Head Amasser said. "Lilly Thurman represents the Madam. Joseph Banbury represents the Devil. Rafael Von Thorburn represents me. As for the Absolute, he has ignored my summons, refused my request for an audience. He has done nothing to address this crisis. So he will not be seen as an ally, but as an adversary, if he chooses to oppose us in the battle to come. And rest assured, the battle is coming. Even now, the Abstract gathers its forces and prepares to assault your universe one last time."

Its white, glazed eyes stared into the distance, as though piercing dimensions to gaze into chaos itself.

"I demand my due when the time comes," the Head Amasser said. "When the battle is finished, whether won or lost, I shall take all the souls that die."

Joseph Banbury's heart sank with the Christian realization that in the great fight ahead, people would die. Inevitably. No matter what he did now, there would be no stopping it. Against the inevitability, he felt helpless.

The Devil laid a comforting hand on Joe's shoulder. "Come now. Now is not the time to second-guess yourself."

Joe exhaled, steadying himself, then raised his voice to address the Head Amasser. "Very well. You may collect whatever you wish at the end of this, if there remains an 'after this.'"

The Head Amasser pointed a bony finger at him, warning. "No matter what you do in this battle, if the balance remains broken afterward, there will be no point. The universe seeks balance. And presently, without a God, and with only two devils walking the earth—you and your father—there is a dearth of balance. See that it is restored once all of this is over."

"I can assure you, Lord," the Madam said. "We will do our utmost to right the wrong."

"With that, and the matter concluded," the Head Amasser intoned, lowering its hand, "you may take your leave."

The black mist surged back, all-consuming, and in an instant they were banished from the Bone Orchard, returned to their own worlds. It happened with such great abruptness that it could be construed as rude, but that was how the Collectors operated.

They did not mince words nor did they waste time.

As they were flung across dimensions, Lucifer grabbed hold of Joe and ushered him toward Hell, for he had something to show his son. The Madam brought Lilly to the Axis Mundi to counsel her one last time before Armageddon.

As for Dr. Rafael von Thorburn, he hurtled through time and space, reconciling with his lost soul as it found him, its name freshly scratched off from the ledgers of Hell. A man rendered whole, yet still a vampyre, Rafael sought refuge in

Bridgewater, enjoying his consolidated self, even if it was for just a few moments.

Joseph Banbury was never happier to be in Hell than at this moment when he sat on the terrace of the Devil's idyllic Tuscan home, staring into this peaceful mirage that Satan had built within all of scorch and flame.

At least here, where he resided, there wasn't any of that blistering heat, or any of the screams of torture or vestiges of punishment hanging heavy in the air. Joe sat with a cup of tea in his hands. He could have asked for wine or any of the spirits or liquors in the world if he desired, but at this moment, some Moroccan mint tea with honey added into the mix was all his soul craved.

The Devil sat quietly beside Joseph Banbury, no longer dressed in a black suit, but in a more luxurious burgundy one with a crisp crimson tie and ruby cufflinks. His form had returned to its glowing and brilliant demeanor. As he sat beside Joseph Banbury, he did so with the regality that befitted the name Lucifer Morningstar.

The father and son did not talk, for there were no more words to say, other than to soak in each other's presence and enjoy these fleeting moments of calm. Even in hell they could feel the tremors of the Abstract's chaos resonating throughout the known universe.

And for all intents and purposes, Hell was within the universe, not something that existed outside it.

Joe sipped on his tea, trying to reason with himself about what he had seen in the Bone Orchard. He had seen many things, both upon entering the realm and upon leaving it. He had heard faint whispers, the voices of all those he had held dear, all those who had passed.

While he hadn't actually seen any of them, he had felt Tasha's presence from beyond the black mist, just as he had felt Joph's presence, and his mother's. It was an impalpable feeling, something that clung to him like sweat to hot skin, or spit on the back of your throat when you are battling fever.

Going to the Bone Orchard had filled him with a sense of loss and dread, leaving him hollow, as if he had left part of himself in that realm. The spectacle of all the Collectors by the thousands gathered there in their great assembly, ranks upon ranks of them cascading and staring with their ghastly eyes and hooded faces at Joseph Banbury—the dead center of the axis upon which the fate of the upcoming battle was to turn—had not been a light feeling.

In that world where the floor was made of human bones, he had learned something. Something he was meant to do. But how he was to do it was the tough part, because right now he wasn't sure he had it in him to make the right decision at the right time.

The Devil turned his head to Joe and gave him a squinting look, one of a little frustration mixed with surprise.

"So, for someone who has charted most of the known universe, including Heaven, Hell, the Axis Mundi, and the Bone Orchard, you are far too quiet, son. Tell me, what are you thinking of?"

Joe's eyes were hazily looking out into the distance at the rolling green hills and the olive trees in the valley below. He wondered if the olives in the Devil's martini, which he was holding in his hand, came from those trees.

"Oh, it's nothing," Joe said quietly. "It's just, when you came to me first, I did not know that an interview with the Devil would entail the unraveling of the entire universe."

The Devil threw his head back and laughed, clapping his hands.

"What did you expect, Joe? That you would win a Pulitzer and then be on to the next notable personality in the Forbes Top 100 list? That maybe you would get to interview Bill Clinton after me? Oh no, an interview with the Devil is as high as it gets, because God does not give an audience to those who wish to meet Her and ask questions. The rest of the bunch are a basic and boring breed, too serious about their roles. Whether it is the Collectors or Madam, you would not have had any fun talking to them, as I'm sure you observed. No sooner were we done than the Head Amasser banished us out of his realm without so much as a cup of tea.

"And yet here you sit with me, as relaxed as one gets, enjoying creature comforts."

"Well," Joe said, "I guess what you're trying to say is an interview with the Devil is the best thing that could have happened to me."

The Devil looked Joe deep in the eyes with an intensity that made him unnerved.

"An interview with the Devil, Joe, is an interview with the universe at large, for I hold all of its knowledge within. Who knows? Maybe after we are done, you'll write another book about me."

Joe laughed. "No, I'm not falling for this again. I'm not writing any more books for you, Satan. You better know it well."

Satan looked a little disappointed.

"Then I'll just have to start this all over again. Find another writer. Tell the part of my tale that hasn't yet been put into words."

"Oh really?" Joe asked. "Which part would that be?"

"The part that is happening right now," Satan said, grinning. "This is as uncharted as it gets. To think that I get to stand as lead character, center stage, and call the shots, not be the adversary that the Bible made me out to be. That's something, isn't it?"

Before the two of them could talk further, Delphine trotted out onto the terrace wearing her black garbs. Nothing as playful as what she used to wear before. These garbs were long and unassuming. The black robe clung to her body, but not in a way that aroused attention.

She was sullen, as one would be when they were destroyed and recreated, then destroyed again, then recreated. This was her third time coming into existence. Being unarmed and remade had a price upon one's soul, even if it was the soul of a demon succubus.

"You called, Lord?" she said to Satan, standing there morosely.

"I think, Delphine," Satan said, "that given what is going to happen very soon, you should make your peace with Joe. I have, and I would very much like you to make it with him as well."

"I don't think I have anything to say to Joe," Delphine snapped. "Not after what he did."

"What he did is nothing that wasn't part of his nature. After all, he's a chip off the old block."

"Yes, Delphine. It has taken me this long, and yes, it has been long, but I have finally accepted myself for who I am."

"Good for you," Delphine said, giving a mock clap with her hands.

"I am sorry for what I did," Joe said.

Delphine was not expecting an apology. When she heard those words from Joe's mouth, she was surprised, her lips parting a little, familiarity trickling through her eyes as she stared at Joe not as what he was now, but as he once was, the scribe who had finished writing the book in this very house.

"If Satan and you are fine, then who am I to hold any qualms?" Delphine said.

Then she bowed and walked away.

"What's her deal?" Joe asked. "I mean, besides the obvious."

The Devil chuckled.

"Well, Joe, creation and uncreation is tough business. She has been through a lot, as I'm sure you can tell. When Hell fractured upon the Abstract's leave, I had to rebuild it all. In that regard, I feel like I am not much different from the Greek myth of Sisyphus. I keep rolling this boulder up the hill. And one must imagine Sisyphus happy, as that French philosopher said."

"Are you happy?" Joe asked.

"I can't complain. I have been thrust into a role very different from the one I had been playing until very recently. I cannot consider myself Satan any longer. For Satan is a word that means adversary. I am not man's adversary anymore, not if I am helping him save the universe and his place in it."

"You are still the adversary," Joe said, raising his cup at the Devil. "Only this time, it's the Abstract you are the adversary of."

"Ah," the Devil said, "we can banter back and forth on nomenclature and labels all day, but that isn't going to get us anywhere. What will get us somewhere, Joe, is if I show you what I have accomplished."

The Devil stood up from his chair and beckoned Joe to do the same. Joe wasn't done with his green tea yet, but sensing the impatience in the Devil's tone, he got up and followed him out of the house.

The two walked down the stone path that led to the door on the other side of the Tuscan hills. They crossed in silence, Joe making sure to take in every little detail—the rumbling hills, the yellow flowers, the scent of the olive trees, the streams that ran alongside him. He reminded himself that a thing of beauty is a joy forever, and the Devil was nothing if not an appreciator of things of beauty.

Satan opened the door to the rest of Hell. Its scorch burst through, but Joe had already braced himself.

Together they traveled into the fiery bowels of flame and cinder. Their forms changed, no longer resembling humans but their real selves: wings, pale scaly leathery skin, horns, and red glowing eyes.

They came through on the other side, standing on the terrace of the tallest tower of Pandemonium.

Joe had never seen a sight like it. He had never been to this city before, only glimpsed it in passing when he had visited Hell. The castle tower stretched high, and the sprawling building beneath it held all of Hell's glory in its vastness and scale. And below, in the field of flame, stood tens of thousands of demons, dukes, lords of Hell, Nephilim, monsters and mayhem alike.

"They are yours to control. They are yours to lead, Joe," the Devil said. "For this battle is as much theirs as it is yours. And when the Abstract comes, you will find that they will heed your every order."

"Is that not right?!" The Devil turned to address the horde.

The hell-horde resounded with a thunderous, "Aye!" Roaring, stomping their feet, clashing their chains, unfurling their wings, spitting flame into the sky.

Joe did not know whether to be more petrified or in awe, standing there watching rejuvenated Hell awaiting his orders. For the first time in his life, he saw demons with hope in their eyes. He did not see them as demons any longer, but as comrades. Fellow kin and kith in this kiln, eager to join the fray and sacrifice their lives for a battle that would undoubtedly claim many lives.

"And where will you be in all this?" Joe asked the Devil.

"Oh, Joe," the Devil said sympathetically. "I will be where I've always been, right beside you. And whatever you do, I will help you do. No matter what it is, no matter what it costs me. Just so you understand, this whole business has cost me dearly."

The Devil placed a hand on Joe's shoulder. "I have never said this before. I have never said this to anyone. Especially not in a cadence like this. But here, at the end of everything, Joseph Banbury, I am glad to call you a friend."

Joe stood there, soaking in the silence and gravity of the words. He understood their weight. And with his eyes, he witnessed the entire army of Hell standing resolutely, not breaking ranks, not breaking formation, awaiting his orders.

So he addressed them. Pressing both hands on the balcony, unfurling his own wings so even those in the far back could see he was no mere human, but the spawn of Satan.

And he spoke. He spoke with a ferocity that did not belong to the meek and mild Joseph Banbury of once upon a time. He spoke in a tongue steeped in all of Hell's scathing. He spoke loudly, as befitted a leader. And he spoke the truth.

"Defeat is not eternal. Victory is not permanent. The only thing we have that can be called forever is effort. Effort is permanent. Effort is eternal. It does not matter that we fought against the Abstract and failed once. The Abstract itself does not know that the principalities of order demand repetition until perfection is achieved. And with you alongside me, my brethren, we shall achieve that perfection together.

"This time, it won't be us who drag the Chaos into Hell. This time, we bring Hell to Chaos itself. Flame shall mete out justice against darkness. As it once was, so shall it be now. As above, so below. And with that, I do indeed declare with all my being, Ave Satanas! Hail Satan! Hail yourself!"

The armies assembled below roared in unison, the name of their master shaking the air, screaming, "Hail Satan!" at the top of their lungs, every lick of flame billowing bright, all of Hell an incandescent orchestra with the tips of each infernal Hell streak burning bright blue-purple, shedding a deep neon shadow upon the army.

And for one second, letting go of ego and devil-hood, the Devil felt great joy. Great joy welled in his chest, even bringing a tear to his eye, seeing everything he had accomplished, witnessing his true reflection in his son, Joseph Banbury.

11

PARADISE LOST

Lilly Thurman could not feel the hold of the Madam on her as she hurtled through the portal. Though someone else had grabbed her, a presence that she had never felt before. Panicking, bracing herself for the worst (in her mind, she anticipated the Abstract to make its move, but she had no idea that the Abstract would make its move this fast), and landing on the other side, not in the Axis Mundi but somewhere else entirely.

She had not been here before.

This place, with its green grass and its dense foliage marked by a boundary of palm trees and waterfalls cascading off verdant hills, seemed like a caricature a lesser being might consider Heaven.

She stood up from the grass, her heart beating fast, readying herself for a fight as she turned around and faced whatever had pulled her here. To her surprise, it was not the Abstract as she had imagined it to be.

It was a dark-skinned man in a corporate Sunday dinner getup, plaid shirt tucked into cotton pants, an effervescent smile on his face, his fingers interlaced.

"I have watched you all your life, Lilly Thurman, or should I call you Lilly Frost?" he spoke.

"You may not address me before you tell me who I am addressing," Lilly said, hands up, ready to dole out a flurry of spells, her white blouse marked with green blotches where she'd been grazed against the grass.

"Is it not apparent?" he asked, unfolding his hands, as if that would help clear it up somehow. "I am the Absolute."

Lilly lowered her hands, but did not lower her defenses. "Why did you summon me?"

"You are close to Joseph Banbury," the Absolute said without so much as making an attempt to hide his all-knowingness. "I have tried to reason with him, but that reasoning—"

"You set loose one of your horrors in my house, and if Joe hadn't stepped in at the right time, that *thing* would have killed his sister and his friend," Lilly snapped. "It can hardly be called reason."

"Nevertheless," the Absolute said, losing patience quickly, his mild expression disappearing, frustration taking its place. "It was a challenge that I set for him, one that he passed. But he has not chosen to side with me, even when I am offering him back his godhood. I was hoping that you would..."

"Bend his ear?" Lilly said, looking around, hands on her

hips. “What the fuck is this place anyway? Your idea of paradise? You know, it’s pretty pathetic.”

“Whatever this place is, is not your concern,” the Absolute said, trying to smile despite his anger. “I have a task for you.”

“I am not yours to command. Unless you’d rather go toe to toe with the Madam, that is. I am her champion. Go find your own,” Lilly snapped.

“You did not hear the task.”

“I have no interest in hearing it.”

“I have decided to bestow his godhood back to Joe,” the Absolute said. “And I need you to convince him to take it. If he wishes to win this fight, he is to be my champion.”

“A little too late for that, don’t you think? You should have considered it before taking his powers away,” Lilly said.

Around them, light without an apparent source shimmered, making the surface of every leaf, every water body shine and glow, sickening Lilly to her stomach that someone such as the Absolute would conceive of this as their idea of a good time, a peaceful place.

“What do you recommend I do then? If he is not to be my champion. If he won’t even meet me. I tried to pull him, but his father’s reach on him was strong, preventing me from getting a hold of him,” the Absolute said.

“Somehow, that does not seem like my problem. Contrary to what you think, there are bigger problems in the world than your little snags.”

“For your insolence, I could smite you where you stand!” the Absolute shouted.

"Try me, motherfucker!" Lilly shouted back, hands raised once again, spells tingling at the tips of her fingers, making blue sparks fly. "You think I'm scared?"

"No. I think you're foolish enough to challenge me," the Absolute said, backing off. "And I do not want to contribute to the increasing imbalance of this universe by engaging with you. It saddens me that you would not see reason. After all, I am not the enemy here."

"And yet, all of us are handling your mess for you. If you really are the Absolute, you'd be able to take care of the Chaos that encroaches upon your universe. But you're incapable of doing that yourself," Lilly said, still ready for the fight.

"I have assembled my own army, witch. And contrary to what you think, I am going to fight alongside the rest of you. This threat is mine to face as well," the Absolute said. "It would have been easier if... But since when have any of you humans made anything easy?"

The Absolute raised his hand, revealing the source of all the light that this place was bathed in. Thousands of rays of bright luminescence stood tall like spears. "My army of light would have been his to command, but it seems that I must step into the fray myself as my own champion."

"What on earth is that?" Lilly asked, shielding her eyes.

"The brilliance of a thousand suns, and you shall find that it will burn the Abstract wherever it appears," the Absolute said, marveling at his work.

But his marveling was short-lived. The ground shook, making trees tremble. Lilly held onto the palm's trunk beside her. A black rupture crackled through the lush grass floor, breaking rapture in two.

"Seems like the Abstract has decided to take you up on the challenge," Lilly shouted over the deafening sounds of chaos bleeding through the cracks in the sky, the crack in the floor.

"And so it begins," the Absolute said grimly, witnessing the destruction of Heaven, but not standing idly to just let it happen. He sent forth beams of blistering light wherever the black tendrils of chaos appeared, impaling the parasites on each light-spear. They writhed and died, but more appeared from each crack and rift that now had Heaven surrounded from all sides.

Lilly Thurman did not know if her magic was strong enough to escort her away from this place, but she tried anyway. She conjured a portal and jumped through it, watching Chaos fall upon the Absolute.

It was nighttime in Bridgewater as she landed safely on the roof of her home. Rafael was already standing there, looking at the sky.

"It's begun."

Rifts upon rifts had broken through the night sky like claw marks made by a monolithic beast, and from each of those crackling black rifts, out poured a fresh flurry of parasites, descending upon Earth.

"Where is Joe?" Rafael asked. "I do not see him with you."

"I don't know," Lilly said, her heart sinking.

Rafael clasped her hand in his.

"You are not alone, witch."

Lilly turned to Rafael and saw that his eyes were aglow a

ghastly white, the same shade as that of the Collector who had once come to her on the stake, the same shade as those of the Head Amasser.

"We fight with you," Rafael, prophet of the Collectors, spoke in the gaunt drawl of his new masters, a voice distinct from his mild-mannered tone. "And although you may not believe me when I say this, but I saw this day all those hundreds of years ago when I saved your life and granted you your immortal life on the pyre in Salem."

"What happens now?" Lilly asked, looking up at the sky, at the increasing amount of rifts.

"The pieces are all on the board. The game has begun," the Collectors spoke through Rafael. "Armageddon is nigh."

Lilly lowered her gaze to the town, witnessing the lit windows behind which people lived their little lives. Tomorrow, they might cease living those lives. All these little streets, the quaint homes of Bridgewater.

Rafael opened his mouth, his eyes shining bright, his hands raised, and let out a shriek that sounded like a trumpet, a trumpet that suddenly resonated from the mouths of the ranks and ranks of Collectors that stood on the slope of the hill below, all of them robed and afloat in the air, signaling the start of the war.

The time for protection spells was long past, but Lilly was surprised to see the familiar streak of protective spells fly into the sky. This was not her doing. She ran over to the other side of the roof, the part that overlooked the pasture and the stables below.

Black-robed and numerous, they stood, witches of every

caliber, assembled from all over the area, here to be led under the charge of Lilly Thurman, casting spell-work in the sky, once upon a time burned to save the world, now saving the world from burning.

The battle for the fate of the universe began on a fateful night in late August, and everyone was witness to this great calamity.

12

APOCALYPSE

There was a woman standing on the porch of Amy Banbury's house. As for who she was, she hadn't introduced herself, but from what Amy could gather, the haggard black clothes, the hood pulled low, she must be one of Lilly's witches. From what Amy could see in the murky night, there were others like that woman standing equidistantly across the entire city. She could see another one on the edge of the street.

Amy watched from behind the curtain of the living room window as the woman flung spells into the sky, and corresponding to her spells, other spells rose into the sky, confirming Amy's suspicion that there were more witches out there than just those that she could see.

Her father, a confused soul, did not know what was happening. Despite everything Amy had tried to explain to him in the short time she'd had, all he had been able to say was, “Joyce was one of the last good people on this earth, and now that she is dead, this is it. Apocalypse has come.”

He had still not come out of the grief of losing his wife, and now he was forced to deal with the reality of the world coming undone. He watched alongside her as the sky ripped open into one rift after another, purple-hued darkness pouring down like billowed, corrupt rain.

Amy’s heart throbbed with terror, knowing this was it, that anything after this might as well not happen at all, because this was the end. As for what was going to happen, she had no knowledge, but while she could, she would stay with her father and protect him in whatever way she could.

“Where is Joe?” Tommy Banbury asked Amy. “Where is your brother? Shouldn’t he be indoors?”

Amy’s heart wrenched as she heard these words of worry from a father’s mouth for his son. “Dad, Joe is occupied somewhere. I’m sure that he will make his way to us when this is all over.”

“When what is all over?” Tommy said irritably and with plausible deniability. “This? This is just a thunderstorm, nothing more.”

Amy realized, with growing desperation, that no matter how much she tried to explain, it was beyond her father’s ability to grasp a reality that was more akin to madness.

With that, Tommy Banbury went back into the living room and did not let himself be bothered by the fluctuating electricity, or the fact that no channel played on the TV, or that the ground shook every now and then. A man confused, a man dazed, a man drenched in sorrow, he just sat there, beer in hand, cigarette between his fingers, staring at the sofa where his wife used to sit.

In that moment, Amy Banbury thought it best to just join him and be with him, because what else could she, a mere human, do in a battle that had all of the cosmos stirred to riot?

"I miss Joyce," Tommy said. "She would know exactly what kind of prayer to pray in such times." His voice broke.

"Well, I know a prayer, Dad," Amy said, even though she didn't believe in it anymore, because now she had lived to see evidence contrary to its words.

"Oh yeah? Which one?" Tommy asked.

"The Lord's Prayer," Amy said.

Tommy gave her a troubled look. "I always felt that prayer was a little too grandiose for my taste. I could never really pray to God the way your mother could. Let's just say I was in it for your mother. Me, personally, I couldn't care less."

"Well then," Amy said softly, "there's nothing better than a moment of silence to serve as prayer for our disturbed thoughts."

"Ah," Tommy said, ignoring the deep rumble that shook the living room and sent flower pots tumbling from the shelf, breaking as glass shards and petals scattered across the floor, water soaking into the carpet. "Let's say a prayer to Joyce instead. A prayer to Joyce."

Amy kept one eye on her father and the other constantly flitting to the woman standing on the lawn, trying to hold back the flurries of chaos from falling on the Banbury residence in Red Bank, New Jersey. Both father and daughter closed their eyes and said their prayers, and in that moment, as the world came undone around them, they found their prayers a strange source of soothing.

Not because they expected the prayer to be answered in any way, but because they were both remembering a loved one. A mother. A wife. And in that regard, the prayer served its purpose. While both sat there, eyes closed, they could each imagine Joyce in the room with them. And even if they didn't have faith, *she* had faith.

She *was* faith, just as she was Joyce.

After a while, once the tremors had settled and the electricity returned, Amy took a beer from the fridge and, against every inhibition and every caution, went out onto the lawn where the woman still stood. Like her, there were others equidistant across the town.

Amy handed the woman the bottle. "Here. Something to calm your nerves," she said.

The witch took it and smiled at her. "Thanks."

Together, the two women stood and watched as the sky became a tapestry of chaos. The rifts had crackled into the many hundreds, long slits showing the blackness beyond the dark night's expanse, the blackness of chaos itself.

"I just hope we make it through the night," the witch said. She was a young girl, her robes far too big for her, no older than in her early twenties.

"How did you come about this witch business, if I may ask?" Amy asked.

"Oh," the girl said, "my mother was a witch, and her mother before her. We come from a long line of witches. I woke up with a strange dream tonight, one that I am sure all the rest of the women had too, otherwise why would they be standing there like sentinels? A woman called Madam told us that we were to protect the earth tonight. That's what I'm doing. That's what all of us are doing, all over the world."

"You must be quite lucky," Amy said, "to have such powers."

"Sometimes they're a curse. Especially when I'm trying to pretend to be normal. I still haven't graduated college, and I have to skip class whenever I get one of my episodes. People think it's epilepsy. But I get visions, things about to happen, things long past. But that's neither here nor there. I have a more pressing task at hand, and we've been delegated this task by the Madam herself."

"I'll leave you to it then. You know which door to knock if you need anything," Amy said, giving her a gentle pat on the shoulder.

"Hey, take this back," the witch said, handing the beer bottle back. "I'm not old enough to drink yet."

"Drink it anyway. I'm sure nobody's calling the cops tonight."

The witch laughed, and with her, so did Amy, before going inside and locking the door.

IN THE NIGHT SKY, it wasn't just the Abstract anymore, nor were there only parasites. Collectors hovered in the air, giant spectral figures with arms out, their hoods and robes flailing in the winds.

They found their prey in the sky, and for each Collector there were tens upon tens of parasites to subdue. The Collectors rose and covered entire skyscapes above the cities, preventing the parasites from entering the atmosphere or slipping through underneath.

On a rooftop in Bridgewater stood Rafael, directing the Collectors as to what they should do. For each parasite the Collectors apprehended, they isolated it in the Bone Orchard, where it would remain until the end of time itself, isolated, starved, depleted, comatose.

But while this was happening over the sky in Bridgewater and Red Bank, New Jersey, another rift, this one longer and resembling a hurtling vortex, appeared over New York City.

Observing it from the window of Billy Hawthorne's apartment was Blake Weston, dressed in his army uniform, holding his service rifle. His heart skipped a beat, his mouth went dry, his feet shook, and his hands tremored. His wartime PTSD came back in flashes, reminding him of his dead compatriots on the battlefields of Afghanistan, of gunfire and bomb roars, as the sky rattled and the foundations of the apartment building shook, making every single frame that hung on Billy Hawthorne's wall clang and fall to the ground.

Amidst all this, Billy Hawthorne sat with the stoic confidence of a man who knew he would not die. Whether that knowledge was true or not did not matter to Billy. He held the Remington rifle in his hands and was just biding his time, waiting, waiting for the madness within to finally unfurl and uncoil, allowing him to become his true self. The one that would have to go out in a matter of moments and deal with the parasites, the Abstract, the Absolute, and everything else.

"You know," Blake Weston said, "we've been in this for quite a long time. You and I. And everybody gets a champion, isn't that so? The Devil has Joe Banbury. The Madam has Lilly. Who is the champion of the human beings? Who represents us in this fight?"

Billy Hawthorne looked at Blake Weston with a sly smile. "Are you saying what I think you're saying?"

"Damn right," said Blake. "I think we were in this journey for a reason. I think we need to be the ones representing humanity in this battle. And I, for one, am not going to sit still in this apartment, hoping everything dies down without us even contributing. I'm sure there are many like me, in the thousands of apartments and houses and condos all over New York, all over America, all over the world, who are gathering their firearms at this very moment. And I will not wait until the last moment. I will not wait for all of them to rush out of their houses for this great battle. I will be the first to join them. And you, my dear friend, are more than welcome to join me."

"Blake Weston," Billy Hawthorne said, a strange cheer in his voice, "I thought you would never ask."

"So be it then," said Blake.

"So be it," said Billy.

Together, armed with their rifles packed with ammo, the two men headed out of the trembling apartment building and into New York City, where a fresh hell was descending from the sky, a hell that had nothing to do with the Devil.

Above the New York skyline, the parasites had overpowered and outnumbered the Collectors. They slipped past them and descended upon the tall buildings, Central Park, the houses, the stores. They broke through glass and found prey in the form of vulnerable, susceptible humans cowering behind sofas, hiding under beds, locking themselves in cabinets.

As a parasite hurtled through a deli window in Brooklyn, the shopkeeper hid behind the counter with his daughter, both of them clinging to each other, weeping helplessly. The parasite, a gargantuan, cancerous thing with grotesque proportions, like solidified sludge, traveled through the store, touching everything and turning it black with its withered presence. It climbed over the counter, eager to swoop down on the defenseless father and daughter. But as it reared its head, a bullet pierced the air and struck the parasite.

The parasite screeched, lashing out, reeling away from the counter.

In the doorway of the deli stood Billy Hawthorne, his rifle aglow with a strange light. The bullet had hit true and killed the parasite. Its corpse lay splattered and defused, as if the bullet had more than just killed it; it had deflated the chaos creature.

Billy Hawthorne was glad, though he kept his cheeriness controlled, because there were many more parasites falling from the sky into the streets. He barricaded himself and Blake Weston inside the shop, boarding up the broken window with benches.

"Do you have any weapons?" he asked the shopkeeper.

The old man, brown-skinned with a long white beard,

nodded and revealed a sawed-off shotgun from behind the shelf.

Blake Weston said, “Now would be the time to use it, old man.”

They watched from behind the boarded window as more men and women appeared in the street with their own weapons.

All of them shot at the parasites like there was no tomorrow. And while the bullets might not have done as much damage as they would have wanted, they made the parasites retreat, at least temporarily, escaping the onslaught of gunfire flying from every direction on the street.

“I told you the people would rise,” Blake Weston said. “I told you, didn’t I?”

“Damn right, you did,” Billy Hawthorne said.

Together, on this Brooklyn street, the people gathered, driving away the parasites. And above them in the sky, a host of archangels appeared, led by none other than Gabriel, along with an army of lesser angels eager to aid the Collectors in this great battle.

The Collectors noticed the angels fighting alongside them and gave their approval, as the archangels slashed with their weapons at the agents of chaos.

The rift above them doubled in size, now a proper vortex resembling a black hole, and from it came maelstrom winds and a storm of rain and thunder, encapsulating New York City in a blaze of chaotic weather. It heralded the arrival of the Abstract itself.

All around, parasites clashed—in the air, on the ground, on

rooftops, in the park, in the streets—against Collectors, angels, and human beings, all fighting for the same cause.

Back in Bridgewater, Lilly Thurman had finished casting the last of the protective spells with the rest of her witches, and was bracing herself for the army of parasites now falling upon the little town.

The invisible barrier of protection kept the parasites from entering, but it was only a matter of time before the spell gave out. Lilly looked upon the assembly of witches below and said, "You're going to spread out. Help anyone who's stuck, tend to the injured, take care of yourselves and the people. This battle will not mean anything if there are no more people left to save."

With that, the witches dispersed, and Lilly Thurman found herself looking toward New York City, because that was where the heart of the battle was. She conjured a portal and traveled through it, leaving Rafael standing on the rooftop of her house, directing the Collectors.

Now that she was in New York City, she could see the chaos here was far more menacing than in Bridgewater. Parasites crawled all over the buildings as if they were aware this was the place to make their stand. Lilly cast a flurry of spells from the roof of a Manhattan tower, obliterating the parasites as they came near her.

On other rooftops she could see other witches holding their ground. And on the streets below, she was surprised to see that ordinary people with ordinary weapons had joined the fight. Though they were not winning—many of them shooting at the parasites had been killed, dismembered, feasted upon, their corpses strewn across the sidewalk and road. Traffic was jammed, cars bumper to bumper, abandoned by their drivers as they fled for safer places.

It was a cacophony of sounds: children crying, women weeping, men screaming. Lilly realized she had to hold her ground here, do only what she could from where she stood, lest she fall herself.

To the north, in Central Park, a great pentagram as wide as the park itself seared into the grass, burning away leaves, scorching the bushes. And as the pentagram glowed bright red, Hell unleashed itself from below.

Demons, imps, Hellions, cambions, succubae, dukes of Hell, lords of flame, all flew out, meeting the parasites in midair, thrashing them with chains, slashing with swords, impaling with spears and tridents, setting fire to the sky. Burning parasites came crashing down, screeching as they died. But even that was not enough.

Smaller rifts in the sky ripped open and merged with the larger vortex, from which more and more parasites poured through. And as Joseph Banbury and the Devil flew out of the Hell portal, they realized that no matter how many armies their side conjured, the parasites would keep coming, the Abstract would keep throwing soldier after soldier from its endless reserve of chaos.

“Don’t lose heart now, Joseph, my boy,” said the Devil. “Look, the angels have joined the fray, as have the Collectors. And witches. We are not alone, and this night is far from over.”

Joe nodded at the Devil, who wasted no time flying high into the sky, sending blistering infernos into the vortex itself.

The vortex pulsated, absorbing the fire. For a moment it seemed there would be no more new parasites. But then the vortex threw the flames back, directing them at Satan himself. The fire struck him, and he crashed into the Empire State Building's rooftop. His wings scorched. His body broken.

Joe flew after him, but before he could reach the Empire State Building, he saw something dark, black, and humongous rise from the roof. It was Satan, flying skyward in his unhindered, menacing, demonic form. Fifty feet tall. A giant trident glowering black in his hands. Wings like those of a great dragon. Horns curving fiercely.

This Mephistophelean manifestation of Satan flew into the sky, tearing through the fresh hordes of parasites pouring from the vortex. He cut them down without effort, charting a burning trail through the heavens, a blazing sign for all to see: the Devil had come to Earth.

Up till now, there had been only one vortex in the sky. But upon seeing the Devil in all his prime, more vortexes opened. Now the sky above New York held no fewer than seven gaping holes, with chaos on the other side and a crumbling Earth below.

And then, while Joe was still gathering himself and trying to think of a course of action, brilliant luminescence burst through the night sky, turning it into day. From high above came rays of sunlight, and upon them, the Absolute—descending as though the rays themselves were his steeds. With grace he came down onto the lower clouds, the many rays he commanded piercing parasites, impaling them midflight.

Lilly Thurman, from her Manhattan roof, spotted the Absolute.

But she had her own battle to fight, for a fresh batch of gelatinous, dark, oozing creatures had reached her roof, surrounding her.

Lilly, recalling she was no ordinary witch but the champion of craft itself, unleashed a wave of flames, burning the parasites before they had a chance to close in.

But it was to no end. The world was drowning fast in the darkness of this parasitic hive mind, and it was clear that unless something was done about the Abstract, the parasites would keep coming.

Lilly sent another beam of electricity into the sky, targeting a fresh batch of parasites, watching their dead bodies thud against the ground.

It was then that she saw Billy Hawthorne and Blake Weston on the street, standing with other human beings like them, survivors of this war, fighters with their makeshift weapons and rapidly depleting ammunition. She watched as they held their ground, sending bullet after bullet into the parasitic horde surrounding them. Lilly lent them a hand from the rooftop, sending bursts of lightning that electrocuted the parasites, striking them dead and giving the humans an edge in the fight.

From other roofs, she saw other witches doing the same, helping those below. This did her heart good, though she wished the Madam were here herself.

"You called?" the Madam asked, appearing behind her.

"You... You're here?" Lilly said, surprised.

"I will heed the call of my champion. Tell me what you need."

"They're outnumbering us. Can you help us somehow?"

"Let me see what I can do," the Madam said. She raised one hand toward the sky and curled it into a fist. Several of the vortexes resisted, but eventually closed down, their presence blotting away from the night sky.

The Madam panted, one hand on her knee, the other on her chest. "That took a lot out of me. The Abstract is strong, and he is angry."

Despite the toll on the Madam's health, it achieved a greater goal. Now there weren't as many parasites in the sky as before. Only a couple of vortexes remained open. The angels, the Absolute, and the Collectors dealt with whatever hordes poured through those rifts.

This was the lull in the fight everyone desperately needed, even the Abstract, who, for the first time since the onslaught, did not send more forces, but waited, watching.

Joe Banbury, all flame and burning wings, rushed from one roof to another, cutting down any parasite foolish enough to cross his path. It tore at him to see that New York City, the city that he had loved ever since he was a little child staring at it from afar from the shores of Red Bank, was coming undone because of this battle. The Empire State Building's rooftop had crumbled. The Chrysler Building was shattered from one side. There remained only fallen rubble of the Flatiron Building. From up in the air, he could see the smoldering ruins of Madison Square Garden. All of the places that he had loved, all in ruins.

"You fight as well as your father, boy," Gabriel the archangel said, swinging his sword and cleaving through another wave of parasites, distracting Joe from the sight of dead bodies and destroyed buildings.

"Thank you, Gabriel," the Devil said, now back in his more palatable form, landing beside Joe. "You're not corrupting my son, are you?"

Gabriel only laughed and flung his sword again into a fresh batch of shrieking horrors. "No. Only admiring his handiwork. Or, rather, yours."

The Devil's eyes gleamed with something that looked like pride—dark, sinister pride—as he kicked away any parasites that dared climb to the roof of the building, while Hell's legions around him pushed back wave after wave of airborne chaos beings.

"How long until this is over?" Joseph asked, his breath ragged.

Michael descended, his wings vast, landing on the roof beside him. "Fights like these never end," he said. "Unless someone does something drastic."

"And what would be the fucking right thing here?" the Devil snapped, crushing a parasite in his fist, catching his breath.

Michael didn't answer him. Instead, he turned to Joe. "I heard you turned down the Absolute. He was scrambling at the end, desperate for anyone to be his champion. But nobody came to his call, because everyone had realized what he is. An arrogant fool. Even when he called out to us, we ignored him. We're here representing ourselves."

"Good to know," Joe said, his eyes on the remaining vortexes. They had stopped spitting out fresh horrors for now. "But what difference does it make if more of them keep pouring through? Look at how many have died already."

He gestured toward the city below. The angels and the Devil followed his hand.

Thousands lay dead in the city, in the streets, hanging limp from shattered windows. Women. Children. Men. Expressions of fatal horror etched on their dead faces. The survivors clung to life by threads, battered and broken, retreating within buildings, boarding up what could be boarded up, or else seeking refuge on the upper floors. Some of them started flocking to the roofs, where the parasites took some time reaching, giving them enough time to recuperate.

"This is the consequence of war, Joseph Banbury," Raphael said coldly. "What's the matter? Is this your first?"

"What does it matter?" Joe snapped back, catching sight of the Absolute descending in his beam of blinding light. "Even now, he can't resist."

"You don't have to deal with him alone," the Devil said, his mouth curling.

"Oh, this I have to hear from him," Joe muttered.

"Then I'll take my leave," the Devil said.

"And so shall we," the angels added. They soared away, throwing themselves once more into the fray of parasites, of which there were still thousands.

The Absolute landed, blazing, raising a finger at Joe as though he were casting judgment. "This is all your fault," he said scathingly.

Joe only shrugged. He looked down at the roof beneath his feet, the building once home to a literary agency called The Avernus Collective. It was fitting that he stood in the literary heart of New York while the world burned all around him.

"I think we're both equally to blame," Joe said. "You should never have stripped godhood from me."

"You should have taken it when I offered it. You should have taken it back," the Absolute retorted.

"I cannot be both God and Devil. And I've already made peace with who I am. The Devil I am is better than the God I never was."

The Absolute's face twisted, as if he would curse Joe or strike him down. But instead, he dismissed him with a wave, turning back to the fight, flinging his spears of light into the swarms pouring through the city.

Joe watched him work, watched his lonely army of flickering light cut through the dark. He disagreed with everything about the Absolute. But still, he respected one thing.

At least he had shown up.

"Is that all you can do? Are these mere efforts enough to warrant the name Absolute?" Joe called out. The Absolute turned back to look angrily at Joe, and then hurled one of his light-spears at the largest vortex open in the sky above the city. This rift had thunderclouds around it, lightning crackling as it traversed across the skyline.

Everyone stood still to watch the Absolute's work—the angels, demons, Collectors, and witches—and watched as all the beams of light converged on one point, becoming a larger beam, and penetrating through the clouds, obliterated the vortex, making it implode upon itself, killing all the hundreds of parasites that were coming out of it, and disappearing from the sky after an ear-splitting explosion.

"Is spectacle your desire, Banbury?" the Absolute growled from the roof across the street. "Because spectacle won't be enough to win this battle."

"But it'll buy us some time." Joe nodded.

"Do you really think the Abstract is short on time?" the Absolute glowered. "Or space, for that matter? It brought the battle to me, and I was all too kind to bring it to those who were responsible."

Joe Banbury stood there listening to those words of betrayal.

"Had you become my champion, we could have taken the Abstract in some far-flung corner of the universe, away from all this. But you were smug, adamant in your pride, stubborn as your father. Let this be a lesson to you." The Absolute possessed none of his mildness as he spoke these words. He sneered at Joe as he ascended into the sky, flying toward one of the smaller rifts.

Joe looked around helplessly, trying to locate Satan.

As it happened, Satan was holding a conversation with Lilly Thurman on a roof five hundred meters away. Joe flew there, and landed between the two of them. He explained, as well as he could given his state of mind, what the Absolute had just said.

"I was there," Lilly said gravely. "When the Abstract attacked Heaven. He was tempting me to become his champion. I refused, same as you. No one wants to be under the favor of that son of a bitch."

"This isn't on you," Satan said. "This is all on him. He could have fought with the Abstract there and then, and perhaps the two would have duked it out for many eternities until one of them got tired or rolled over. But no. This had to happen, Joe. When too many prophets prophesize the same thing, when all the seers and oracles in the world manifest Armageddon, Armageddon must happen. You'd have become his champion, and the battle would have happened here regardless. For it was written."

"That does not mean that the Absolute is not to blame," Joe growled. In the absence of the largest portal, the nonstop onslaught of the parasites had ceased. The sky was a diverse array of flying demons, airborne angels, hovering Collectors, and the Absolute flying from one end to the other, piercing whatever parasites remained. "He cannot come swooping in and act as the world's savior."

Rafael emerged on the roof, eyes still aglow a ghastly gray-white, channeling the Head Amasser. He acknowledged the presence of Joseph, Lilly, and the Devil before speaking his piece.

"The Bone Orchard is not confined by space or time, but heed this, Joseph Banbury. My Collectors have accumulated more parasites in the past hours than they have human souls. This cannot go on."

"Any bright ideas?" the Devil chided Rafael. "Or do you think we don't see that already?"

"Hit the heart, smite out the blight," Rafael said, pointing to the sky, to the remaining vortex.

"I know now what I must do," Joseph whispered.

"What's that?" the Devil asked.

"On my count!" Joe Banbury roared in a loud voice that rang all over New York and was heard by everyone partaking in the battle. "Let loose all arcane cannon fire you have upon the remaining portal!"

He did not wait for anyone to follow him. Joe pushed his wings and bolted into the sky, turning into a billowing ball of flame as he rose toward the remaining vortex.

"Now!" he roared.

All along him, illuminating the night sky, tampering the darkness of the thunderclouds and the abyss that lay ahead, thousands upon thousands of beams of magic, light-beams, fire both infernal and angelic, and the brilliant burning rays of an Absolute sun, all rose with him, on collision course with the final vortex.

Joseph Banbury, burning, raced ahead of the bombardment, sweeping any parasites in his path, and to anyone, anything that watched from the other side, it seemed that Joseph was going to hurtle through the rift, but at the last moment, he held back, and let the artillery hit the portal, collapsing it upon itself.

He watched it all explode, the last of the portals sealing up against a destroyed world, and for a moment thought that his cleverness had worked out, dead parasites all around him falling from the sky, leaving him there all by himself to witness the sight of the smoldering city beneath, angels alongside demons, the Absolute standing there with the Madam and Lilly and Satan.

There was no victorious glee on any of their faces. There was panic and terror upon beholding something fiercer than all of them put together.

He sensed the ruptured vortex stir in the sky behind him, and was too petrified to turn around to see what he had stirred in the chaos dimension that was now stepping through the cracks.

13

AZATHOTH

When it first appeared, all went quiet. Every single thing, living or otherwise, bore witness to the grand spectacle of Azathoth's arrival through the vortex.

As for the vortex, having been freshly bombarded with every kind of magical artillery, it was pulsing like a hurt orifice, a throbbing open wound, bleeding not blood, but waves upon waves of parasites. But as Azathoth appeared, as the Abstract took form, everything became still.

The shadow of its large presence fell upon all of New York City, distinct from the shadow of the night, because while the night cast a dark shade, the silhouette that the Abstract cast was colorless, taking away the essence of things it touched, leaving the colorful ruins of Manhattan drab and lifeless.

As for the Chaos Being itself, it stood in the air, unperturbed by such trivialities as gravity, having no ground beneath its feet. Its presence was five flames, radiating in five directions, burning in jets as if from torches, and all of these flames were of the utmost blackness, dissolving matter where they touched, turning the world around itself gray. The anti-matter to all matter. The black hole to all of existence.

It had no eyes in this true form, nor did it have a mouth. But its form could be distinguished as having limbs, a head, and a body, all of it much larger in size than was imagined by Joseph Banbury. This creature, this anthropomorphization of chaos itself, was both larger than the Head Amasser and yet somehow still perceivable to Joe's senses as one distinct body. Possessing, yet not possessing, space-time. Both there and not there. Both large and small.

Petulant insect, the Abstract spoke, but with no mouth. Its words rang in Joe's head as a chaos-clad arm flung out and grasped his neck, squeezing, its life seeping into him. The black threads of chaos turned him mad, while also suffocating him in its anger.

The Abstract hurled Joseph Banbury down toward the city. Black webbing wove all over his skin, indicating his corruption. His wings curled limply, lifelessly. Joe hurtled like a meteor toward Central Park, where the Hell portal had freshly closed.

Here he fell, crashing headfirst into a stone fountain. His body broken. Unbreathing. Lying there, for all intents and purposes assumed dead by all the forces that stood in defiance of the Abstract.

And of all these forces, the only ones who did not feel immediate fear—for they did not possess the capacity to feel fear—were the Collectors. Their only instinct was to collect. And with that in mind, they sought their prey. Chaos itself.

What a grand end to this tale, thought Rafael, *would it be that they took Chaos, collected it, and then isolated it in the Bone Orchard?*

Rafael von Thorburn, standing on one of the many half-destroyed rooftops of New York City, commanded by the Head Amasser, directed the army of Collectors all gathered around him to lay siege upon the Abstract.

The portal from which the Abstract had emerged had blinked out of existence with a purple blip that shone bright, blinding all temporarily, and now no more of these parasites or any other madness from the Chaos realm poured through. For all that was left to be poured through had already made its way.

On the other side, such calamity and terror the Abstract possessed that everyone who laid eyes on it saw their own worst dread reflected back to them, yet while also beholding its true form. Shapeless flame dissolving everything in its surroundings.

Upon the airborne ranks of its many parasites, the Abstract descended, making its way into Earth's atmosphere, sizing up all of its foes, who were also conveniently gathered in the same place so it could smite them.

Hundreds of Collectors soared, shrouded, hooded, robed, skeletal eyes aflare, claws held out to subdue the Abstract.

The Abstract watched them with merciless apathy as they formed a circle around it, slowly closing in.

And as the Collectors closed in, the thunderclouds that

had gathered around the vortex now hearkened to the call of the Abstract, obscuring it from view, and along with it, the Collectors who disappeared into the furling clouds.

This gave the others an opportunity to gather themselves.

The Devil first located Joseph Banbury, unbreathing, and rushed to him while his armies assembled on top of the remaining roofs, demons, fiends, Hellions, all awaiting their next order, yet apprehensive of the form that had once fractured Hell without even lifting a finger.

"Joseph!" the Devil cried out, flying like a bolt of lightning, crashing to a sudden stop beside his son.

The Devil was joined by Lilly Thurman, who also knelt beside Joseph Banbury, feeling for his heartbeat and finding none.

"He's not breathing," Lilly stammered. "I cannot feel his pulse!"

"Forget his pulse! I cannot feel his life force!" the Devil said frantically, pushing against Joe's chest, his wide eyes observing the way Chaos had left its mark on Joe's body, penetrating every vein, turning them scorching black, ruining Joe's visage and making him look undeniably dead.

Despite the Devil's futile attempts, Joe did not resuscitate.

For he was elsewhere.

Touched by Chaos, he was now in Chaos. Chaos himself. All too aware of what Chaos wished to will upon this world. Stuck in this deathless catatonia, Joe could still witness the fight as it happened, from the Abstract's point of view.

Hundreds of feet in the air, hidden in clouds, the Abstract, center of all dark things, stood suspended and fought off each of the Collectors that had come to contain it.

The moment a Collector even so much as touched Azathoth, it would disperse into a mist of black smoke. Azathoth waved its deadly limbs, undoing the Collectors, making them dissolve into wisps of air under the sky. And those that it did not touch, it stared them into oblivion.

On a rooftop, Rafael stood with waning strength, his eyes flickering as terror found its way for the first time into the Head Amasser's consciousness.

And he was forced to whisper a confession with desperate finality: "The Abstract is uncollectible."

Despite that, Rafael kept sending the ranks of the Collectors to subdue Chaos, only to discover, as the clouds parted, lifeless shrouds of dead Collectors falling from the sky. And those that were not falling were disintegrating as they touched the Abstract.

Their hollowed-out, skeletal bodies crashed all around New York City, shattering into pieces, laying waste to those who once laid waste to entire empires, collecting the souls of emperors and kings. Now their lives ceased to exist.

The Abstract now stood unchallenged, having taken care of all the Collectors that had dared challenge it. What little remained of the Collectors flocked around Rafael, not intent on fighting, but on choosing a course of retreat.

"AZATHOTH!" Satan bellowed, soaring into the sky, his flight a signal to the demons under his command to follow him without question, no matter how afraid they were.

The Devil, since the moment he had existed, had never really felt the need to transform into a form that would truly reflect all of his terror. Not when he fought in the war in Heaven that had resulted in his fall. Not when he became the ruler of Hell. And not when he was banished into nonexistence.

Until now.

Seeing Joseph Banbury in that state had brought out Satan's true fury, one that was every bit deserving of the title of Lucifer Morningstar, because as he ascended, his form transcended anything that anyone had ever imagined the Devil to be.

His wings spanned across an entire borough of the city, his body not ablaze with fire but burning with brilliant light that returned color to everything the desolate shadow of Azathoth had touched. He burned brilliantly, not letting any label hold himself back. Fallen angel he might have been once, but not anymore. His horns pierced up and out of his skull, shining brighter than any halo with all of his channeled might, and his hands grasped the trident fiercely, the weapon growing to abnormal scale in his grasp. The rage of Satan unleashed him as the nightmare that every poet and prophet had ever penned down, and then unleashed him beyond that, into something that rivaled the Abstract.

And sensing it, the Abstract retreated from where it hung in the sky, its black flame being doused by bright fire, the entirety of Hell ascending to subject their eons of perfected torture upon him, only this time, basking in the intense light of their master, they were sure they would not fail.

Legions fell upon the formless existence, avenging their

fallen leader, Joseph Banbury, Hellions biting into abyss itself, cambions plunging their fiery swords into the stark nothingness, fiends ripping into the fabric of chaos, singeing it with their scorch, and at their head stood Satan facing Azathoth.

"You should not have gone after my son," the Devil said, not giving the Abstract even a second to respond. He skewered the illuminated spear across the black fire, perforating it with lightning, fire, and his own unholy red hue. Reason ceased to exist, for reason would have told the Devil that if the Collectors had failed, there was no chance in Hell that he was going to succeed. But Satan was not concerned with such trifles as reason. He wanted to exact his revenge, his rage, upon the endless presence of chaos.

He brought the trident out, pulled it all the way back, and impaled it through the Abstract's body once more, making it bleed muck and black mulch. Wherever this dreadful liquid fell on Earth, it scorched the surface into nothingness, leaving behind holes looking out into the expanse of space. Witches, still on the ground, rushed to remedy this, filling the holes back up with their earth-magic.

The Abstract bore that torture, its body pulled in every direction by fiends, its robustness coming undone as its limbs ripped, as trident blows shredded its body, and all of Hell's legion was upon him, this time without any subduing intent, but with the will to kill.

And they would have killed it, if the Abstract was killable.

But it only reared its head and allowed itself to explode, sending forth waves of undoing black blaze that wiped away every single demon that had sought to kill it, until just the

Devil remained. The Devil, incredulous, realizing that despite all he had done, there was nothing more to be accomplished, and that his fire could've only driven Azathoth away—as it had on the first day of existence—but never completely eliminate it.

Reap the same fate as your son, Azathoth spoke with menace before snatching the Devil's trident and piercing his chest with it. To add insult to injury, Azathoth, ever-present in the night sky, kicked Satan's body to knock it far beyond the initial trajectory.

And then it descended with great surety in Times Square, with the Collectors gone, all of Hell's legions gone, the Devil out of the play. With less and less adversaries left to fight, it was certain that its dominion upon this world was only a matter of another few more finite moments.

Perhaps it spoke in the favor of the infinite hope that was instilled in angels when they were created, a hope that was perhaps borrowed a little too much from Satan, leaving little for himself. That they all, despite seeing what had just happened to the Collectors and to Satan and all of the armies of Hell, attacked the Abstract in Times Square, the ruins of flickering billboards and collapsed brickwork and fallen metal staircases.

Gabriel the archangel, with his sword, struck furiously at Azathoth, who stood impassively at the center of the square, blocking the attacks of every angelic being that struck him from every direction—Uriel from above, Raphael from behind, Michael from the side, and from the front, Gabriel.

Around them, throngs of the lesser angels, still potent yet

nowhere near as powerful as the archangels, dispersed the parasites that had come with the Abstract. Their presence was favorable to the archangels, as these lesser angels, accompanied by the witches atop the rooftops, smote and destroyed parasites, giving Gabriel, Uriel, Raphael, and Michael an opportunity to attack the Abstract, not with the intent to kill it, but to at least get some semblance of revenge for felling their other, Satan.

At this point, with its many limbs working in unison to fend off the attacks, the Abstract was amused and commented, *What pathetic excuse do angels have for existing? All the power in the world, and yet none of the will to use it.*

Gabriel shrieked, rallying a battle cry as he attacked the Abstract. "You shall find that I have plenty of will, Chaos." His sword struck the Abstract's dark shoulder, drawing out blood.

All that will for a few drops of blood, the Abstract taunted, and then pulled on Gabriel's sword, which was still stuck in its shoulder, with Gabriel holding the other end. And as it pulled the sword, Gabriel realized that he could not save himself in time. So he pushed his brothers away and allowed himself to be taken as sacrifice.

The Abstract grabbed the archangel's head and crushed it into a fine mist, throwing away the archangel's dead body. As Gabriel's headless corpse struck the ground, it lost its luminescence, the quality that made him an angel, and he just lay there limply, unknowing.

The other angels, not knowing how to process both the grief of losing their brother and the terror that the Abstract kept menacingly sending forth, did not retreat, but bravely charged forward, only to meet the same diminishing end as their fallen brother. The Abstract dissolved Uriel, stomped upon Rafael's body, and tore Michael into two.

It stood there unchallenged in Times Square, hovering upon angel corpses and broken wings. It looked to its surroundings for the next challenger, wishing they would come forward so that the matter of its adversaries would be concluded all the much faster, leaving the Abstract to power this world, and with it, every living thing that called it home.

Without skipping a beat, as if eager to continue this fight, it set its eyes upon the witches still standing like silent guardians on the roofs.

The Madam came forward, resplendent, graceful, standing on the other side of the corpses of the striven angels, and stood addressing the Abstract.

"Is this not enough, Azathoth? Or will you only relent when there is nothing more left?"

Sister, Chaos said, *my hand has been forced. From my exile, I have merged, and I do not come in hopes of restoring any balance. I am the balance to all life in that I am anti-life. To death, I am undeath. And to everything that even remotely resembles the Absolute, I am in defiance of it, Abstract.*

"Defy this!" the Madam said, and upon her call, all of the assembled witches, including herself, sent forth runic spells, binding spells, in every manner of magic to bind the Abstract into place, even if it would be a momentary victory.

But in response to that, standing there in the ruins of this once-great city, over the corpses of these once-brilliant angels, the Abstract just waved away all of the spells without so much as lifting a finger. And as it waved away the collective might of the Madam and her witches, it left them standing drained, having soaked up their power and consumed it for its own.

The Madam breathed laboriously, descending on all fours, knowing full well that if the Collectors had fallen, and Satan, and the angels, then it was not going to be much longer—not even a few seconds—that she would remain. And so, accepting the inevitability of her death, she readied herself for the final blow that would seize her existence.

The Absolute boomed from above. "Brother."

The Abstract lifted its shade-shrouded, formless head, matching its gaze with that of the Absolute, who was standing on the wreck of the Flatiron Building. Those who had died while the building was collapsing and had tried to escape were still stuck half in, half out the windows, their dead bodies hanging limp, arms out, heads down, covered in dust, drenched in blood.

"I think you have made your point," the Absolute said. "And I think there is no more need for any further bloodshed. If you cease now, I shall relinquish this universe unto you, as well as all the universes that are under my domain. But only if you cease now, and let the fallen and the defeated have their moments to wallow in their sorrow."

You think I came here to barter? the Abstract derided. *And you think I shall stop when my victory is so near, so close at hand? I have waited patiently for eons for this day. But everything that you've built will be laid to waste under my feet. Look upon your order, your empire, your word—and weep, Absolute. For I have laid face to it, as I will lay face to you.*

"Then you shall find your strength evenly matched," the Absolute roared, and descended upon the Abstract.

But the Abstract was not one to take it from lower ground.

It flew like an abysmal bat, colliding with the Absolute midair, their collision sending forth explosive shockwaves, breaking windows, loosening the rubble, crumbling buildings.

Both of them wrestled in eternal conflict, soaring high above New York City into the sky. Light clashing with dark. Order encroaching upon disorder.

Chaos consuming creation.

Creation undoing chaos.

THE BATTLE on the ground that had raged so fiercely had pushed Billy Hawthorne and Blake Weston farther toward Manhattan, as they had fought wave after wave of parasites that were appearing from the woodworks, from the roofs, from the streets. They tried to save as many people as they could, but in the face of terrible odds, they were only able to save themselves, and whatever survivors they came across in the city, they told them to lock the doors, keep themselves inside, and hold fast for dear life.

Now, after hours of fighting the grotesque, macabre creatures that wouldn't quit despite how many bullets you put into them, Billy Hawthorne and Blake Weston had sought refuge in an abandoned building near Times Square. And as the spectacle that was happening in Times Square unfolded, both of these men feared from behind a boarded window, watching the Abstract mercilessly, ruthlessly murder the angels and then drain the power of the witches and the Madam.

"I don't like our odds," Blake said, his ammunition all but gone, only two more rounds in the chamber of his rifle.

"Neither do I," Billy said, staring at his rifle. There was only one more bullet left in it, and there were no more ammunition caches for them to access.

"But so much for being the people's champion, huh?" Blake asked, chuckling. "Really, there's no way we are coming back from this. After everything. Where's Joe? I mean, we all saw the Devil fall. Fuck it. Even the Collectors, they're scrambling."

"Yeah, but," Billy said, "this doesn't have to be as terrible of a loss, if you really think about it."

"What do you mean?" Blake asked.

"Consider this. In another four billion years, the heat death of the universe was bound to happen anyway. If you and I had any children, maybe their ancestors' ancestors would still be alive, you know, billions of years later, and they would have to face the inevitability of the heat death of the universe. And mind you, it would be the heat death of the universe, not just of the Earth. The entire solar system would collapse. Entire star systems would implode. And there would be nothing. Right?"

"I don't know what you're getting at," Blake said.

"I'm just getting at the fact that sooner or later, death for all of us is inevitable, so it literally doesn't matter that we are about to die."

"Well, thanks for the cheery nihilism," Blake said. "But I'm gonna take one last shot before I call it quits."

"How so?"

"Give me your rifle. I wanna try something."

Billy Hawthorne, very fond of the rifle that had saved his life on several occasions tonight, hesitatingly parted with it, giving it to Blake.

He stood. They were on the top floor of the building on the other side of Times Square, easily 300 yards away from where the Abstract and the Absolute were.

"I'm going to do something. And I know there's no cause to believe in deus ex machina or anything, because all the deus that were supposed to be there are literally down here fighting for their own lives. This is, you know, a little token of humanity's collective effort against the colossal fuckery that is the Abstract."

And with that, Blake Weston put the Remington rifle scope to his eye and aimed true. He aimed at the rising black mass that was the Abstract and held his hand steady as he aimed for the heart of Chaos, regardless of if Chaos had a heart or not.

Around him, Billy Hawthorne realized with increasing dread that the parasites they had been outrunning all night had finally caught up with them and were barging on the other side of the bolted door, their formless bodies leaking in from under the door and seeping into the room.

"Whatever you are doing, Blake Weston, do it fast, because we are out of time," Billy Hawthorne said, a mad laugh escaping his deranged sensibilities as he grabbed Blake's rifle, the one that still had two rounds, and shot futilely at the two parasites that had appeared in the room. The bullets struck them, but only served to hinder them, not eliminate them.

The two parasites screeched and clawed their way across the room filled with filing cabinets and bullpen desks littered with corporate paraphernalia that all seemed pointless in the face of this universe's extinction.

Blake Weston breathed out through his nose and watched the trajectory of the Abstract as it flew above the skyline, clashing with the Absolute. And then, with all of his soldierly accuracy, he pulled the trigger.

The bullet, an ordinary bullet, not silver, not infused with any alchemical substance, but carrying within it the resolve of all of humanity, soared through the air, and as it soared, it adjusted its course, guiding itself toward the Abstract.

And while the Abstract was still clashing in battle with the Absolute, light and dark sparks rising from their friction, the bullet struck it in the torso.

It did nothing to stop the Abstract.

But, surprised that something as minute and as vain as a human would choose to strike it in the face of its unending power, the Abstract paused and turned, scoping the horizon, locating the point from where the bullet had come.

Blake Weston, still looking through the scope, grinned and said, "Made you look, motherfucker."

He was all ready to accept his death, seeing as how the parasites had flooded the room and now there were more than just two. But Billy Hawthorne, inspired by Blake's action, had now seeded all thoughts of going quietly into the night. He grabbed Blake by the scruff of his neck and plummeted out the window. Both men flung out of the building and landed upon the roof of a car, crashing it, shattering its windshield and laying there, tired, bruised, broken, their breath shallow, and their eyes beholding the sight of the sprawling parasites oozing out of the shattered window from where they had jumped.

But that bullet, as pointless as it had seemed, had done something the Abstract had not expected. For just one second, and nothing more, it had broken the Abstract's resolute focus, releasing from its grip the psyche and consciousness of Joseph Banbury.

In Central Park, drenched in the water of the fountain, Joseph Banbury woke with a start, whispering something that he had learned from the depths of Chaos itself. He saw Lilly hunched over him, her eyes swollen red, her cheeks puffed, and he could not bring himself to say anything consoling to her other than, "*So long as even one cinder is lit of Hell, Hell cannot be quelled.*"

"What?" Lilly gasped in disbelief upon seeing Joe come back to life miraculously.

"Where's Satan?" Joe panted, his body in deep pain as it fought off Chaos's claim upon it.

"The Devil fell," Lilly stuttered, still incredulous, but getting over herself quickly by wiping her eyes. "He fell right after you."

"Nope, that can't be right. I'm still alive, and I don't know where he is, but he cannot die while I still live."

And so it was that the inane bullet, which had momentarily broken the Abstract's focus, brought back Joe Banbury from the clutches of Chaos.

He stood in the coarse remains of Central Park, his arm around Lilly's shoulder for support, comprehending the incomprehensible, that all the forces they had brought to war had failed thus far.

In another sunken part of the city, where his fall had plummeted him through the road and had landed him in the sewers, Satan's body stirred.

"Joe," he whispered, realizing that the only reason he was alive was because so, too, was Joe. It took him some time to gather himself. Fighting the Abstract and then living to tell the tale was not an easy feat, as he was sure the world around him was learning. He watched from underneath broken sewer pipes and broken chunks of asphalt as the Abstract and the Absolute thrashed each other in the sky.

It sank his heart to see that another vortex was piercing open in the sky, and he wondered what further nightmares Azathoth had in store for this fight.

The Devil slowly crawled out of the hole, witnessing his dead demons laying by his side, their wings burnt to a crisp, their red skins turned black and dead. He punched the ground in despair, and set out, with his weakened form, to search for his son.

"I WAS...TRAPPED," Joe panted, looking to the sky. "When it attacked me, it trapped me within itself. I saw...things...Lilly. I thought I was going mad, but every deranged thought was a perfect premise in the vast consciousness of Chaos."

"What did you see?" Lilly asked.

"I..." He paused. He wasn't sure if he was going to tell her this. "I saw Chaos's intent. It does not wish to stop. Not now. Not ever. So long as it exists, it does not matter if it's days or centuries, it's going to keep coming back. There is no end to Azathoth."

Above them, the Absolute was holding his own against the rapid flurry of blows the Abstract hurled at it. Wherever the Abstract's blows landed, the Absolute ceased to be, but then he would recreate himself, and inflict a similar fate upon the Abstract, trying to create something out of the nothingness, only for nothingness to consume said creation.

Their battle had taken them high up into the sky, well into the stratosphere, away from the city and all those who were in it. As of this moment, they appeared only as clashing bolts and flashes of thunder.

But the dark rift that opened in their background was large enough for all to see.

Joe looked helplessly around the destroyed city. Fire hydrants gushed out water. EVAC and paramedics still operating despite the circumstances, running around with bandages, stitches, the millions of New Yorkers witness to this great cataclysm from behind the windows of their wrecked buildings, from within their cars, from the rubble underneath which they were buried, and in the park, where they had run for safety, away from all the falling debris.

"Come on. We can't stay here," Lilly said, tugging at Joe's arm. "The Collectors have failed. The angels have fallen. The witches have retreated in defeat. Only the Absolute remains, fighting the Abstract. There is nothing more that we can do. Joe, we tried. We did everything we could."

"Not everything," Joe said, nodding at a figure that had appeared in the park's entrance. Satan, disfigured, drowned in his own diminished wingspan, walking slowly toward Joe Banbury.

"So long as one cinder is lit…" Joe muttered. "Well, I count two cinders."

14

ASHFALL

Given all he knew now, Joe was certain that Azathoth never meant for its psyche to connect with Joe's the way it had, giving Joe a deep understanding of everything going on in the mind of Chaos itself. However, despite his intelligence and his grasp of concepts far bigger than himself, peeking behind the Abstract's mind was something that had left Joe feeling fractured-minded.

He felt as if he had gone insane after witnessing too many horrors, too many atrocities, all at once. And that was only half of it. The other half being Chaos's intent, its destructive will as it wanted to instill upon the universe. Joe thought that he knew hatred, being in such close vicinity to the Devil these past years, but what pulsed in Chaos was something for which there existed no word. Malice would come close, but it would still diminish the scale of loathing that the Abstract possessed for the ordered world, for the other Cornerstones, for the Absolute.

Within that formless malevolence, Joseph Banbury had beheld all of the history of existence, not from the perspective of creation, but from the point of view of Chaos itself. How there was nothing but endless havoc everywhere, and in its many permutations it existed without form, satisfied, senseless, possessing no will to conquer anything, for there was nothing to conquer.

All there existed was the will of the Abstract swirling from one part of uncreation to another, outside of the bounds of space, outside of the limitations of time. These trifles had yet to come into existence.

But then something happened that the Abstract and all of the principalities of chaos that it dictated did not expect. Out of the billions and billions of probabilities and permutations of ceaseless disorder, order arose as a consequence. At first, it was so miniscule in its existence that the Abstract altogether ignored it, thinking that it would dissolve in the rest of the sea of unbridled anarchy. How this order had come into existence, the Abstract did not know.

In its long dreaming slumber, several things had come into creation. Strange, parasitic beings that clung to its formless form, devouring its dark as their nourishment, growing strong, multiplying. It did not bother the Abstract that these parasites existed, for it saw them only as its own extension. What bothered it was the speck of light in the dark, a glow that existed far beyond the bounds of the Abstract's domain.

Who are you? were the first words spoken in the known

universe, and not, *Let there be light.* It was the Abstract interrogating this remote speck, which, even though it was small, blinded the Abstract with its light.

I am all you are not, The Absolute spoke in response, freshly birthed, a consequence of chaos, an anomaly that should not have existed under any circumstances but somehow, because of the strangest chance, the nth+1 infinite combination of chaos creating matter out of un-matter, thought out of thoughtlessness, form out of smoke.

And so it was that the Absolute willed itself into existence through the vey laws of Chaos itself, undefinable laws which eons later would be recognized as quantum physics, chaos theory, stating t hat within the apparent randomness of chaotic complex systems such as the Abstract itself, there are underlying patterns, interconnection, constant feedback loops, repetition, self-similarity, fractals, and self-organization, all of which resulted in the existence of the Absolute, a nondeterministic counteracting agent to Chaos, an antidote born out of the very poison it rendered useless.

I am everything, the Abstract tried to reason with this immovable, incandescent speck.

Not anymore, The Absolute said.

And thus started an antagonistic effort against each other that marked the first moment in time, the first opacity of space, the Absolute creating from unto itself, resisting the will of Chaos. When threatened, the Absolute clashed with the Abstract, their friction giving birth to sentient fire that singed Chaos and made it retreat. That sentient fire, dubbed Light Bringer, was quickly capitalized by the Absolute, who appeared to it as an ally, giving it grand titles such as Lucifer, such as the Most Beautiful.

And upon the retreat of this looming black cloud that had covered the entire blank canvas that was someday to be the multiverse, more order sprung forth from the vacuum, giving shape to Craft, ushering the Collectors into existence, and prompting the Absolute to keep on creating while he still had momentum.

Everything that happened afterward, the creation of God, the creation of the universe, the demarcation of boundaries between the prime universe and its imitative universes, springing forth the multiverse into existence, was a long, painful unfolding that the Abstract watched from the far flung corners of inexistence, where it still held domain, where its endless parasites writhed in agony, as the nourishment that they were getting from their maker was bitter with resentment, hatred, and a sense of loss of control.

Locked out of a large chunk of its domain that was now steeped in order, where atoms formed molecules that formed distinct structures of minerals, gems, ores, metals, nonmetals, where the collection of these chemicals turned into masses of celestial bodies bursting forth from the initial explosion, the one that scientists would one day dub the Big Bang, the Abstract sought revenge.

But above all, it sought to reclaim its territories.

However, there was the inconvenience of finding a flaw in the system, a system that was ordained by the Absolute, held accountable by the Collectors, and imbued with power by the Madam.

And so the Abstract waited, not patiently because patience was not a virtue that Chaos possessed, but with increasing desperation as the universes expanded, further diminishing the reaches of chaos.

And after time immemorial, the Abstract, dissolved into its desperation, forgot that once it had an ambition to reconquer what was once its unshared domain.

Until the balance—the great counteracting force that served as a repellant to chaos—was broken, and news made its way to Azathoth that within the prime universe, God had fallen, and the sentient flame that was Satan was banished.

Here, after epochs, it had finally found the chink in the armor of the fabric of existence. And here, the Abstract attacked, first sending forth its parasites to subdue this universe, and then finally, when its time was nigh, Azathoth itself entered the fray.

What it did not expect was the resilience of those who stood up against it.

It had tried to eliminate the main player on the board by trapping him within chaos, but somehow, in a moment when the Abstract's defenses were down for the briefest of seconds, Joseph Banbury had escaped the clutches of the Abstract, his mind filled with secrets that, up until now, only the Abstract knew.

Such as the secret that the Sentient Fire could never be quelled; so long as even one cinder of Hell is lit, Hell cannot be quelled.

SEEING Joe come back to life had greatly charged Lilly Thurman with power. Now no longer hunched defensively over Joe, she was on her feet, sending forth bolt after bolt of incinerating spells toward the last wave of parasites that had ambushed Central Park.

The surviving witches joined her blaze, and sent forth their own spells from the rooftops, giving the survivors in and around the park a fighting chance. Two of those survivors were Blake Weston and Billy Hawthorne, who, against all odds, had survived their fall from the building, and had staved off the attacks of the parasites thanks to the witches who had swooped in at the last moment.

Bruised, their clothes ripped, blood trickling from the cuts and slashes on their skin, the two men ran into the park. At any other time, it would have been impossible for them to spot Lilly and Joe from the other end, but this battle had seared away the trees and the bushes that populated the park, leaving it a flatland, charred with a giant pentagram, all of it visible other than for the little crests and troughs that were the natural elevation.

Blake Weston, bloody-faced, broken-bodied, was relying on Billy Hawthorne to see him through to the middle. When they had both thought that this was it, that the swarm of parasites would consume them whole, Lilly had let loose her magic, giving them the momentum they needed to finish the sprint.

"He's badly hurt, Lill," Billy said, laying down Blake Weston by the broken fountain. Joseph Banbury looked at Blake with great rue on his face. And then, he approached Satan, who was having quite a difficult time walking up to Joe.

Lilly paused her spell slinging for just enough time to cast a healing spell on both Billy and Blake, then went back to eradicating the parasites. Their numbers dwindled gradually, and when she was sure that the witches on the periphery of the park could hold their own, Lilly stopped for a breather. The celestial dogfight didn't seem like it would stop any given moment, and the vortex appearing in the horizon only grew in size.

"It's going to swallow earth whole," Joseph Banbury said once he was close enough to the Devil. "No more parasites. The minute that vortex is big enough, Azathoth is going to—"

The Devil did not care about what Joe was saying. Weakened, he fell upon Joe, giving him a frail hug, whispering, "I thought you had died."

Joe was still experiencing alarming jolts from the chaotic reverie that had been coursing his system. His eyes were wide in incomprehensible shock, his mouth hanging open as he gasped. "You couldn't die if I was alive. The Abstract knows this. It knows that you're the sentient flame at the beginning of time."

"Come now, Joe. Enough of this genealogical nonsense," the Devil sighed. "This is where we cut our losses and exit stage while there is still a stage. The offer extends to all of you," he said, looking beyond Joseph, to where Lilly, Blake, and Billy were. Rafael von Thorburn had also found his way into the park, and was standing there without the influence of the Head Amasser upon him. His eyes had gone back to normal, although his body was haggard, tired, and hunched over.

A circle comprising witches and Collectors had formed

around these survivors, ready to fend off any further attack. Beyond the circle, survivors of the battle were setting up emergency stations for rations, medicine, and first-aid.

"I do not promise that you shall all have an excellent time in Hell, for that is not what Hell is," the Devil said, his sunken face reflecting his real age now, a withered old man, graying at the wings just as he was graying at the hair. "But if it means that you will survive another day, is Hell so bad?"

"No." Lilly shook her head.

"Your Madam has already ditched and absconded to the Axis Mundi, leaving you in charge, witch," Satan said with none of his usual malevolence, but only in a matter-of-fact tone that conveyed the acceptance of his own defeat. "As for the Head Amasser, he was never here. And what does it matter? Our entire hope of the Collectors playing a pivotal role did not pan out. Come. Let us mourn our losses in Hell, where there is still some semblance of order."

"Joe?" Lilly whispered. But Joe did not turn back.

"You once likened me to the Horsemen of Apocalypse," Joe said, staring into the sky. "What if the Horsemen were not supposed to bring the apocalypse, but end it?"

"What are you saying?" Satan, more tired than ever, sunk by the fountain and sat on its steps, his suit covered in ash and dust.

"I was in its head," Joe continued with his deranged monologue. "It knows that it is not invulnerable. That is why it's fighting us all at the same time. It fears you, what you can do. What we are capable of."

"I guess you were passed out when the Abstract thrashed

me to within an inch of my life." Satan grimaced. "There is *nothing* I can do, Joseph, that can turn back the tide this late in the game."

Joe shook his head. "It's not something you have to do."

Lilly yanked Joe by the shoulder, making him face her. He had blood dripping down his face, leaking from his eyes and ears. The toll of trying to contain insanity.

"Joe. You're not making any sense," Lilly whimpered.

"In the beginning, the Abstract and the Absolute were evenly matched, an unstoppable force pushing against an immovable object," Joe whispered hauntedly. "Until he came. The sentient flame. He said it himself. It was Satan that drove Chaos beyond the universe's bounds.

"Then call me a one-trick pony, son," the Devil said. "Because I do not think that it can be done again. I fought it. It defeated me. I fought it again. It nearly killed me. I will extend this offer one last time. All of you, cut your losses and flee with me."

"I never knew you to be such a defeatist," Joseph snapped. "I always thought that you were unstoppable."

"Alas, dear boy, this is where I have to give up. If only so that I can regroup, come up with another plan of attack, and then, maybe, just maybe, in another thousand years, when Azathoth's fury has simmered down, I can attack once more," Satan said, some hope still in his despairing tone.

"And what of these people? What of this planet? Why must they be subject to the consequence of my actions? Your actions?!" Joe yelled.

"What the fuck is going on here?" Billy Hawthorne called

out. Blake Weston held his side and sat up, grunting. "The world is ending, in case the two of you didn't notice. Now is not the time for a father-son squabble."

Above them, the vortex had opened so wide that it stretched all over Manhattan. What was on the other side of the vortex was obscured by a layer of sheer blackness, or maybe it was just sheer blackness on the other side of it, and if that blackness had a name, it was chaos.

"You fool. He's not fighting me," Satan said with great sorrow steeped in every word he uttered. "The rest of you don't understand what he's talking about, and I'm not letting him do it."

"Joe," Lilly cried, tears rolling down her cheeks as understanding dawned upon her, understanding that she wanted snatched away for blissful oblivion. "What is he talking about?"

Something lessened in Joe's seething intensity, the blood ceasing its trickle from his eyes, ears, and lips. He wiped it away as well as he could, not wanting this to be the way Lilly would remember him for the rest of her life. He walked closer to her, knowing that there was nothing he could do about her tears other than wipe them off her face with his thumb.

"I have loved you since the day I first met you," Joe whispered, his face close to hers, the enormity and finality of what he was about to do making terror course through his being. The only thing that stopped his palpatory fear was holding Lilly in his arms, his hands on her cheeks as he brought her face close and kissed her wet lips.

Lightning crackled in the sky above, storm clouds assembling in confusion, not knowing how to deal with the torrential winds and the vacuous pull of the vortex that was now so near New York City that it was beginning to pull the very air in the city in, yanking air conditioner units and fire escapes from buildings, sucking them in, its roar building as it grew bigger.

Joe did not care. He kissed her again, all of his passion distilled into this last kiss, tasting the succor of her pout, then parting her mouth open so he could feel all of her on all of him. She kissed him back, not out of denial but in grim acceptance, her hand on the back of his head, her arm around his waist.

When they pulled back, Joe, whose face was wet, and not just because of the pouring rain, said, "I regret the fact that you and I couldn't have more time. A god and an immortal witch, short on time. I guess the universe runs on irony batteries, huh?"

She laughed as she cried, her forehead against his forehead, raindrops pouring on top of them as the world unraveled around them.

"I love you too," Lilly cried into his face. "I have always loved you. Even when I thought I hated you, I couldn't stop myself from caring for you. And now, too little, too late, I'm realizing I never hated you. Just hated your absence."

"What are you doing?!" Billy Hawthorne yelled at the top of his lungs. "Why am I the last one to be in on anything?" he shouted, nudging Blake's injured shoulder, but Blake only looked away. However his relationship with Joseph Banbury was, he did not want this fate for him.

"I guess I'm giving you something to remember me by," Joe

said, kissing her quickly on the cheek one last time before plucking out a little glass bottle from the pocket of his tattered jeans. It had an unbreakable spell upon it, some of Joe's own handiwork, and inside it was a flash drive. "I never did stop writing, you know. Not even when I was...up there. I think there's plenty in there for you to read, but it's just for your eyes only."

He handed it to her, and closed her hand around it. "I know it's pretty fucking stupid, but if you ever need a message in a bottle..."

Lilly laughed despite herself, and then hugged Joe close.

When he'd parted from her, he put his hand on Blake's shoulder and gave it a squeeze. "Hang in there, traveling soldier."

Blake patted Joe's hand, looking up to him with pursed lips, cheeks pulled morosely.

Billy Hawthorne gave Joe a bear hug. "I can't bear the thought of losing you again, you motherfucker. Was it not enough that you ditched me at Stonehenge that you gotta pull this shit on me again?!"

"I'm sorry, brother," Joe said, holding Billy close.

Rafael stood a little afar. He reached out with his hand and said, "I have had the misfortune of losing one too many friends in my long life. This is one of those moments, and there is nothing I can do about it."

"You did everything you could," Joe said, shaking Rafael's hand.

This left only Satan, who had been soaked in the rain, all the dirt and ash washed off his body. He stood there battered, head lowered, unable to look Joe in the eyes. He said, "I raised you to be many things, but I never raised you as a pig for the slaughter, Joseph."

"I never said you did," Joe replied. "This is *my* free will that I am choosing to exercise."

"Why? What do you gain from it?" Satan asked, lifting up his face, curiosity mixed with grief marked in every fold, every wrinkle.

"I do it because it's the right thing to do. I do it so that people don't have to pay for my mistakes. So that the universe can live on," Joe said.

"Do you even know if you can do it?" Satan asked. "This'd be the first time something like this happens."

"You know what they say, first time for everything," Joe said, breathing deep, readying himself for his flight. He deeply wished to meet Amy and his father one last time. If he were to stand here and gather regrets, there were one too many for him to count, but not seeing his sister one last time was at the top of that list.

"Goodbye, all," Joe said, lifting off the ground, traveling against the pouring rain, witnessing the grand majesty of this beautiful, cultural capital of the world one more time. Even in ruins, it retained all its grandeur, the many fires that had erupted all over Manhattan now being doused by the rain.

He wanted to linger, just for a little longer, in the hopes that this was all a nightmare that he would wake up from, and find himself a little boy in his bedroom in Red Bank's quintessentially American suburbia, but when no such waking impulse presented itself to him, Joe ascended higher into the sky, leaving everything behind, the people he loved, the places he had called home, the Devil he knew as father.

Joe looked up to where he was headed, and discovered that he was not flying as much anymore as he was being pulled in by the ever-growing portal, the gaping maw of the Chaos Realm.

And in front of it, still clashing in their brilliant blaze and bursts of dark energy, the Absolute and the Abstract engaged in combat. The closer Joe got to them in the stratosphere, the more he realized that these two were probably enjoying themselves, both equally powerful beings finally having something to do instead of just scheming from distant corners of the universe.

"Look who joins us," the Absolute boomed from above, watching Joe rise. "What conceited idea rattles in your head now? What is it that you can do in the face of such destruction?"

He wishes to vanquish us, brother, Azathoth commented, still not breaking away from the fight, its many limbs fending off the Absolute's attacks, landing blows on its body, both forms spinning around like yin and yang. *Or perhaps he has come to simply request us to leave his premises.*

"Leave, Joe," the Absolute commanded. "Everything that you tried to do failed tonight. It's too late to ask to be my champion. If it is eternity that it takes me to fight with the Abstract, eternity is what I will give this fight."

How poetic, how sublime, the Abstract resounded.

Joe did not respond to either of them, did not even deflect the light rays as they pierced his wings, or the void tendrils as they slashed from the Abstract's body. He let himself feel each sting of pain, reminding him that in this colossal match between deities, he was just a human, but perhaps that was not a flaw as much as it was a redeeming feature.

He rose until he was level with them, which gave both of these beings considerable pause.

"Leave, Joe! What do you think you're doing?!" the Absolute growled, confirming Joe's belief that they were two sides of the same coin, that the Absolute was just as terrible as the other.

He hazarded one last glance below, and could see, even from up close, the kindled light of Hell lit up like a beacon in his father standing below, witness to the grand scene above.

And then, once finality had dawned upon Joseph Banbury, and the vortex was right upon him, he thrust himself forward, coming between the Absolute and the Abstract, holding onto them both, feeling one burn away his very skin, and the other dissolve him into nothingness.

"Stop this foolishness!" the Absolute commanded, now no longer fighting the Abstract but trying to get Joe off him. Joe dug his scorched nails into the Absolute's skin, and wound his arm around the Abstract, plummeting toward the vortex.

It had always made him curious as to what was on the other side of this portal. It would be the last thing in his existence that he would find out, and maybe that was not such a bad thing—to end his life on a studious, inquisitive note.

The two ends of the spectrum that were tethered to his rapidly depleting body pulled away so that they wouldn't be whisked through the portal, but Joe held on with every last ounce of force he had, knowing that if he didn't succeed now, then all would've been for naught.

And then, carrying both of them with him, he plunged through the vortex, coming out on the other side in the dense, suffocating nothingness of inexistence. Here, where there were no stars, nor sounds, nor any meaning to the concepts of time, space, and bounds, he could finally let go, thinking to himself, *If the first spark of the sentient flame, borne from the friction of these two, brought forth a fission that created the universe, then my act shall, at least theoretically, bring forth much needed fusion.*

Hell was within him, unrulable, burning eternal, never to be quelled so long as there was one cinder yet lit, and he had left that cinder standing in Central Park in another reality far, far away.

Joseph Banbury let his scorch consume him, still not letting go of the Absolute or Azathoth. In his final moments, he could see just how terrified both these beings were, their forms fusing together in the sweltering temperature that Joseph Banbury had conjured one last time.

When the heat crossed its threshold, when Joseph could no longer contain it within his disintegrating body, he closed his eyes and imagined himself standing on Red Bank's beach, a young child with eyes filled with wonder, a head full of ghosts, and the rest of his life laid out before him, just like the city across the water with its tall towers and its shapely spires.

And with that last thought—a comforting thought—Joseph Banbury ceased to exist in the eruption that turned him into a sentient blaze himself, that blaze consuming the Absolute, eviscerating the Abstract, and, with its heat and shockwaves, dissolving away chaos wherever it hid in this dark dimension, shattering the vortex, causing it to implode upon itself with great finality, leaving nothing behind of the Absolute, the Abstract, or Joseph Banbury.

Only Absence.

Amy Banbury had watched the witch stationed outside her house fearlessly, tirelessly battle away hordes of parasites, assisted, of course, by those that had joined the fray with her. Her father, drowned in his sense of loss, drunk on beers, was asleep on the sofa, and slept through the entire thing no matter how many times the house shook or the roof quaked.

She kept checking in on him every now and then to ensure that he was breathing.

The vivid clashing display in the sky was visible to all who were witness to it in Red Bank from behind the windows of their homes, from the roofs of their houses, the vortex growing in size, looking like it would absorb the entire planet at any given moment.

Amy braced herself, still watching from the window, when she saw a streak of brilliant light soar up into the sky, pull away the two antagonistic forces with itself, and hurtle through the portal. It was hard to miss that sight, being in such close vicinity to it, and because it was the only visible thing in the entire night sky.

She could not fathom what had happened, wouldn't fully know of it until the next morning, when the survivors of the

Morningstar Tribe would make their way to the Banbury residence.

But the moment the vortex shuddered implosively and shrunk within itself, leaving behind nothing but one last deafening shockwave that traveled all over the sky, making every remaining parasite still standing drop dead, Amy Banbury felt loss.

Deep, plunging loss within her body, making her heart squelch. Her hands began shaking violently as she burst into tears, not realizing why she was experiencing such a torrent of emotions.

"Ames?" she heard from behind her, and for a second she thought it was Joe calling her name out. But it was her father, stirring from his sleep. "Why are you crying, my dear?"

"Dad..." Amy wept, falling into her father's arms. "I don't know...I don't know...something...terrible has happened...and I don't know what it is."

Tommy Banbury held his daughter in his arms, gently running his hand in her hair, letting her quiet down before finally saying, "I don't know what's happening outside, but I just had the most amazing dream. I saw your mom. And I didn't see her like she was a week before. She was young, Amy. She was like I'd met her the first time, her hair short, just past her neck, and she was wearing one of those polka dot dresses that were all the rage back then. I wanted to join her. She felt so real. Like I could just reach out and touch her. I wonder if this is the fate of all widowers across the world. That they spend the rest of their lives dreaming of their dead wives."

Amy wept harder, and was inconsolable no matter what Tommy Banbury did.

There was a knock on his door.

Strange. At this hour? he wondered as he opened the door. A young girl in a black dress stood there, looking tired, covered in dirt and blood.

"Halloween's not for another two months, kid," Tommy Banbury said.

"I just wanted to check in on my friend." The witch nodded toward Amy on the sofa.

"You're a friend of my daughter?" Tommy Banbury asked, stepping aside.

"We all are," the woman said, stepping forward, revealing that she was not alone. But only she walked in the house, and gave Amy the comfort that she needed. One last spell for the night, a calming cantrip that would put her to sleep, or at least make the horrific bludgeoning realization not hit as hard when she'd discover in the morning that the painful sense of loss she'd felt at night had been her brother's death.

Tommy Banbury stood in the doorway, staring at the sky, now clear of all clouds and thunder and strange phenomenon other than the ash which kept falling from the clear night sky, almost as if somewhere close by, a volcano had erupted. If he squinted his eyes, he could imagine it snowing in August.

EPILOGUE

Three Months Later

Lilly Thurman sat in the study of her Bridgewater home, having just finished doing a favor for a friend, even if that favor came at a terrible cost. She closed the book down, having read through the whole damn thing cover to cover in a single sitting. When you lived as long as an immortal witch, you picked up a thing or two along the way, such as the astute reading speed of a jaded literary agent who had once been the force majeure behind a literary agency nestled in New York called The Avernus Collective.

It had taken her several hours to get through the book, but Billy Hawthorne, as impulsive and brash as he was, had tried to be very patient with her up until the very final moment when he called her late last night and said, "If you're not even going to read it, why did I bother sending you the ARC?" She'd then placated him by telling him that she had a lot on her plate, and that he should rest assured that she would get around to reading it as soon as possible.

November was a joy in Bridgewater, because the town hadn't truly accepted winter's arrival, and fall's tail end was still there, its foliage shining deep yellow, crisp orange, and bright red as far as she could see, and she could see *all* of Bridgewater from her study's window. It gave a panoramic view of the town below and the lake on the left.

She had finally gotten around to removing that unnatural fog from the surface of the lake, and had rid the waters of any lurking magic that remained. There hadn't been any more souls to usher into limbo in quite some time. She remembered Maggie, the meek whom she had saved a long time ago, and the other sinister ones, who were beyond all saving. Lilly smiled with a sad weight, looking at the book's back cover that now lay in front of her.

Billy Hawthorne had aged quite abruptly, as was evident in the back cover image of the book. But he leaned into his whiting hair, his lined face, and had even grown a small beard to commemorate his coming of middle-age.

As for the book itself...

Lilly looked around her study, trying to ground herself in sensations, sight, and sounds so that she could do away with the panic attack that the book had brought on. Little glass jars filled with water, carrying within them money plants, snake plants, and ferns, lay upon a shelf above the door. Decoration, sure, but also a protective remedy. The plants repelled bad energy and invited positive vibes as well as plenty of oxygen. Lilly Thurman, still recovering from the events of Armageddon, needed all the oxygen she could get.

She turned the book over, frowning at its title. If she were his literary agent, or if Sean Gainey was alive, the title would never have been so terrible.

Apocalypse: A Story of Sacrifice.

She cringed internally, looking at the title. On it, old apocryphal, biblical black and white pictures stitched together depicting the Horsemen, Hell, and the Old Testament's bearded version of God formed a collage that could be dismissed as derivatively collegiate.

And in it, just as with his previous book, Hawthorne had spared no detail, talking of the Devil, writing about the Collectors, the vampyre Rafael, and how Joseph Banbury's selfless act of self-immolation with the Abstract and Absolute in tow was the defining moment that saved the universe and prevented apocalypse, or rather, brought an end to Armageddon itself.

She could never remember all the other details by herself, and in that regard, the book was a curse as much as it was a factual account of everything that had happened. She had not wanted to remember.

Because remembering hurt.

Because remembering meant still feeling the ghost of Joe's kiss on her lips as she watched him soar across the sky, drag the two cosmic beings with him, and blip out of existence. The whole world had witnessed that. But she, she had felt it deep within her bones.

Just as Amy had, the next morning, when Lilly had gone to tell her that her brother had fallen. They had wept in each other's arms, trying to reason with their sense of loss, but no reconciliation came. Only more confusion.

The book talked in great length of what happened the days after the battle that had shattered New York. But Lilly only remembered that she had descended into the depths of denial, and from what she learned later on, she was not alone.

Satan was nowhere to be found. She had not heard from him nor spotted his signs anywhere on the planet. The Parks and Recreation Department of New York City had taken great pains to uproot all the dirt and grass where the behemoth pentagram was etched, and had tried their best to recreate the park, restoring it to its old glory in as little time as they could with a hamstring budget.

The rest of the budget, naturally, went toward restoring the city, dealing with the bodies of the people who had died, and disposing the corpses of the parasites that were festering with swarms of flies hovering around them. It was a joint effort, one in which the local government was aided by the volunteers and witches alike. It was not as if their existence was a secret any longer.

There was still the point of dealing with the world population's memory, a point that would be discussed in today's meeting, the first meeting of its kind after Armageddon, with the others present. She had been summoned, and any time now she expected a portal to the Axis Mundi to open, and the Madam to come beckoning.

Lilly Thurman put the book in her crammed shelf, then

sent a text message to Billy, saying, *Read your book. The only person I can think of who could have done a better job at writing this is the main character of your story. 4/5 stars.*

Billy replied the very next second, saying, *Thinking of Joe. Thinking of you.*

How's Blake? she sent. Billy was the only one who had kept in touch with Blake afterward. From what Billy had said, Blake had stayed with him in his broken Brooklyn apartment for a little while before heading out.

Haven't gotten in touch with him. He didn't even respond when I asked him for the book review.

Hope he's well.

Hope so too.

With the obligatory texts out of the way, Lilly reclined in her leather seat, closing her eyes for a moment. It was a terrible gamble, being still and doing nothing, for if she did nothing and allowed herself to sit with her thoughts, the trauma from her past thrashed against the jagged cliffs of her mind, making her relive every horror, every torture, every loss that she had ever experienced all in one concentrated moment where she wished for the sweet release of death.

Lilly breathed deeply. She was still here, and for better or worse, so was the world.

Some minutes later, there was a knock at her door.

"Come in, Chloe," Lilly called out. The young girl who had stood resolutely in front of the Banbury residence, defending it from parasite attacks, stepped in, wearing a green blouse and faded jeans. She carried a cup of tea in her hands.

"Your tea, Ms. Thurman," Chloe said, putting it down on the table.

"You don't have to make me tea, Chloe," Lilly said, opening her eyes.

It had been a month since Chloe and the other younger witches had flocked to Lilly, seeking leadership, guidance, instructions, whatever they could get. Lilly was still pretty shell-shocked at that time, but seeing all these young witches who had risen to the call of the Madam on the night of Armageddon filled her up with something that had been lacking in the month following apocalypse.

Purpose. She could teach them what she knew, pass on her legacy in more meaningful ways than just overseeing a small town in New England. And it felt good to be in the presence of others like her for a change.

"I like making you tea," Chloe said, smiling, her hands folded nervously in front of her. "In a non-capitalistic cohabitation space, one must circumnavigate the payment of rent by doing favorable chores for the proprietor of the house."

Lilly rolled her eyes. "Oh no. Is this what they've been teaching you at college?"

"No, but it's a personal interest of mine," Chloe said, blushing red.

"Well, you don't have to do anything for me. Your staying here is just fine. It's company, at the very least. And it gives me something to do."

"Speaking of, I mastered the spell you taught us last night."

"I don't think anyone can master levitation in a single day," Lilly said, drinking tea, wishing it was anything but tea. She had actively decided to stay away from alcohol until she was in a better headspace. Liquor, in her experience, should only be imbibed when there weren't demons lurking in the dark corners of your consciousness. Otherwise it was only fuel for their fire. For now, she doused them with tea.

"Well, me and the others were wondering what...comes next."

"The next spell."

"And then?"

"The next spell after that. There are more spells and magic to learn than one lifetime can allow," Lilly said, feeling authoritativeness course through her as she spoke the words. She'd always wanted to have a coven of her own, or at the very least, witches to teach and practice with. In the absence of Mallory, and the bare minimum communication from the Madam, this was a good role for her, she decided. Even if it was an interim role.

"I guess I'm just being impatient," Chloe said, her eagerness brimming from her eyes. She was barely able to hold herself in one place.

"I kind of envy your youthful enthusiasm," Lilly said, cheering her on with her cup of tea. "But you must pace yourself, dear one. There is such a thing as practicing too much magic. We only have a limited supply of mana in our bodies, and that mana requires replenishing every now and then before you go out and do more spells. Is that clear?"

A little disappointment showed up in the girl's eyes. This was Lilly Thurman after all, the witch who had held the world together when everything was coming undone. But, she nodded, keeping her thoughts to herself, saying, "Yes."

"Good. You are dismissed."

"See you soon, Ms. Thurman."

"Call me Lilly," she said, but a little late, as the door had already closed, leaving her alone. Ms. Thurman sounded like the name of a very angry, old librarian.

She finished her tea, and then, when she was certain that there was no more putting off the inevitable, she stood up, admiring her reflection in the tall mirror in the corner of her study. A white dress with a beige shirt. She looked elegant, another idea that did not altogether sit well with her. Now that so many people knew who she was, she had to come up with an air of elegance. There was a time when she'd just put on a t-shirt without even a bra underneath, and a pair of jeans shorts, and that'd be her attire for the rest of the day. And now, even though she looked quite young for her age, it was quite difficult for her to carry on with that old nonchalance, especially when deep sorrow had touched her and left her permanently scarred.

"I'm ready," Lilly said, and in response, quite promptly, a portal appeared, emitting green radiance. She stepped through it and came out on the other side in a drab, gray, underground altar room-esque space that she had always associated with the Madam.

Except there was nothing on the altar, and against the barebone slabs of it, the Madam stood, an ageless woman somehow reflecting all of her age, her hair both black and shiny and yet still feeling *ancient*, her eyes wide and green, but weighed down with worry.

"Lilly," the Madam said, turning around, stretching her arms in welcome.

"Remodeling, are we? What happened to this place?" Lilly said, greeting her back, looking around the drab surrounding. "I remember there was much more light in here, and a panorama of the Axis Mundi."

"The Head Amasser is not fond of trifles like decorations and views," the Madam said.

"So he's definitely coming?" Lilly asked.

"Yes," the Madam said. "This meeting pertains to all of us who survived. He's coming."

"Will he fit in this small room? I mean, I remember him being—"

Lilly didn't get to finish that thought. A door appeared in the gray stone wall, and from the other side, Rafael stepped out, looking fresh, clean shaven, and quite healthy for a vampyre.

"Lilly," he said, smiling at her.

"Rafael. Still performing your role as the Collectors' champion?" Lilly asked, taking his cold hands in her own, and greeting him back.

"It's the only living for someone of my kind that makes any sense. When I require sustenance, I am provided sustenance without having to spill any living person's blood. And..."

"And in exchange you've turned into the Grim Reaper?" Lilly chortled.

"It's only temporary, until things start making sense again," Rafael said, standing close to her so that the Madam wouldn't overhear. "And between you and me, it's quite peaceful, lulling a dead soul with comforting words as I take it to the Bone Orchard. As if I'm atoning for my past sins." Then, stepping back and clearing his throat, he finished, "I shall now serve as the vessel of the Head Amasser for the remainder of this meeting."

His eyes flashed white as his body paused, the same white light also shining through his open mouth, making for a menacing sight.

"Three are present, while there should be four," said the Head Amasser, his deep voice booming from Rafael's mouth.

"Yes, Head Amasser. I was assured he would be here," the Madam said, taking her seat on one of the four chairs in the otherwise empty room. Lilly remembered reading somewhere that in order to channel the purest of magic, a witch would remove everything from her surroundings, even the paint on the walls of her room. This would allow her to invite magic as magic really was, unadulterated, pure. Perhaps the same could hold true for this plane of existence within the Axis Mundi.

"If this is a meeting for the Cornerstones, I do not see why I need to present here," Lilly said, taking her seat.

"All will be clear in time," said the Head Amasser quite patiently, sitting down as well.

They sat in silence, waiting on the Devil, but with each passing minute, it seemed that the Devil would not appear.

"Are we sure if he's even there anymore?" Lilly asked, tapping her feet impatiently. She had not remembered seeing the Devil leave that night. There had been no parting words between them. After the implosive closing of the vortex, when eventually she had taken her eyes off the sky, she had looked around only to find Blake, Billy, and Rafael around her. There was no sign of Lucifer, and there had been none ever since that night.

"Believe me, the Devil's incendiary signature is one that still exists in the universe," the Madam said. "If he wasn't there any longer, we would know. But it does seem that he has abandoned us."

"I have a question about that night," Lilly said, trying to muster the courage to address the Madam and all of Craft itself. "Where were you?"

"I fought beside you all," the Madam said, looking perplexed.

"But near the end, when we were all standing in the park, where were you?"

The Madam breathed deeply, then sighed, closing her eyes. "I was in woe. In a single night of existence, I had witnessed a massacre as which I'd never seen. I was drained, Lilly. I had to seek refuge within the Axis Mundi while there was still an Axis Mundi."

"I see," Lilly said, and said no more.

"Was I supposed to have done more?" the Madam asked, her tone that of hesitation and uncertainty.

"Neither of you were there when it mattered. You only channeled yourself through Rafael, Head Amasser, and when the battle was at its thickest, you absconded, Madam," Lilly said, the rage that she had been doing a good job of repressing these past months finally coming to the surface, as if aided by something.

"There is the matter of the balance we need to tend to," the Head Amasser said. "The importance of restoring the balance, should there be an after. This is the after."

The Madam rose from her chair and walked slowly around the others. "I have been observing you these past few months, Lilly. The way you rose to the occasion in my absence, took all those witches underneath your wing... I did not call you here to ask you to take the mantle of God. I wanted to ask you if you would become the caretaker of Craft. Would this be something you'd be comfortable doing? That you were the Axis Mundi's Madam?"

Lilly did not know what to say. What she was being offered was something that she had never imagined acquiring. To hold dominion over all of the magic in the entire known universe.

"Will...will my life change?" Lilly asked, thinking of Bridgewater, of her friends that were still there. Of Amy, Billy, and even Blake.

"Only in that you will not be answerable to anyone above you. You shall rule over the Axis Mundi, from wherever you wish. And that will leave me to pursue godhood," the Madam said.

"Remind me again, what interest is godhood to you?" The Devil laughed, walking in the room confidently with his cane that he didn't need.

Satan continued. "Now that Joe, my boy, has somehow killed both Abstract and Absolute, I do not hear any chaos squirming anywhere. To my knowledge—and if you're eager to know how I attained that knowledge, I will let you know that I went looking for my son beyond the bounds of the universe, and I found nothing there. There is no Absolute alive. Nor, for that matter, is the Abstract. Which brings us back to my question. To my knowledge, nothing out of the ordinary has happened, so why this meeting?"

"They wish to elect a new God," Lilly said exasperatedly. "That is why they have called us here."

The Devil froze, saying nothing, but looking upon each of the presences in the room with great judgment, as if sizing them up.

"*That* is my interest in godhood, Lucifer Morningstar," the Madam said with a warm smile on her face. "I observed the old god make as many mistakes as one can expect, and because of my role being so different than hers, I could not intervene. At her best, she was an absent deity. At her worst, she was a macabre nightmare leveling entire civilizations in her unchecked rage. And let's just say that in the short tenure Joseph was God, he overcorrected so much that the universe cracked open. You need a level-headed god, one who can nourish humanity while also keeping it in check."

"Spoken like a true diplomat, Madam," Lucifer continued.

"You and I go way back, Lucifer. I have never looked at you with judgment, or with scorn. You will find that there will be all the leniency extended from my side as is possible," the Madam said.

"How quaint!" the Devil said. "I do, however, find something amiss with all of the above, and I think, Your Excellency, you know what I'm talking about," he said to the Head Amasser, exhaling smoke through his nose in two thin lines.

The Head Amasser said nothing, it only continued to look in Satan's direction.

"When Joseph destroyed both the Absolute and Chaos itself, he did so through the Sacrifice," the Devil continued, his voice amused as he walked around the room admiring the walls as if something beautiful hung from them. "And here's the part you've all been too afraid to speak aloud: When there is no chaos through the Abstract, there is no need for balance. Balance only exists as a leash between order and disorder. Take one away, and the leash snaps. What remains? Free will, baby! And what does that mean?"

He tapped ash onto the floor before him from his cigarette, savoring the silence that followed.

"It means the game ended the moment the boy slit the board in half. There are no scales to tip, no thrones to contest. Balance has no teeth without chaos to grind against. Which means the only law left is will itself. And will, dear friends, is mine."

Lucifer turned around, his eyes glinting in the dark. "That's the joke I've carried with me since the boy died. You've been arguing about restoration, elections, mantles. But I knew the instant his blood hit the ground—the wager was over. Free will reigns. And free will was always my side of the coin."

He lifted his head and looked at the Head Amasser.

"Clever," the Head Amasser said. "The question before us is not whether we can restore what was. The question is whether what was is permitted to be restored."

"Permitted by whom?" Lucifer said as he tipped forward, as if pressing his ear to some imaginary wall.

No one said it for him. The Madam didn't. Instead she passed a glance over to Lilly as if to borrow a little steadiness, then returned her gaze to the vessel the Amasser wore. "Say it."

Rafael's eyes filmed white and the Head Amasser spoke again.

"In the beginning—of this universe, not all—agreements were sworn because only agreements hold when strength fails and logic differs. You can call them wagers if it pleases you. I do not. Its terms were not written in one tongue. Each power used its grammar. What you call God wrote obedience, what you call Devil wrote rebellion, what Creation wrote we later called law, what Chaos wrote we later called entropy, what Craft wrote we later called possibility, and what I wrote you can hear now: if either party removes itself—by choice or by defeat—the surviving party holds the field until a countervailing will arises from within the field itself."

"Which is a lovely way to say what I already did," Lucifer murmured. "They left. I didn't."

"Do not confuse sequence with victory," the Madam snapped.

The Head Amasser did not look toward her. He had no need to; his next words faced everyone at once.

"Sequence is not victory," he agreed. "Endurance is."

The Devil's grin was smug. "There it is."

The Madam's jaw tightened. "We can appoint function," she insisted. "We can elect roles suited to the need now. New God, new balances—"

"Silence. It falls upon us all," the Head Amasser went on, "to accept what has already been written. The cosmic wager agreed upon before time began cannot be undone by those subject to it. Its clauses for dissolution are explicit. One side obedience. One side rebellion. The Absolute is erased. God is dead. Chaos has been subsumed by the act of the Sacrifice. Only free will remains within the field."

He paused before he continued.

"Therefore, it is granted that the realm belongs to Lucifer," the Head Amasser said, and there was no ceremony left to hide in. "Free will reigns supreme. Congratulations, Lucifer. You've won."

The words rang once and then disappeared into the chamber's cracks. The Madam did not move, as if movement would concede something her words still refused to.

Lucifer didn't smile right away. He looked, for an indecent heartbeat, almost embarrassed—like a man who hadn't expected the punchline to his own joke to make him laugh. He flicked the ash from his cigarette with a small satisfaction.

"Well," he said. It was almost gentle. "There you have it. How very bureaucratic an apocalypse turns out to be at the end.

"I will not gloat," he lied politely, and somehow managed it. "I will not sermonize either. I am too old for sermons. The boy bought this verdict with his life. If you think I could love the price, you've misunderstood me, just like humanity has all this time."

The chamber had never been more silent. The Head Amasser resumed his customary pose of stillness. The Madam stood firm—she wasn't mad at Lucifer, she was mad at herself for not seeing the truth.

"Function remains to be assigned," she said, and the voice she found was steadier for having been cut. "Not the throne. The throne is dust. If free will reigns, it will make bad kings of us all unless some part is tended. Craft does not require God. It requires stewardship. The Axis Mundi cannot run on memory and hope."

She turned then, fully, to Lilly. It wasn't a flourish; there was no pageantry left in her. Her eyes were tired, and the tiredness made them honest.

"You have been doing the work already," the Madam said. "Without the title. Without the mantle. You gathered the ones who were not ready and made them almost so. You strengthened the ones who thought they were ready and were not. You built a set of hands where there had only been intent. I am not asking you to be a god. I am asking you to be a gardener."

Lilly's first instinct, what with everything else gone to ash, was to laugh. What sound came up made it only as far as her teeth. She looked down at her own fingers, as if to check if dirt lived there already.

"What would it change?" she asked.

"You would not be answerable upward, to any God!" the Madam said, as she stared at Lucifer in defiance.

"And the Bone Orchard?" Lilly asked, still to the Madam but angling the question toward the white-lit eyes wearing Rafael's face. "Do the Collectors consent to a Craft that is not shored up by obedience?"

The Head Amasser took a beat that felt like the pause

between judgments and sentences, between swinging a door open and stepping through.

"Consent is a human concept," he said. "I will allow it because it aligns with charge. I collect endings. I do not require you to generate them faster, and we do not care who you answer to."

"You're so romantic," the Devil drawled, and there it was again: that flick of humor that held at its back the thing that made humor cruel when wielded by others. His grin turned; it wasn't for the Head Amasser anymore. "Let the witch tend the ground. If I am to inherit a realm, I prefer it planted. Otherwise it gets boring too quickly."

"Are you saying you'll stay out of her way?" the Madam said, and if there was steel left in the world, it lived in the question.

"I'm saying," Lucifer answered, "that I won the right to move as I please, and this pleases me. If I wished to meddle pointlessly, I would have arisen as a philanthropist."

"God forbid," Lilly muttered before she could stop herself. It won her, inexplicably, the Devil's briefest, truest laugh. And in the sound of it she heard nothing comfortable and something honest.

The Head Amasser slackened inside Rafael's stance but did not surrender it; this was what the borrowed body had been for.

"You'll want a formal," he said, and the Madam, with the weary minimal nods of someone who had signed documents while entire towns burned, gestured permission.

The Head Amasser conjured a golden scroll, brighter than

any of them had ever seen, and within its parchment lay fields for each of their signatures.

"Craft requires a caretaker. The office does not assume the throne's obligations. The office assumes the Earth's. The Axis Mundi recognizes Lilly Thurman, lately witch, lately war-worker, as its steward. She may call herself Madam. The Bone Orchard will treat her environs as outside the field of harvest during the hour of making and the hour of teaching. All other hours remain as they were."

The candles along the wall leaned a little toward her in a draft that hadn't existed a moment earlier. Lilly felt nothing descend; nothing rested on her head, nothing slid onto her shoulders. If she had expected weight, she found instead a place to put her hands.

There were no cheers. It was not that kind of room. The Devil inclined his head the precise amount that mocked and honored at once. He walked toward the scroll and ignored the floating feathered pen that hovered beside it. Instead, he stabbed himself in his wrist with his fingernail and proceeded to scribble *Lucifer Morningstar* in blood on the parchment, causing the paper to shake and shriek. The Madam and Lilly followed suit, using the pen provided.

"Welcome to management," the Devil said as he clapped his hands.

The Madam drew a breath that wanted to be a sob but came out as air. For a long moment she only studied Lilly. Then Lilly found herself asking, quieter than she meant to: "And you? What will you do now?"

The Madam's lips curved faintly, not into a smile but into

something like memory. "I will be around. Watching. That has always been my nature. I intervene little, but I see much. When the world begins to forget itself, I remind it. When it reaches too far, I steady it. But I will not rule. That was never my gift, and never my desire."

Her eyes softened. "Consider me the ghost at the edge of the garden. You may not hear me, but you will feel when I am near."

She looked for a second as if she might reach for Lilly's hand. She didn't. She returned instead to the business the Head Amasser's verdict had pried from her.

"There will be no God," she said. The sentence did not tremble when she said it. "We cannot write a new script atop the grave of an old one. We can write footnotes. We can write addenda. We can maintain what refuses to be broken. That is what is left to do."

"Look at us," Lucifer said. "Revolutionaries who turned into custodians."

"You're the king," Lilly said.

Rafael's eyes lost their film, and he was just himself again, blinking, his throat moving as if swallowing someone else's last words. He focused on Lilly.

"If you ever need," he began, and stopped because declaring aid while wearing the voice that had just declared a victory for the other side struck him as poor taste. He settled for a nod that referenced centuries and ended with now.

The Head Amasser did not add anything further. He had said the part that could not be unsaid. The Collectors along the wall thinned, a visual plural turning back into a singular abstraction; the room brightened by the extent they left.

"You asked what I will do now," Lucifer said later, almost quietly, when the procedural scraps had been sorted and menial bindings tied off and the last curious witches had been shooed away into sleep by someone's good sense. It was to Lilly he said it, which surprised no one, least of all the Madam. "I think I will go home and see if the furnace still listens when I call it by its true name."

"And then?" Lilly asked.

"Then nothing," he said, and for a beat it was not flippant. "Then I wait to see who you all make yourselves into when you think no one is grading you."

"You'll meddle," the Madam said, not a question.

"Of course," he said, with the honesty of a man who'd just been given the deed to a city and still promised to use the sidewalks. "But not—" and here he glanced down to the ashtray where his cigarette had died "—not today."

"What will you need first?" The Madam broke the silence.

"Wands," Lilly said, and smiled a tired, crooked smile at her own joke, which was not a joke.

She did not look toward the doorway where the Devil had gone. She didn't have to. The room had shifted in that direction just enough for anyone with a spine to feel it.

Outside, beyond stone and tired flame, the night over the Axis Mundi was calm in the particular way that only comes after a long storm.

Later, after they'd sorted the pattern for who would tend what and where the first circle of apprentices would sleep and which books could be trusted, Lilly walked out of the chamber and followed the hallways she already knew by heart back to the door that made the shortest line to Bridgewater. She opened it and walked directly into the hallway of her manor.

She stood for a long minute there, listening to the particular hush that only houses with memory keep, then walked to the study. From the window, the town sat quiet, like the world hadn't nearly been ripped apart by chaos. She flicked her fingers up and down, as if remembering her magic once more. Yet she could not pray to the man who had just inherited a kingdom he did not have to invent. She would not pray to the woman who had just asked her to carry a garden through winter. She would not pray to the ledger-keeper who had spoken law tonight and left with it.

So she did what she had done the first night the sky tore—she sat, and she let the quiet come.

"Free will reigns," Lilly said to the empty room, the words flat and true. "All right then."

And then she went to find a wand.

Back in the Axis Mundi, the Devil and the Madam had stuck around, as if sending their young daughter off to college.

"She'll do well," the Devil said to her.

"She will if you make good on your promise to leave her alone, let her craft her own path."

Satan rolled his eyes and shifted his cane to his other hand—he then proceeded to walk toward the door.

"And what of Earth?" the Madam called after him. "The cities that burned, the people who saw too much? Do we scrub their minds? Would it not spare them?"

Lucifer paused, his head turning back to face her, his cane firmly in his hand. "Let them remember. Every scream, every claw, every inch of the sky torn open. It's not a curse, it's a gift."

He then turned fully to face the Madam...

"But mark my words, and mark them well. They'll make scripture out of it by sunrise. And scripture, my dear, has always been the best leash."

And with that, the Devil walked out of the room.

www.ingramcontent.com/pod-product-compliance
Lightning Source LLC
Chambersburg PA
CBHW060556310726
48982CB00008B/1142/J
9798993289526